Stella Does Hollywood

Jed Blacksnake, King of the Road, Indian chief, enigmatic warrior, eased himself on to the bike as if he was about to fuck it. It was an Enfield Interceptor – 736cc, four-stroke, parallel-twin, cast-iron barrel, alloy head – a model with serious bike cred and a top speed of 110 m.p.h.

I eased myself as provocatively as possible on to the seat behind him, grasped his waist with tight arms and pushed the bone of my crotch into the small of his back so that he could feel it like a female hard-on.

He took perfect control. Slowly, my hand slithered down the front of his trousers. He continued riding the bike as if nothing was happening. I closed my fingers around his cock which, of course, was as hard as it could be: full up and ready to go.

By the same author:

Shameless

Stella Does Hollywood

Stella Black

BLACK LACE

Black Lace books contain sexual fantasies.
In real life, always practise safe sex.

This edition published in 2007 by
Black Lace
Thames Wharf Studios
Rainville Road
London W6 9HA

Originally published 2001

Typeset by SetSystems Ltd, Saffron Walden, Essex

ISBN 978 0 352 33588 3

Penguin Random House is committed to a sustainable future for our business, our readers and our planet. This book is made from Forest Stewardship Council® certified paper.

Printed and bound in Great Britain by Clays Ltd, Elcograf S.p.A.

Chapter One

I sat in a traffic jam on Wilshire Boulevard. There were police cars shrieking around a mall on Beverly. Four children had been stomped to death in the fight to buy Beanie Babies and there was an unseemly fracas of emergency services. Funeral directors and life insurance salesmen had gathered on the spot, along with the usual procession of television crews, film crews, cable crews and agents from film companies. Los Angeles loves a disaster. Los Angeles loves a disaster as much as I love my car, and that is a lot, my friends. If anything happened to the car, man, I wouldn't know what to do with myself. It would mean years of therapy. And mourning. And a veil. Everything.

I pictured myself briefly in a veil, sniffing dramatically, red-lipped through the black net. It would be difficult to smoke a cigarette through a veil, though Faye Dunaway managed it in *Chinatown*.

There are a lot of people who are possessed by the spirit of the first-generation Firebirds; that early breed – all Camaro class and four-barrel powerhouse. I was driving a 1969 400HO, straight out of Detroit, the darling Ram Air, convertible of course, and, as any porch-sittin' lager-loving ol' fool knows, the '69 is one of *the* great classics. Big, purry, no vulgar fins – rarer than those Mustangs everyone drives round West Hollywood, classier than your average Chevy Chevelle, and more muscle than any boy-zone four-wheel.

Some say it's too bulky; the purists stick with the '68, but I have to disagree. The flash gits worship the 1973 Trans-Am. Certainly the GTO is smaller, more manageable – a girl's car, some might say. But I say big is better and less is less. The '68 is a straight's car – all modified modicum and anal twits on cruise nights. The '69 is the decadent beauty, the symbol of that final year of excess, the year of Woodstock and the Family, when Peter Fonda was a pin-up, the hippies were shot and the angels went mad at Altamont. 1969. I have seen its relations dressed up for hot-rod nights like big birdy slags – painted Corvette yellow, beefed-up sub-frames, pinchweld braces, idiotic axles; but mine was an original four-bolt main-block, one hundred percent rust-free meta goddess. Colour? Deep, dark red. Not pillar-box, not fire-engine. Blood. And yes, the nails matched.

Some sure had ordered those options. The Firebird had power steering, power brakes, power top, power windows, power seat and a power antenna. There were integral bumpers in Lexan plastic, chrome grille, spooky tail lights, rally wheels, and wide, soft, double-bed bucket seat giving up the space, the wide-open space, for any sexual position available to the thinking and fucking people of this great free world. And the bonnet? The bonnet was a metal bed made for it.

This girl has seen a lot of action on and in this good old car. I mean, there was Lonny, who liked me to ease myself up and down on the gear stick, and that cowpoke from Austin who tied me up, pushed me face down so that all I had was that smell of black leather in my nose as he took me from the back. Leather. Darkness. Screaming-out orgasms. I can't recommend it enough. And there was a man named Sebastian, about whom I can remember very little except that he had a thick dick and looked like one of Gene Loves Jezebel.

Most everybody likes it over the bonnet. Face up, face down, panties on, panties off, who cares? It's all metal and fuel and come and heat.

Some drivers wound down their windows and waved at me. I snapped open the gold compact and reapplied a deft slick of major red. Red lipstick, red car, red nails. I looked so good I wanted to fuck myself.

'Nice car,' said a punk in a passing Packard.

'Marry me?' said a beard sitting in a Lexus.

'Madre de Dios! El coche! La guapa! Magnificissimo!' said a short Mexican peering over the wheel of a 1976 Cadillac Eldorado.

'Whore!' shouted a plaid shirt in a Ford pick-up.

'Is that a compliment?' I gazed at him coldly through cat's-eye shades as black as the night.

'Sure, honey.'

Jealousy. Jealousy. Wherever you go there is jealousy.

I turned on the radio. The Eagles were standing on a corner in Winslow, Arizona. Hot metal stretched out towards Santa Monica, heat wavered off bonnet tops. There was the thumping of radios and 'Cam An!' Then honking and distant gunfire. To the right a mini-mart offered Donettes, Bageldogs and Beauty. To the left one Marlboro man said to the other, 'Bob, I've got emphysema.' The heat burned down on the top of my head. I sipped a white grape-'n'-cranberrry ginseng soda.

Looking up, I saw twenty red parakeets sitting in a palm tree, still, like scarlet jewels on the green leaves. Then, without warning, and as one, they soared into the air and swooped away, one scarlet streak across the cloudless blue sky.

A ponytail in a suit cruised past, wound down his window, and flipped a bunch of roses into the back seat of the convertible as the traffic finally began to move slowly forward.

'I love you!' he shouted.

Gad. Everyone is a romantic.

I had met Bleak Hardcourt at a barbeque in Bel Air. He bore down in mirror shades and told me to attend his 'little pardy', or else. He had enjoyed the peak of his acting career and was now settling down to enjoy the luxuries of its rewards. Over the years he had sustained hundreds of car accidents, nuclear explosions and alien attacks, but now, as the years were making his face more distinguished and endowing him with an illusion of worldliness, he was devoting less time to work and more to squandering his enormous wealth. And so, as all ageing action heroes must, Bleak had retired to his sauna, where he sat and planned his run to presidency. He lived underground, where he hoped to be safe in the event of Armageddon.

'If it worked for the pueblos, it can work for me,' he told me.

A team of pot-holers and interior designers had created a subterranean labyrinth underneath the Hollywood Hills. A masterpiece of engineering, the network of caves and grottoes protected the inhabitant against fire, flood, hurricane, riot and all the other hallmarks of life in California.

Living underground and in the dark did not suit everybody. Hedy Hardcourt, Bleak's third wife, had had to be readmitted to a treatment centre on Bob Hope Drive, where qualified counsellors promised to 'supply a unique environment in which she could regain control of her life'.

The entrance was hidden near a lake, its secret presence was indicated by the limousine gridlock that had built up around the edges of the water. Suits, implants, highlights and teeth poured out of cars and swirled through the maze of candle-lit tunnels towards a central cavity that constituted the banqueting hall.

A charming youth ambled towards me. He was fresh and dark and brown-eyed and blessed with all the things a youth should be blessed with, such as a smile that said I could do it with you anytime I liked. You know it, I know it, the world and his nubile niece knows it.

'Good evenin', ma'am,' he said. 'I'm your parking valet for tonight.'

He opened the driver door for me and I allowed him a full view down my cleavage, whose crevice had been pushed up and enhanced by an underwired leopardskin bra. He observed with a mixture of curiosity and admiration, as if he was looking around a house that he knew he could not afford.

'Nice car,' he said, still staring at my chest. 'Late 60s?'

'Yes.'

'I've got the Bonneville, hardtop coupe . . . ever had sex in it?'

'Of course.'

'Are you wearing panties?'

'No.'

'Good.'

He pushed me backwards over the bonnet and kissed me very hard on the mouth while pushing his hand up my skirt. As he shoved three fingers into my fanny I oozed all over them.

'Man. You godda shaved puss . . .'

His eyes closed and he pushed his fingers further into me, bringing me to the first orgasm. Pressing the bulge in his jeans firmly against my pelvis, he then pushed me back over the banquette that joined the passenger and driver seat and burrowed his face between my thighs. Separating the lips of the labia with his fingers, he pressed his tongue firmly down on to my clit, flicking relentlessly and licking voraciously.

I love LA.

A young man, a good, hard, confident cock. He gave me a simple banging, no hanging around, no small talk, no lies. And I yelped because I liked it. He would not let me get away with three or four climaxes, but went on and on until I was trembling all over him and wondering if I would ever stop. Then, he came, suddenly and without comment. It was enough. The size of that dick made it so.

He zipped himself up. 'Give me your keys and I'll park your car for you.'

'You certainly provide a good service,' I said.

Smoothing my clothes down into something that resembled their original positions, I checked the make-up in the wing mirror and ambled casually towards the party with his smell still on me, and the fading memory of the tough shaft still tingling in my cunt.

Bleak Hardcourt was wearing a white shirt split to reveal a brown chest that was sprouting grey hair much as an old wall sprouts lichen. He leaned towards me, squinted painfully, and advanced his perfect brown nose so that it hovered in front of my face. He was short-sighted and, in dark nightclubs, had been known to go home with a hat stand.

'Stella, honey,' he said warmly. 'Good evening.'

He was standing with two people. One was the Dalai Lama and one was a man named Vinny Paladino.

'I love LA,' said the Dalai Lama.

I bowed my head in reverence. 'The shopping is fabulous,' I said.

'Fabulous,' he agreed.

His Holiness and Bleak disappeared into the swirling crowd, leaving Vinny Paladino behind. He smiled a mouth full of postmodern teeth that sat unnaturally in his worn features. Two tall blondes towered over us, bending and swaying like palm trees.

'Tomenicole are here,' one of them drawled.

'Cute tits,' said the other. 'Are they real?'

'Yes,' I said.

The conversation moved mysteriously towards obesity and whether it was genetic.

One of the girls swept ecru extensions from her forehead to reveal a large brown face, at the centre of which there was a nose so small, so *retroussé*, and so out of proportion to her natural physiognomy, that any observer would think the doctor's hand had slipped during the operation.

'Cocaine is good for slimmin',' she observed.

'Or a death in the family. I dropped ten pounds when my granddaddy died . . .'

'You should not starve, though. Starving is very, very bad for you. Starving makes you fatter, my doctor says. You become distended like those poor little babies in Band Aid and your eyes bug out and then you don't have your period any more.'

'Gad. Who cares about periods? I had mine removed years ago . . .'

'On insurance?'

'Yeah . . . Well, the doctor put it in as an emergency hysterectomy.'

'Good idea.'

Ecru extensions suddenly seemed to notice Vinny Paladino, whose face was seven inches in front of her bare midriff and therefore not in her immediate line of vision. She inspected him closely as one might inspect a child to see if he looked like Auntie Rhonda.

'And who are you?' she lisped.

'I am Cher's eyebrow consultant,' said a man in green silk who thought that the question was addressed to him.

'Not you, honey, this one here.'

'You mighta seen me in *Murdering Hoodlums*,' he said. 'I was shot in the face.'

I looked around.

A young man wearing a grey Armani suit spoke into his StarTac 6500 Motorola mobile phone.

'Jesus, Drue, go up to three thousand dollars, then. I've to got to have them. Yeah, three thousand. I don't care, just do it.'

He snapped the telephone shut and noticed that I was staring at him.

'I'm bidding for Cecil B de Mille's cricket socks,' he explained. 'I could have had Captain Kirk's original space suit but I went for the socks. I think I'm right, don't you? They have provenance and a name tag ... Say, honey, cute tits! They got representation?'

'I don't think they really need it at the moment, thank you,' I said politely.

'Pity,' he said. 'Still, take my numbers, anyways.'

He pressed his card into the front of my T-shirt and ebbed away. A bald person wearing yellow-tinted contact lenses appeared. He held his hand up in front of my face so that I could see that each of his five digits was in a metal splint.

'Never,' he said, 'leave your hand in a chick's mouth while you are bringing her to orgasm.'

He snapped his teeth together dramatically.

'You know what I mean? Lockjaw ... Say, cute tits. Are they real?'

'Yes!' I said, beginning to feel slightly exhausted.

I went to find a bathroom. There was a long queue.

'Is this the line for the ladies'?' I asked a willowy brunette

'Gad, no! This is the line for Alector Anderson. He's so cute! Everyone wants to do it with him. He's in the john right now with Demonica del Rio.'

She stabbed me in the chest with a long red fingernail.

'And you'll have to wait your turn, girl, because *I'm* next!'

A crack in the open door revealed two bodies wound in a medley of breast and buttock, tattoo and hair gel, platform boot and erect cock, cheekbone and groan of gratitude.

She was getting what she wanted and she was getting it good and hard, from the back, as she bent like a slut over the seat of the loo. It looked good but, as the brunette had said, there was a queue for it.

I slumped into a pink leatherette sofa. A waiter bought me a vodka, an oyster and a sliver of yahimbi, a tree bark thought to be imbued with energising qualities. I swallowed all three.

Vinny walked past chatting animatedly to the two blondes.

'I think I saw you in *Filth of Society,*' one of them said. 'You had blood coming out of your mouth.'

'Are you sure it was that one, sugar? I had blood coming out of my mouth in *The Man in the Fedora,* in *Mario's Gang,* in *Smashed Teeth,* in *Mothers Against the Mob,* and in *The Scar*. Then I had blood coming out of my ears in the *Maim Game,* and blood coming out of my head in *Ice-Pick Massacre III,* blood coming out of my nose in *Neopolitan Nightmare,* and blood coming out of my eyes in *They Only Live to Kill*. Plus I had my foot cut off in *Terror,* I was crucified in *Christians out for Revenge,* and I was hung, drawn and quartered in *Sicilian Blood Bath*.

'Dear me,' she said, 'you must be very brave.'

'Well, it goes both ways. I've shot Steve McQueen in the leg, John Wayne in the back, and I once gave Olivia de Havilland a good slap.'

He jangled a gold watch to emphasise this point.

The yahimbi bark stuck in my teeth and I maneuvored my tongue around the inside of my mouth in a gesture that Vinny translated as provocation. He waved at me, and was about to occupy the sofa when a voice said in my ear, 'In fact his name is Keith Noakes. He was born in north London.'

I turned around and saw a fifty-year-old man with a

grey fringe combed over his forehead and a tough body of the type sometimes seen by Jean Genet when hanging out on the dockside in Marseilles.

'I'm Doug,' he said.

He sat down beside me and talked a lot of rubbish, so I assumed he was an artist.

I was right.

'I am interested in cultifying the commonplace presence,' he said. 'I want to be able to reproduce a suggestive atmosphere.'

He studied my breasts with unembarrassed scrutiny like a squirrel wondering if he should pick some nuts up and put them in a store for winter.

'... symbolise it and by so doing neutralise it. I want to study the detachment of distortion and art's pathological enchantment with total retinality, thus questioning whether the woman/object, addressed in an antithetical way, can achieve authentic non-objectivity. And I wanna make a lodda money.'

Half of my face started to go to sleep as I contorted my muscles into a stiff pose designed to disguise boredom. Soon the features stiffened into a rictus and I knew that the blood was ceasing to oxygenate the vital veins.

Doug gently stroked my nipple with one soft finger. It stiffened immediately.

But I did not seem to be a part of it.

'You may ask me what this means psychodynamically, but, as I tell my students, it is axiomatic that My Art must be about an objective relationship with vital forms that are Spinozan in their intellectuality. The breast, or the ankle, or the knee, reduced to mere geometry, can be made to represent a statement on the history of appropriation as well as man's inability to repress instinct. Or emotion if you will.

'And then, of course, there are all the dictums of abstraction, the questions of definition and irrelevance, of art and commerce, on inward decadence and outward religiosity; the question of whether the consolidation of universal concepts can be made through symbols, and whether the de-equilibrated whole has a valid position in any universal principle or whether one must still provide the shock of fragmentation. This is complicated, of course, by the fact that in studying the female form we are hoping to empathise with the pre-adamite, but we are also having to address the pleasure principle and all the Freudian machinery of understanding.'

'Of course,' I said nodding and trying to stay awake. I could not help noticing that, as Doug was in a position to look down my breasts, two primates behind him were not so lucky and were punching each other in order to gain a better view.

'Are you English?' Doug asked.

'Yes,' I said.

'I'm English as well, grandfather's side. I've got relations in Chipping Sodbury. Where do your folks live?'

'I have no idea. My mother disappeared when she heard there was a warrant out for her arrest.'

'Oh. Then I would like you to model for me . . . *nood.*'

'Why?'

The two primates had given up the struggle and were now kissing each other.

'Well, honey. You have a lovely shape. It advertises antepatriarchal balm and it speaks to me; it speaks to me of radically different versions of natural illustrations; it tells me that it can help me to realise My Art and help us to know that there is no such thing as uniform deification. Your shape, honey, your body, will represent Unawoman – the woman who can authenticate the important, indeed the life-giving contention, that the universalisation of the organic aesthetic has destroyed all possibility of integrating the self, which, as I am sure you will agree, has enormous and dangerous repercussions to all of humanity, and to the progress of civilisation itself. You can help save us from this disintigration.'

I tried to be polite. Proud though I am of my body, and keen to be generous with it, I knew that modelling would be boring and uncomfortable. I have often been asked to comply with this trade. Art students have told me that I resemble all kinds of things and was thus of great use to honing the skill in recumbent Venuses that it is necessary to perfect before graduating.

I have subjected myself to their stares and to long discussions about the traditions of design and whether birth control was responsible for the obsolescence of the fertility symbol as the great female icon and why, since then, the female icons had male bodies, and why men liked looking at women and women liked looking at women.

These experiences had taught me that I was a tiny and almost useless part of their cause. They could utilise geometry, fad, classical training, matriarchal nightmare or genuine vision there but they were not interested in reporting the nature of the model; to see me would confuse them. Their heads were full of concept and composition, the problems of tone, the pressure of modernity and their gambling debts.

So I knew a bit about art and I knew I would have to contort myself into some unnatural posture for hours on end and stare glassily into space and know that the mere blink of an eye would be seen as a seismic upheaval in the atmosphere of artistic concentration. I wouldn't be allowed to smoke or watch the television and I would have to pretend to eat cherries.

Some might have been flattered by Doug's request. Indeed, in the years stretching from the Aphrodite of Milos, there is no documented record of such an appeal being turned down. For hundreds of years men in smocks have said to women to whom they have not been introduced, 'Will you please take your clothes off so that I can stare at your naked body for hours on end.' And, because he lives in Paris and owns a couple of paintbrushes, she has clattered up the rotting wooden stairs leading to his garret and marched, clickety-clack, into a chamber whose only source of heat derives from the tension between the voyeur's unbridled desire and his compulsion to relieve himself through images.

I am able to flatter myself, and I often do. I do not need attention from others to make me feel beautiful and I am not drawn to the distance created by Art Man. I did not wish to delve into his aura of secluded personal privacy. I do not see him as an interesting challenge and I do not think that I can change him so that he will love me and me alone, for the only truth is that he must love himself alone if he is to paint the picture properly.

I am bored by Art Man. He is never present and I like people who are present. I am not interested in his image of me, except at the very basic level of fleeting entertainment, because I knew it could never be me. Furthermore, my experience of Art Man has shown me that he paints, he eats, he paints. There is little pleasure involved in his scenarios. Sometimes he even forgets to fuck you.

'I am quite busy at the moment,' I lied.

'I could paint you having sex with my dog,' he said.

At this point I perked up and began to warm to the idea but, suddenly, from nowhere, a huge female appeared: a mud-wrestler type, six foot at least, arms bulging with muscles, head erupting a storm cloud of huge grey hair. Silently she pulled Doug out of the sofa and dragged him into the swirling crowd.

I was left on my own, chewing the yahimbi and wondering if it was time to go home.

'Stella Black!'

I jumped. Nobody knew me here.

I looked around and there was Leon. The face was older, the hair had been helped with a black dye, but the voice was still the same: that voice that delivered sad observations from the side of the mouth.

'Leon!' I said, genuinely pleased. I had always liked

Leon. He was so cynical and clever and liberal and Jewish.

'Stella,' he said. 'Darling . . .'

He hugged me closely, pulling me into the soft melt of his casually ageing body. I tried to remember whether I had slept with him in the days when Mel and I had thought that he was like Elliot Gould. A flickering of some scene with a bong in a tent at Glastonbury passed my mind's eye but did not pause to allow intelligent reflection. It must have been a false memory. Leon would never have gone to a pop concert. He never went out in those days. Lived in his limo. Held parties in his limo, as I recalled.

'Leon,' I said studying the familiar features: the long nose, the deep brown eyes, the tragic shirt. 'How nice to see you . . . How are you?'

'Well,' he said. He stared down at his gold signet ring and then up into my face, smiling in a way that I did not know he was capable of, and displaying teeth that he had not owned in the 80s. 'I'm off the Lithium and I'm very very rich.'

'Rich, Leon?' I said. 'How nice for you.'

'Yes, Stella. I have plundered the mines of iniquity and I have dug the gold; I have danced with the devil of DVD and played in the playground of filth. I have sold pagan sex, anal sex, animal sex and sewage sex. I have made magazines and books and websites and now I have an empire. I own a fourteen-storey corporate superstructure off Rodeo Drive and a gold-plated bulletproof Mercedes Benz with the company logo on it. I have three Chagalls. I am Gatsby, Stella, but I have well and truly sold out.'

'Ah.'

I recognised the implications of this, for Leon was no ordinary porno king driven by the pumping of hot totty and the main chance. He had been dragged screaming into adult entertainment, for all his dreams had been made in the art house.

Tarkovsky, Suzuki, Tavernier, Cocteau – these had been his idols. He had spent his youth watching black and white films with subtitles by directors whose work could been seen only in way-out places on tiny screens. He sprang out of the London School of Cinematography in 1970 with a signed diploma and the confidence that he would harvest his vision as an independent activist and intellectual. But it is not like that, of course. It is a cruel casino and Leon's number never came up. No one had wanted his art. There had been years of producers and Soho and debt and terrible ads for things that were related to ladies' freshness.

Beaten down by panty pads and drained by sadness, he had finally succumbed and made a porno flick entitled *Naughty Nancy*. This opus, unfortunately for Leon, was the bestselling video of that year and made a star of its heroine, the short but dynamic temptress Candy O'Belle – a lady whose cavernous cleavage seemed to unite with her permanently open mouth so that it was often difficult for the fan to ascertain where one started and one finished. Not that it mattered, as they both performed approximately the same function.

So Leon made money from porn. The devil had taken his art soul and returned a treasure chest full of gold. Leon could buy the isolation that he liked, the wives that he fancied, the first editions that he felt he needed, and the scripts that kept him on top.

'I am,' he said, 'the most successful pornographer in America. Bigger than Flynt, Guccione, any of them. I am worth more than a billion dollars!'

'Christ,' I said.

'I have been on the cover of *Executive* magazine, Stella.'

'Blimey.'

'I own eight mansions, including the Steckmest place, a yacht, a private jet, and an island in the Pacific Ocean.'

'Blow me down.'

'Yeah, well it won't make my dick any bigger.'

'I can't remember how big your dick is,' I said honestly.

'No, my darling, I don't think you ever saw it, did you? Only that beastly Mel was honoured with that privilege.'

'You had a scene with Mel?'

'Well, various things went on in the back of the limo and she seemed to be at the bottom of the pile somewhere. Where is that queen bitch and witch of the universe?'

'Pregnant,' I said gloomily. 'And living in Ipswich.'

This was a tragedy that I did not want to talk about.

'Jesus, an accident I suppose.'

'Yes, she was very upset, but now she has gone all smug and Mothercare, so I don't see her any more.'

'What a waste,' he said, looking genuinely devastated.

'Yes,' I said. 'Sometimes I think it's as bad as seeing a friend run over by a car.'

He looked at me with his sad brown eyes.

'Stella,' he said. 'You were always lovely and now you have become even more beautiful. I don't think I have ever seen such beautiful breasts.'

'Thank you,' I said. 'They are my own, in case you were wondering.'

'I wasn't,' he said. 'I've been in the adult entertainment industry for fifteen years. I know an implant when I see one.'

'Good.'

He took my hand, held it, and continued to look at me with avuncular affection.

'You wouldn't consider working for me, would you?'

'In what capacity?'

I didn't really think that I was designed for a job. I

had never had one, in the official meaning of the word. My father had organised a complicated network of off-shore accounts and trusts, some of which sent me cheques on a regular enough basis to allow me both constant leisure and perfect autonomy.

'I'm looking for a new star,' he said. 'We've had real problems casting *The Ordeals of Emmeline*. It's a good project. Even I like it. God knows I'm throwing two million at it. You'd be Emmeline . . .'

'What would I have to do?'

'Not much, really. There'd be tying up and buggery, a bit of oral, a lot of flagellation, machinery, serious PVC costumes, spikes, chains, horses, that kind of thing. Very up your street, I would imagine.'

'Yes.'

'And a lot of money.'

The vision of a pair of emerald, gold and diamond earrings popped into my head as easily as breathing. There's nothing like a vision of genuine jewellery to stimulate career moves.

I didn't have much else to do. My father was in prison. My mother was supposed to be in Ascot but she could have been anywhere. Certainly the police had never found her. I didn't mind lounging around in LA. I wasn't bored. I was a girl who owned a baby-pink turban and a pair of mules, after all. And the best kind of Ann Klein swimwear. My life was a holiday.

'I have never acted,' I said. 'Or even been in front of a camera, actually.'

He laughed uproariously, shoulders shaking, light flickering in his eyes, nearly becoming hysterical.

'You won't have to act,' he said. 'You will just be as you are. And Stella, my dove, you are Emmeline.'

I heard myself agree to visit Leon at his house and look at the script of which he was so oddly proud.

* * *

The next day I drove high up into the hills, where his mansion hung on the edge of a canyon looking over the Franklin Reservoir. It was a quiet neighbourhood populated by those who had availed themselves of everything that Hollywood had to offer and now lived in gated palaces, manned by armed armies and surveyed by cameras.

You name it, you can have it, and, in this neighbourhood, everyone had it: his 'n' her bathrooms, media rooms, marble floors, retractable roofs, mirrored gyms and huge houses for the servants. Style? No problem. French country mansion, Spanish four-plex, Taj Mahal folly. All these could be seen as I meandered slowly up the narrowing road, further and further to the top of the canyon, so that soon there was only a tiny track with a vertical drop down the mountainside.

I had lived in Hollywood long enough to know something about Leon's house, for it was famous in its own way. Many houses in Hollywood become known for their sordid and fantastic histories as these serve to increase their value in a market where celebrity and horror are considered to be more commercial than attractive architectural detail.

The site had once been owned by Gracie Feelings, the silent-movie star who had choked to death on a banana. The mystery surrounding Miss Feelings's death was centred not so much on the members of Congress who were in the house at the time, but the fact that the banana, which was found halfway down her throat, still had the skin on it.

The Feelings estate sold the house to Tammy-Sue McCorkodale, the country singer, who installed a swimming pool, at the bottom of which there was a mosaic portrait of Rambling Roger Trilling, the singing cowboy superstar with whom she was in love. The house then passed to the Rev. Alvin Binder, celebrated among ufologists as being the victim of an abduction experience known as the Binder Incident. Binder and his black Honda Accord had been airlifted from outside a Futon Shop in Pasadena to the middle of an alien vehicle moving in a manner inconsistent with the Newtonian laws of motion.

The place had then been blown up by Hans Steckmest, a German architect who had bought the property from the receivers because he wanted the site. It looked over a bluff, enjoyed a panoramic view, and was well situated to offset his work of art – a huge glass, steel and stucco construction inspired by the International Style and, in particular, the work of Richard Neutra. Cubist in mode, the house was, in effect, five levels of concrete and glass rectangles built into the cliff side. Utilising horizontal lines, airy interiors and open-plan ideas, it was upheld as an apotheosis of neo-Internationalism.

The architect (usually known only by his surname) received many prestigious awards. His design was said to be a welcome release from biorealism and a useful move towards the new supra-functionalism, although no one, including Steckmest, knew what this meant.

The electric gate purred back to let me in and I eased the Firebird through bougainvillea and palm trees to lawns that glittered under the iridescent showers of endlessly rotating sprinklers. To either side of the long tarmac driveway, placed at regular distances, stood hundreds of life-sized copies of Michelangelo's *David*. Rendered into an army of plaster clones by factory treatment, they all stood with that hand-on-the-hip stance like some flouncing army of sit-com hairdresser homos.

They were an unnerving site, these long lines of *Davids*. One *David*, after all, was quite enough. And here were hundreds of them. I laughed out loud and could not imagine why Leon had bought them unless it was to annoy himself. He had never been a collector when I knew him in London, but then he had had no money when I knew him in London. It was interesting that as he was not happy then, in those fast days of the early 80s, so he was not happy now. He had been poor and now he was rich, but he was still the same lugubrious lamprey.

The glass front door was bordered by towering Ionic pillars. It was open, so I let myself in, not thinking to be on ceremony with Leon, who might have turned into Howard Hughes since I last saw him but was still Leon, who I had once lent money to because he was stealing milk from people's doorsteps.

I entered an atrium adorned with showers of ivy and towering palm trees. Tiny tropical birds darted between dangling fronds to the sound of various tinkling fugues piped through invisible speakers.

In the distance, across acres of grey and white marble tiles, the small figure of Leon appeared from behind a white piano. As it scuttled nearer and nearer, it loomed larger and larger, the muffled sounds of incoherent speech finally turning into audible words.

He bustled.

'Jesus Christ – did you let yourself in? Where the hell are the maids? I was employing five of them at the last count.'

He clicked open a mobile phone and snapped into it.

'Who's that? Domenica? Why can't you answer the front door? What do you mean you will have to ask Jesus? What's it got to do with him? I pay the bills round here. Well, if that's the case tell him to cut the lawn. No. Just answer the bloody door.'

'Jesus?' I asked.

'Gardener,' he said. 'Useless.'

Leon was wearing a white bath robe and a pair of Gucci shoes and he was carrying a silver ice bucket as if it was a handbag. He kissed me affectionately. I could tell that he was morose, but morose was not a mood with Leon: it was a personality characteristic. If he had mood swings they went from cynical to depressed to maudlin to heightened by champagne cocktails to suicidal mania.

'Come through, come through, come through.'

We walked down a landscaped garden where a waterfall flowed down rocky landscapes, through Japanese bonsai, into a koi pond, and, finally, into an Olympic-sized swimming pool which was clean and clear and blue and everything that Hollywood should be.

There was a table and we sat underneath a parasol. Leon had set up his office there – mobile phone, fax, bowl of fruit, cigarettes, champagne, mineral water, piles of scripts.

'Do you live on your own, Leon?' I asked.

'Well. I've got a Siberian tiger,' he said.

'That wasn't quite what I meant. What about women?'

Or men, I thought, but didn't say it.

'Women, women?'

He waved his hand like some sheik ordering in the dancing girls.

'I tend to order them in. It's easier. I am not a romantic, Stella, I have no faith in feckless love. I have seen too much and I know too much. I have none of the illusions that keep the rest of the world from seeing harsh reality. I have seen reality, Stella, and worse; much worse, I have felt it.

'I have been here in Hollywood what, fourteen years now? I have seen geishas with no teeth and rent boys in chains. I have seen babies with tattoos and toddlers in couture. I have seen Greta Garbo's finger pickled in jar and a swimming pool full of hammerhead sharks. I have seen people with no talent go a very, very long way. I have seen the crack, the mould and the rot. Stella, I have seen it all, and I do not need to suffer the unnecessary atrocities that relationships inevitably bring. My needs are simple. They can be bought.'

I drank champagne and orange juice as it was 11 a.m.

and about that time. I was in tight Capri pants (lilac), mules (lilac), and a cute little scoop-neck top (black). The T-shirt was cunningly cut to push the breasts into a nice round affair with a lot of cleavage, which, as any girl knows, can be of great use when one is employed in important business negotiations.

Leon focused his Ray-Bans on me.

'So, Stella. You may be my Emmeline?'

'Possibly,' I said. 'Where's the script?'

He pushed over a bound folio of paper.

'Why don't you read it,' he said, 'while I go and attend to these faxes and Christ knows what else?'

Leon disappeared into his huge glass house and I lay on a comfortable floral lounger, the sun shining down on my brown legs, the smell of honeysuckle and oranges hanging in the air; everything was blue-sky quiet and beautiful, and I opened the file and read about the ordeals of Emmeline.

Chapter Two

THE ORDEALS OF EMMELINE

An adult motion picture
by
Jane Freeman

1. EXTERIOR. GRAFTON GRANGE. DUSK
As the soundtrack plays a requiem superimposed with the sound of howling dogs, clumping footsteps and the crack of lashing whips, the credits roll over an exterior shot of Sir Grafton Rafton's family seat. Beginning with a distant view taken through the opening of a carved stone arch, we see that this structure has been deeply carved with quatrefoils and with the Rafton family crest, two fire-breathing gremlins and a shield under which the motto is inscribed: *We Dominate.*

The camera enters through this gateway, moves in closer, and then pans over a wide shot of a nineteenth-century mansion built in the Gothic Revival style. The walls are notched into battlements, the mullioned windows are in the shape of pointed arches ending in quatrefoil shapes and floriated tracery, the roof is an asymmetrical pattern of spiry turrets and pinnacles carved with decorative layers and flamboyant finials.

As darkness descends the evening mist swirls around the contorted stone features of the mythical figures carved into the eaves. Slowly the camera focuses on monkeys with human faces, monks whose features are hidden under the dark shadows of their stone cowls, and winged devils with gargoyle features, their bodies sculpted to appear as if they are about to leap off the stone-work and fly away into the dark night.

2. EXTERIOR. GRAFTON RANGE.

Shot taken through a window reveals the character of Sir Grafton's historical family home. There is a giant fireplace, portraits of ancestors, suits of armour, all swathed in dust and cobwebs and covered with dramatic dark shadows. The night descends. Somewhere, in the distance, we hear the sound of the lash of a whip, and the shrill shriek of a woman crying out. The sound of whiplash seems to get louder and there is now, also, the clanking sound of old machinery such as that made by rusting cogs when they rotate.

3. INTERIOR. ROOM IN GRAFTON RANGE

The camera pauses to study the scenes in various rooms before showing the main characters. Thus we see, in a small cell in which the light filters through bars, a large black plastic bag lying on the floor. It is tied at the top and it is obvious from its shape that a woman is trapped inside it. There are no noises except for the occasional sigh as the body in the bag shifts its position and the silhouette of the bag also changes.

4. INTERIOR. ROOM IN GRAFTON RANGE

A room lined with mirrors and lit with huge chandeliers so large the bottom rows of crystal pendants nearly sweep the polished parquet floor. This is the scene of a surreal ballet class. A tall, beautiful woman with black hair scraped into a jewelled mantilla is wearing a PVC hobble skirt and a gypsy blouse that comes off the shoulders. Her breasts are pushed up by a padded lace bra, in white, whose structure it is possible to see underneath the shirt. She is wearing long diamond earrings and carrying a walking stick, which she thumps methodically on the ground. In front of her, three pupils, all dark, all with hair in buns, all with bodies sprayed with liquid latex, are on points. Their feet are almost vertical in their tightly ribboned pink ballet shoes; they are dancing, and in synchronicity – a high-step that resembles an exaggerated dressage technique. It requires the legs to be high and straight, the breasts forward, the hands on the hips. They are doing this, standing in a row, perfectly synchronised, their faces turned away from the Madame and towards the mirrored walls to their right.

In the corner, for no reason at all, but completely naked, a young man stands with his face to the wall. His wrists are tied behind his back with thick white cord. The strict Madame continues to beat on the floor with her stick as we go to another room in Grafton Range.

5. INTERIOR. GRAFTON RANGE

A tiny theatre with red velvet curtains and a spotlight shows one individual sitting on a stool on the stage. She is wearing a pair of black kid-leather boots, with laces all the way up the front. These cling to the shape of her calves, knees and thighs before finishing at the top, where the legs of her panties would be if she was wearing any.

Her torso is covered in a tight polo-neck, made of black cashmere, that clings to her 38DD breasts. She is not wearing a bra and the large stiff nipples strain against the taut fabric. Her hair, in the style of the mid-50s, is an immaculate chignon. Her lips are Rita Hayworth red. She is wearing thick black eyeliner and has long dark eyelashes. She appears to have no arms, though this may only be an illusion; her arms may be tied behind her back, but we do not find this out. A midget appears licking an ice cream.

6. INTERIOR. GRAFTON RANGE

A plump young girl wearing only high white pumps and ankle socks, and whose pussy has been shaved and decorated with a tattoo, is lying down on her back in a deep old-fashioned bath. Her arms are pinioned above her head and handcuffed to the silver Victorian taps. The camera, close in, travels slowly across the full length of her perfect body and, finally, to her face and to her open lips, which have been greased with clear gloss.

She is singing an aria from *Madame Butterfly*. We hear a tap on the bathroom door. She stops singing, looks at the door, and pauses. A gloved hand appears around the edge of the doorway. We do not see what happens next. There is no explanation, either in dialogue or narrative, for the strange nature of the above scenes. They are merely cameos, documented to show the perverse nature of Sir Grafton's purpose.

7. INTERIOR. SIR GRAFTON RAFTON'S STUDY

Camera slowly focuses in on the scene in Sir Grafton's study, zooming in closer until the frame is filled entirely by a close-up of a pair of round white buttocks encircled by a frame of delicate Victorian lace. Firm fleshy cheeks entirely fill the screen. We see the dark crevice that separates the buttocks and the delicate stripes that have marked the flesh.

The soundtrack continues to play the requiem, although this is very soft now; the most dominant sounds are that of a woman crying out and the lash of the whip. Suddenly the smooth white flesh that fills the screen quivers and twitches. The thin leather-covered reed of a riding whip darts down and lashes across both buttocks. We see the fresh mark that it leaves behind and hear a woman shriek out. The camera stays still for thirty seconds, framing the white cheeks that fill the screen. There is now no music, only the female arse, the livid line, and silence.

8. INTERIOR. SIR GRAFTON RAFTON'S STUDY

Camera pulls slowly back. Now we begin to see the picture of Emmeline's life. Sir Grafton Rafton's study is a huge room lined with leather-bound antique books. There are gargoyles looking down from the cornices, antique tapestries, high heavy carved chairs, a huge polished antique desk with brass ornamentation, and tiny drawers tricked with brass handles.

The room is dominated, however, not by antiquities, but by an eight-foot-tall wooden wheel which is similar to a Ferris wheel in structure but much smaller. It is operated by a handle similar to the starting crank on a vintage car. This winds up a series of rotating cogs whose sharp teeth combine with each other in order to push the wheel around.

Emmeline is chained face down on this wheel. Her torso is naked. Her legs are wearing a pair of black Victorian stockings with lace garters and a pair of glossy patent-leather walking shoes tied with thin laces. The heels are customised and, being some eight inches tall, disable the wearer so that she is unable to walk. The first impression, then, is that if Emmeline wishes to transport herself, she must crawl.

Hanging from her waist and around her buttocks are a pair of short frilly cotton bloomers which are split at the back, Victorian style. The lace falls on either side of them, like curtains, drawn to expose a full bottom exposed to the angry ministrations that they must receive.

Emmeline's wrists are chained and manacled on to the wheel. She is blindfolded but her mouth is free to allow her cruel guardian to hear her apologies or shouts, and so that he (or whoever he delegates) may kiss her long and hard on the mouth – a habit to which Sir Grafton is prone in the middle of punishment, often stooping forward to kiss his ward while sliding his fingers deep into her fanny, knowing that it will be very wet.

A beautiful female servant, older than Emmeline, but handsome in her demeanour, is dressed in a long Victorian dress with a bustle, low neck and leg-o'-mutton sleeves. It is made of rubber that has been treated to look as if it is wet and which allows every curve of her form to be revealed. She is sitting on a stool and rotating the lever so that the wheel moves around at Sir Grafton's command.

As the wheel goes round, Emmeline's bottom reaches the place where her guardian is standing and, as it does so, he swipes it accurately with a long thin riding whip, once each time as the bottom comes round the full circle.

One slick swipe, and then Emmeline's body goes on, around the wheel, as the pain from his whip seeps into her nether regions, becomes warm, then begins to stimulate erotic desire just as her arse comes round to the whip again.

The turning of the wheel is slow and Sir Grafton's stance is relaxed. It is not a demanding practice and he leans casually on his desk, sipping a glass of champagne, then placing it down on the polished surface. From this distance we see that he is a tall lean man wearing jodhpurs, leather riding boots and a tailored tweed jacket.

9. INTERIOR. GRAFTON'S STUDY

Close-up of the head of a tigerskin rug lying in front of the fireplace on the floor. We see its glassy eyes, its sharp pointed teeth, its gaping maw locked into permanent anger. Again the sound of rotating cogs and the lash of the whip. Camera focuses in on one of the portraits of Sir Grafton's ancestors. It shows a tall lean man dressed in black. Camera goes in on the face to reveal that it is smiling and seems to be staring down on the proceedings with a feeling of pleasure and encouragement. A placard designates the name: *The Black Earl.*

10. INTERIOR. GRAFTON'S STUDY.
Close-up on Sir Grafton Rafton's face. He is a handsome and determined-looking man in his mid to late 40s. His expression, like that of the ancestor that we have just seen, is one of sheer pleasure. As Emmeline's bottom is cranked around to face him again, his expression becomes one of concentration and firm determination.
11. INTERIOR. GRAFTON'S STUDY
Close-up on Sir Grafton's hand. He wears a gold ring and he is holding the whip.
12. INTERIOR. GRAFTON'S STUDY
Camera shows only Sir Grafton's arm, hand, the whip, and the buttocks in front of him. We see his arm draw back as, expertly, the thin black rod swipes cruelly down on its target. Emmeline's bottom wriggles frantically in front of him.
13. INTERIOR. GRAFTON'S STUDY.
Close-up on Sir Grafton's hands as he slowly pulls on a skin-tight pair of short black leather gloves embossed with rows of tiny metal studs at the wrist.
14. INTERIOR. GRAFTON'S STUDY.
Close-in picture of Sir Grafton's finger stroking Emmeline's smarting flesh, which he caresses gently and sensually, slowly easing his gloved forefinger underneath the buttocks and up into Emmeline's vulva. He pumps her with his leather digit for a few seconds. The arse wriggles, convulsively now, and there are groans of pleasure. Sir Grafton withdraws his finger and licks it slowly, smiling as he does so.
15. INTERIOR. GRAFTON'S STUDY
Sir Grafton walks around the wheel to Emmeline's face. He takes the glass of champagne and pours some into her mouth.

SIR GRAFTON:

Ah now, little Emmeline, it's not as bad as all that. You

know full well that you do not leave this house without permission, not even to walk in the garden. Now then. What do you say?

EMMELINE
(defiant)
I hate you!

SIR GRAFTON
Josepha – rotate the wheel faster please. This girl still does not know who is boss.

16. INTERIOR. GRAFTON'S STUDY
Camera shows Josepha working hard at her labour. The wheel is heavy and she is having to put her back into it. We hear the noise of machinery as cogs and chains wind around each other. Josepha cranks the speed up. The wheel starts to go round faster and more easily as it swings into its natural rhythm and needs less physical exertion from the operator.
17. INTERIOR. GRAFTON'S STUDY
The picture now shows the full scene with all three characters and the wheel. The wheel is going round very fast now. Emmeline's body is propelled around on top of it, and her buttocks come towards Sir Grafton much quicker so that he hardly has time to collect himself between each lash of the whip. And this is how we leave them, the wheel going round and round, as Emmeline remains tied to it, her bottom being switched by her guardian. Fade out.
18. INTERIOR. GRAFTON RANGE. CORRIDOR.
Camera shows point of view of person walking slowly down a long dark corridor where the walls are made of wooden panels. Suits of armour gleam in corners and tapestries shiver on the walls as if somebody is breathing underneath them. Camera stops in front of the door of Emmeline's bedroom. Door opens to reveal . . .

19. INTERIOR. EMMELINE'S BEDROOM

There is an old-fashioned Victorian washstand with a floral jug, an ornate wardrobe, expensive rugs and a bell pull. The room is dominated by the four-poster bed, which is covered with white cotton trimmed with lace. Emmeline is wearing only a short lace nightie made of white cotton and a pair of high-heeled white mules trimmed with white marabou.

She is lying face down on her bed. The blindfold is off now. So are the Victorian drawers. Her arse is lifted from the bed by a pillow that has been placed underneath her stomach. Both wrists are manacled to the posts of the bed with silk scarves.

Close-up of her buttocks shows the lashes left by Sir Grafton's riding whip. A female hand gently, slowly, lovingly, rubs cream into the flesh. The hand has no jewellery and short immaculate nails.

Close-up on Emmeline's face. Her eyes are closed and she is smiling with pleasure.

Close-up of Josepha's face. The expression is one of love.

Close up on Josepha's hand slowly easing the cream into the wounds and then sliding down into the dark crevice of her cunt, which she starts to finger with erotic intent. Emmeline's pelvis jolts towards her and she emits a loud sigh of pleasure as Josepha's now places three fingers deep into her with calm and expert skill. Emmeline is now writhing and pleading.

JOSEPHA

You are very wet.

EMMELINE

I know, I know . . . Please finish me off, Josepha. If you love me, let me come.

JOSEPHA

You know I love you, darling, but he will punish me if he finds out that we have been playing without his permission.

EMMELINE

(still writhing)

Oh God, Josepha – go and get permission, *please*!

20. INTERIOR. SIR GRAFTON'S STUDY

Sir Grafton is sitting in a high-backed leather chair reading the *Racing News*. His legs (still in jodhpurs) are stretched out in front of him. We see that there are spurs on his riding boots, and at his feet, and where a dog might be, a woman lies asleep. She is wearing an all-in-one body suit made out of short-haired black fur. It is cut low at the front allowing a glimpse of the structured bra that pushes up her breasts into bullet points. Her hair is long and black, her eyebrows plucked to a fine arch, her lips painted. Around her neck there is an expensive dog collar decorated with diamonds. Her feet are bare and her toenails are painted dark brown.

A servant is crouched on all fours and is poking the fire in the giant fireplace. She is wearing the outfit of a Victoria maid customised to Sir Grafton's deviant vision. That is, it is made of skin-tight shiny black rubber. There is a white lace apron and white lace at the cuffs. As she bends over at her work the rubber rides up over her waist to reveal that her arse is entirely bare, though she is wearing very sheer black stay-up stockings with seams and a pair of immaculately pointed narrow-fit stiletto shoes ornamented with gold buckles. Her wrist is chained to a heavy coal scuttle.

The naked man has reappeared and is now standing silently in the corner of the room, in the same position and stance as before, head bowed, wrists tied behind his back with rope.

Close-up of Sir Grafton's hand. He is flexing his fingers as if getting them ready to punish somebody. He wears a gold signet ring.
21. INTERIOR. SIR GRAFTON'S STUDY
There is a knock on the door. Sir Grafton looks up from his paper, not pleased at being disturbed.

SIR GRAFTON
(shouting)
Enter!

Josepha enters and kneels at his feet, head bowed.

SIR GRAFTON
Yes, my lovely, what is it?

JOSEPHA
Please, sir, I am seeking permission to pleasure Emmeline.

SIR GRAFTON
How exactly? I am not pleased with Emmeline, Josepha. I do not feel that she deserves any privileges, especially those given by your own sweet self. She is to marry the Duke of Orleans in two weeks' time and she is not ready to be a good wife. This is a sad state of affairs for which he will not only blame me, I suspect, but worse, much worse, he might refuse to pay the considerable sum of money that he has promised me for her hand.

He rustles the *Racing News* in Josepha's face.

And I need the money, Josepha! I need the money!

He stands up and slaps the paper down.

What kind of wife is she going to make: pouting, sulking and answering back? She lounges around this house as if the world owes her a favour. I don't know who spoiled that girl. I really don't, but I'm sure as hell it wasn't me. If Emmeline does not start to behave herself, if she does not impress the Duke, we are all done for! We have a lifestyle to sustain, Josepha, a very pleasurable one to us all, as I think you will agree, but there are thirty or so of you girls to provide for. Thirty! I am landed, Josepha, landed and loaded thanks to the Earl (he indicates the portrait of his ancestor with a dismissive wave of his hand) but not *that* landed and loaded. Everything costs money, my sweet, they cost a lot of money. Look at Dee Dee's dog collar! Five thousand pounds, if you please!

The camera moves in to Dee Dee, the dog-girl lying on the floor, pulling in until it focuses closely on the real diamonds sparkling at the collar on her neck.

I can tell you this, I am not selling any of the family acres because one girl is misbehaving herself. Is there anything you can do? Or will I have to whip her like a wild pony? Thrash those disobedient flanks until the blood runs and the pain tames her? I have had wilder than this, Josepha, as you well know, and I always succeed in making the filly submit to all my demands. If necessary she will go and live in the stables!

Sir Grafton cracks the whip down on a small round table causing the ornaments on it to judder. A china dog jumps to the floor and smashes near Dee Dee. The dog-girl jumps and howls out with surprise.

JOSEPHA

I will do my best, sir, but she is a complicated person . . .

SIR GRAFTON

Of that I am sure, and overeducated I suspect, thanks to me. Though God knows, that bloody governess should have pushed her over the desk and rulered her bottom for her. As it was I spent my whole time pulling down the governess's panties in an effort to make her do her job properly. She wore Joy by Jean Patou, as I recall. And her thighs? Her thighs . . .

He stares out of the window. We see a brief memory flashback of a schoolroom. The governess, a neat woman of 36 with a prim expression and dark-red hair smoothed into a tight bun, has been tied, with thick rope, face down, on to an old-fashioned Victorian rocking horse. Her head is positioned over the horse's nose, her wrists and ankles are tied underneath its body. Her long navy-blue skirt with voluminous lace petticoats has been pulled over her back so that the top of her body can hardly be seen and her face is partially hidden by the petticoats. The red lipstick on her lips has smeared.

Being forcibly tied forward means that the governess's generous bottom is pushed up and displayed. She is wearing a skin-tight pair of black cotton high-waisted school underpants and a 50s-style garter-belt with stockings and suspenders. But it is not her bottom with which Sir Grafton is concerned. It is her large, sensual mouth. Emmeline stands at the tail end of the rocking horse wearing a tight school uniform comprising a tiny white school shirt, a tie, and a tight dark-grey hobble skirt which prohibits any step larger than three inches at a time. Her hair is tied high on to her head into a ponytail with a ribbon.

She pulls the tail of the horse rhythmically and, as she does so, the bound body of the governess moves towards Sir Grafton, who is standing at the nose end of the rocking horse. He is wearing tight black-leather jodhpurs, old-fashioned black riding boots, spurs, and a master-of-the-hunt jacket (black) with a cravat and gold pin.

His large hard cock is poking through the zip in the leather and, as Emmeline rocks the governess forward on the rocking horse, so the governess's mouth closes over Sir Grafton's purple-headed knob. As Emmeline pulls the horse back, the governess's mouth withdraws.

Thus Emmeline controls the rhythm by which the governess sucks their master off. Sir Grafton issues commands: 'Slower, slower, faster faster,' and so on. The rocking of the horse picks up speed, becoming almost violent. The bound governess's mouth takes Sir Grafton's cock in with frenzied supplication. Finally he withdraws and his come spurts into her face and into the horse's face.

Fade out

22. INTERIOR. SIR GRAFTONS STUDY. PRESENT.

JOSEPHA
Emmeline is very keen on the Duke of Orleans, sir. She wants to marry him. I will impress on her the importance of doing as you say . . .

SIR GRAFTON
Good.

JOSEPHA
And . . .

SIR GRAFTON
What is it, Josepha?

JOSEPHA
May I screw her with my dildo, sir?

SIR GRAFTON
The leather dong that I bought you back from New York?

JOSEPHA
Yes, sir.

Sir Grafton sits down again, leans back on his chair, and looks over into the fireplace, where the half-naked maidservant is still crouched.

SIR GRAFTON
That thing should sort her out, certainly. Come here, Josepha.

Josepha stands up and presents herself in front of Sir Grafton.

SIR GRAFTON
Lift up your skirt.

She slowly pulls the rubber dress to her knees and then up her long lean thighs until finally it is clinging around her waist and we see a pair of high-waisted pants made out of thin black leather and equipped with a tiny, delicate zip at the front. It is chained with a string of gold links and a small padlock. Sir Grafton unlocks the padlock with a key from his key ring, slowly unzips the zip and inserts his finger into the opening. Josepha arches her back, thrusts up her breasts, and groans. Sir Grafton smiles.

SIR GRAFTON
You are a good girl, Josepha, and very very beautiful. I worship you, you know that. And so, yes, you may fuck Emmeline; you may fuck her hard with that dildo. Ring the bell when you are both ready and I

will come and watch. And you had better please me, the both of you, because if you don't ... If you don't ...

JOSEPHA
Yes, sir.

SIR GRAFTON
What do you say, Josepha?

JOSEPHA
Thank you, sir.

SIR GRAFTON
I should think so.

Josepha slowly draws down her dress, wriggling her thighs and her hips as she does so. Then she curtsies and slides out of the room. Sir Grafton gets up, cracks his whip hard against the arm of the leather chair, undoes the button opening in front of his jodhpurs, pulls out his hard dick and strokes it lovingly with his fingers.

He clicks his fingers.

The girl in the black fur bodysuit (Dee Dee) crawls forward with a condom in her mouth. She kneels on the floor at his feet and places her head in his crotch, sliding the condom over his dick with her mouth in one expert movement.

Then, without saying anything, Sir Grafton goes over to the fireplace where the servant girl is still crouched on all fours, her buttocks bared towards him. He unlocks her hand at the coal scuttle, lifts her up, and throws her over the arm of his leather chair and, as if in one movement, thrusts his dick into her so hard that she cries out with pleasure. He is big and stiff; she has been wanting him to fuck her all day.

Her face and body are covered with coal stains from the fire. Sir Grafton's hands spread her buttocks apart. Swopping condoms, he now takes her anally.

Camera point of view from servant girl's eyes. She looks at the naked man still standing in the corner.

Sir Grafton comes, finishes. He swivels her around, gathers her up, and pulls her face towards his lips with his leather-clad hands. He kisses her hard on the mouth and they embrace with passion.

The woman dressed in the fur bodysuit sits back on her knees and watches this scene with a sulky jealous expression on her face. A close-up on her hand reveals that her nails are long and dark and almost clawlike.

Sir Grafton continues to fuck his servant girl over the arm of the chair. She turns her face to look at the face of the girl in the fur suit. She smiles with triumph. The scene fades out to the sound of her having an orgasm.

23. INTERIOR. FIFTEEN MINUTES LATER.
    KITCHEN

The kitchen is large and very old-fashioned with stone flagging. There is an Aga stove with polished chrome knobs, a long wide wooden kitchen table that could seat at least twelve people, shelves stacked with old-fashioned china, saucepans and so on. There is a pie on the surface of the Aga. It is large and the pastry has been meticulously decorated with leaves. There is a hole in the top through which smoke is piping.

The camera slowly takes in some of the equipment hanging from a rack from the ceiling. There are dozens of long silver knives, butter paddles, wooden spoons and equipment that seems to be more designed for medical practice rather than any culinary purpose.

Dee Dee (the dog-girl wearing the skin-tight black fur

suit) is fighting with the servant girl from the previous scene. Dee Dee is furious that the underling has received favouritism from the master.

Dee Dee is well built. Though she spends much time crouched or lying on the floor, she is, in fact, six foot tall (without shoes). She has long legs, large round toned thighs, and she is big-breasted with muscular arms.

Both women are on top of the large wooden table and they are wrestling. Their expressions are furious and their hair is wild. They are evenly matched. Dee Dee, behind the kneeling servant girl, locks her neck with her thighs.

DEE DEE
Surrender, you bitch.

Fade out.

24. INTERIOR. KITCHEN. FIVE MINUTES LATER.
Dee Dee has won and she is taking advantage of her position. The servant girl is forced face down, crouched over her own thighs. Her forehead lies against the wood of the table; her arse is high in the air. Her wrists have been threaded through her legs and bound to her ankles, so that her buttocks are displayed and she cannot move. She is trussed.

Dee Dee is sitting on top of her with her face towards the servant girl's bare buttocks. Her fur-covered rump is on top of the servant girl's face so that she cannot move, and her thighs are on either side of the servant girl's back.

Dee Dee beats the servant girl's bare behind with a large wooden spoon.

The girl, though muffled underneath Dee Dee's fur-covered arse, is screaming, pleading and crying.

Dee Dee continues to beat down on the reddening bottom with determined zeal.

DEE DEE
That will teach you.

25. INTERIOR: EMMELINE'S BEDROOM. LATER THE SAME EVENING.

Emmeline is naked. She is still lying on the double bed but her body has been moved down so that her buttocks are on the edge, at the end of the mattress. Her legs are stretched wide open and each ankle is tied with silk ties about halfway up the bedpost, causing the crevice of her vagina to splay wide open and the muscles of her thighs and calves to become taut.

Close-up. The camera focuses in so close to Emmeline's displayed genitalia that it is at first difficult to see exactly what it is. It seems to be some red flower made of fleshy folds. Camera gradually pulls back and we see the full spectacle of Emmeline's excited cunt.

Camera pulls back further to show the whole scene. Josepha has changed out of her rubber dress. We see her from the back. Her buttocks are bare. There is a leather strap around her waist. Her torso is encased in a metallic corset made of tiny plates of silver bound together with cord. Her pelvis is pushed forward by the height of her shoes, which are silver and spiked.

Camera moves to the front of Josepha. We see a young naked woman, boyish and gamine, with very short hair. Her body is covered from top to bottom in tattoos, naked except for a tiny diamante cup attached to her pudenda by the thin, almost invisible, threads of a flesh-coloured silk.

The tattooed girl is easing the dildo into the harness that Josepha is wearing around her waist. The phallus is made of black leather and is larger than any size seen in nature. Indeed, it is a fearsome-looking thing, and it is difficult to imagine that Emmeline will be able to take it.

Josepha pushes the tattooed girl away from her and points in the direction of Emmeline's presented clitoris.

The tattooed girl kneels on the floor in front of the bed so that her face is a parallel with Emmeline's labia. She licks it enthusiastically. Emmeline's pelvis twists and thrusts as if to get closer to the tongue of the tattooed girl, wanting her to go deeper and deeper.

Sir Grafton Rafton is watching. He is sitting in a large leather armchair in a corner, which is semi-lit to enhance the impression that he is sitting in a shadow of the room. His riding whip is placed across his thighs. He is delicately smoking a long white cigarette. The smoke wafts up and around his face. He looks through it to the scene in front of him.

SIR GRAFTON
Continue.

Close up of Josepha's pelvis with the dildo pushing slowly into Emmeline's wide gap. She eases the phallus into Emmeline, further and further, until she takes it all and Josepha's pelvis is thrusting, hard, like that of a man, deep into Emmeline.

We see Sir Grafton's eye view. He is looking at Josepha's thrusting buttocks and her long lean back. On either side of her are Emmeline's fine long legs, thin ankles tied to the bedposts, the bed vibrating rhythmically as both girls grown out loud.

Emmeline is now shrieking in the frenzy of pleasure. Tears run down her face. Sir Grafton continues to stare at the scene coolly. He lights up another cigarette. There is no emotion at all on his face. We do not know if he is stimulated or interested or bored. He simply stares and smokes. The naked man is shown again, in the corner of this room now, still with his face to the wall, still with his wrists bound behind him with rope.

Fade out

26. INTERIOR: DINING ROOM. BREAKFAST THE NEXT MORNING.

Sir Grafton, wearing pyjamas and a silk dressing gown, sits at the top of a long, polished, dining-room table covered in antique silver candlesticks and cruets. He reads the newspaper. A cup of coffee is steaming in front of him.

He presses a button on the table in front of him and a bell rings in the distance. The door opens and Emmeline enters, crawling on all fours. A small table has been attached to her back. She slowly crawls forward in order to avoid allowing the china on the table to slide to the floor.

She moves noiselessly to where Sir Grafton is sitting. He looks down, without any expression, and lifts the milk up from the table. Then he takes the sugar and a plate. Emmeline stays where she is, in this position, while he eats breakfast.

He says nothing, but when he has finished, he strokes her buttocks and the tops of her thighs. She is wearing a lacy lingerie set – a flimsy black bra that does not hold her breasts and transparent culottes, made of black gauze and ribboned at the top of the thigh. Her stay-up stockings are very sheer and she is wearing a pair of dark-brown ankle boots with stiletto heels.

Dee Dee crawls towards her, pulls down the culotte, and licks between the crevice of Emmeline's cheeks.

SIR GRAFTON
Stop that, Dee Dee!

Dee Dee takes no notice and continues to lose herself in Emmeline's arse, licking her anus with animal groans. Sir Grafton slashes Dee Dee with his whip. Then he pulls her away, drags her across the floor to the door, opens it and throws her outside. We hear her banging and whining. He opens the door again. We do not see anything but we hear a loud crack. Then there is silence.

27. EXTERIOR. GARDEN AT GRAFTON RANGE. LATER THE SAME MORNING

Camera pans over the garden showing the full view. It is early. The sun has just risen and there is a heavy coat of dew on the grass. Pearl-dipped spiders' webs hang from plants. The overall effect is of the lush private beauty owned by a very rich man.

The garden is large, grand, landscaped and well maintained. The camera records an apparently normal vista with blooming roses, cucumber frames, neatly trimmed pathways and lily ponds. The scene is apparently innocent until the following scenes are documented:

28. EXTERIOR: GARDEN

A huge old tree with many twisted branches and a lush canopy of leaves seems to be ordinary enough until, on closer inspection, it is apparent that it has been doctored to cater for the predilections so liberally entertained at the House of Rafton. Five different girls are tied up in it, all beautiful, all shapely, all wearing black satin mini-culottes, thigh-high stay-up stockings, white cotton panties, and white cotton shirts, a size too small, open at the front to reveal their heaving and well-formed breasts, some encased by lift-up bras, some naked, some actually hanging from the gapes in their shirts.

One girl, blindfolded, is tied with thick rope and an immaculate series of knots, to the branch of the tree itself.

One girl is tied face down on a thick horizantal branch.

One is hanging by her wrists from a harness arrangement.

One, tied to the other side of the tree, has her face to the trunk and her panties down by her ankles as if she has just been casually fucked by a passing stranger.

One has been attached to a child's swing with a complicated network of chains. She is wearing a moulded latex mask with no features. She breathes through a tiny hole made at the mouth. Her shirt has fallen open to her waist and her exposed breasts are heaving. She is not sitting down in the conventional position on the swing. She lies on her front over the seat with her stomach tied down on it. Her wrists and ankles are tied together underneath the seat. She is gagged with a white handkerchief.

Another woman lies underneath the swing. She has been tied up with rope in order to position her face between the buttocks of the girl above her, thus the cheeks in the tight girdle act as a gag. Neither girl can move.

29. EXTERIOR. GARDEN. CUCUMBER FRAME

The cucumber frame looks empty until the camera moves in closer to reveal that two young black girls are lying in it. They wear tight cotton aertex shirts, white stay-ups and white stilettos. One is playing with a cucumber, gently inserting it into her excited gash with moans of pleasure, then removing it, kissing the girl beside her, and pleasuring her, also with a cucumber.

Alongside one flower bed, as if to make a border, is a row of white bottoms, all uniform in size, all placed at regular intervals along the edge. They belong to the women crouched forward, all wearing white gloves, all with gardening baskets, all engaged in weeding. They are sitting on their knees and we see that their feet are wearing customised rubber bootees that fit like skin to their feet and calves and are equipped with small spiked heels made out of silver.

A muscular man walks past them. He is wearing a leather apron and a T-shirt through which his strong biceps can be seen. His feet are in big black boots and he is holding a water can. As he moves slowly past the row of working women he sprays water from the can over their backs and their bottoms, and though we never see their faces, their buttocks wriggle in appreciation.

We follow him to a leafy bower where a woman is attached to a pair of medieval stocks. He lets her free and places her on an old-fashioned hay-making trolley with wheels. Then he binds her with a long ream of soft fabric with a silver sheen so that she looks like a mermaid, legs bound, breasts bare, long blonde wavy hair falling down her back. Once she has been thus immobilised, he lifts her on the trolley and drags her down the garden path towards the house.

30. EXTERIOR. GARDEN. SAME TIME

Long view. From the distance we see Sir Grafton walking down a long avenue of blossom holding Emmeline's hand. They seem to be engaged in pleasant enough conversation until, suddenly, she rips her hand out of his, turns to face him, and we hear the loud word:

No!

He slaps her in the face. She kicks him in the shin and then runs away from him. She can do do this because she is wearing tiny skin-tight shorts made of tartan. Her midriff is bare and her torso covered in a tiny tight jumper made of pink cashmere. She kicks off the ankle boots that she is wearing and runs, feet now only in white knee-socks.

Sir Grafton runs after her, catches her, rugger-tackles her to the grass. They wrestle for some minutes until she surrenders. He sits on top of her, pinning her arms above her head until she is silent. He leans down over her and kisses her on the mouth. She responds with enthusiasm. One of her hands escapes from his and she tries to grab at his cock. He slaps her hand away and restrains it again. With his other hand he rips down her white lacy panties and shoves them into her mouth. Then he picks her up and throws her over his shoulder. She beats his back and screams at him. We see the back view, wriggling buttocks, legs flailing wildly. He carries her to the greenhouse.

31. INTERIOR. GREENHOUSE GARDEN. FIFTEEN MINS LATER

Camera slowly pans down the length of the greenhouse, recording the moist sensuality of the ripe fruit hanging from various branches. There are tomatoes, apples, melons and obscene courgettes. We see that the mysterious woman wrapped up in the black bag has been relocated to the greenhouse, where she lies, breathing and wriggling, in a large clean aluminium wheelbarrow.

At the end of a passage, through a jungle of plants and foliage, there is a doorway with no door. Emmeline is spread-eagled across it. She is naked except for her white knee socks. Her bush is shaved and somebody has placed an orchid betweeen the lips of her mons veneris. She has been blindfolded, but not gagged. Her tongue runs over her moist lips. There are hooks fixed at all four corners of the door jamb and her wrists and ankles are tied to them.

Close-up. Sir Grafton's face next to Emmeline.

SIR GRAFTON

Tomorrow, Emmeline, tomorrow you are going to marry the Duke of Orleans. He wants it, I want it, you want it. You know that. Don't let me down.

EMMELINE

(submissive)

Yes, sir. I am ready.

32. INTERIOR. NEXT DAY. SIR GRAFTON'S STUDY

Close-up. We see the familiar hand of Sir Grafton with the ring, sleeve and cufflinks receive a large pile of cash from another male hand.

33. INTERIOR. WEDDING CHAPEL. SOON AFTER

This is a high-church chapel, with flickering candlelight, rich red velvets, dark carvings, ornamental crucifixes, and stained-glass windows showing the contorted features of the martyrs twisted in pain. Camera lingers briefly over monks whipping each other, and Saint Sebastian, body bleeding with arrow wounds.

The music begins as a Gregorian chant and develops into the pompous orchestration of a traditional wedding march. At first we see only Emmeline, from the front, in a wedding dress customised to suit deviant desire. That is, it is very short, made of shiny white satin, and teamed with a pair of thigh-high white patent boots, laced up the front, and equipped with high stiletto heels so thin, so dangerous-looking, it is hard to believe that they can withstand her weight.

Her veil is a wild affair, bunches of net, that she pulls back from her face to reveal that she is wearing a smug expression. The flowers are the more vulgar type of lily, with phallic stamens. Around her waist on a chain there is a bible. The camera shifts to the back view of the Duke of Orleans, Emmeline's husband, and we see that it is the naked man who has appeared, wrists bound, face to the wall, in the other scenes. Dark hair snakes down his shoulders. He is still naked, though his hands are now freed in order to conduct the ring ceremony.

As the vicar finishes the final words of the service the Duke of Orleans looks down at his bride with tender love and kisses her gently.

34. INTERIOR. HONEYMOON SUITE. NEXT DAY.

A grand double bed with ornately carved bedposts. The Duke of Orleans is kneeling on the floor with his chin on the end of the bed. His ankles have been tied into the kneeling position; his hands are in front of him, chained to the bedposts on either side. The flowers from Emmeline's bridal posy have been forced into his mouth. He is wearing lipstick and a pair of sheer, frilly girl's panties.

Emmeline is standing astride him so that white patent-leather boots are on either side of him and her face is near his. She is holding a long, thin, leather belt and she is viciously beating his back, buttocks and thighs. This scene is being conducted to the sound of 'Perfect Day' by Lou Reed. The Duke of Orleans is writhing in pain and moaning but patently pleased to be dominated by his new wife.

DUKE
I love you, oh Mistress mine.

EMMELINE
(Lashing his arse.)
Ah well, you know, my love, if there is one rule in life it is that you cannot be a good top if you have never been a bottom.

She lashes him again and then pushes her hand (wearing a white kid-leather glove) down into the flimsy fabric of his lacy panties. The bulge of his dick swells and hardens to her touch.

Camera pulls back. One more shot zooms in on her legs, closer and closer, to detail the surface of the shiny plastic of the boots, so that the overall picture is lost as the white background becomes bigger and bigger, providing abstract patterns, as if seen under a microscope. Credits begin to roll up over this to the sound of 'Perfect Day', and the crack of Emmeline's leather belt.

EMMELINE
Ah, my love. We are destined to live happily ever after.

End

Chapter Three

The ordeals of Emmeline were not without their erotic appeal and my hand slipped underneath the waistband of the tight Capri pants as I finished reading the last few pages. There was a tingle in between my legs, and it was beginning to spread. I knew the feeling well. Soon I would need dick, and I wouldn't be fussy who was on the end of it. In Hollywood there was always so much choice. A girl hardly needed to pack her vibrator.

Hollywood had the right to fuck and fuck it did. Degeneration had become a tradition the day that the first orange grove was razed to build a studio. If a 20s girl wanted sex she simply had to fly to the place that Cecil built and go to an orgy up at the Chaplin pad. All this and the Moral Majority too. It was a heady mixture and one on which I had long thrived, revering a legend of louche whose epochs of self-indulgence landed big Errol in court and starlets up the spout.

Who would not surrender to Errol, though? The perfect man for the Tarzan mate in all of us. Who would not be the maiden tied to the mast of the ship, the maiden tied to the railway line, the maiden tied to the inside of a lion's cage, all heaving breasts and frayed cave-lady skimpiness, perfect fit, perfectly lit, perfectly dipped with the free-flow juice of cine-screen youth?

Once the desert had minded its own business. A couple of coyotes and a Mexican, that was it. Then along came pirates, gangsters and sheiks. I could not see myself in a Valentino harem, exactly; I am not made to be Number 34. A pirate's babe? Bit rough.

I would have been a flapper androgyne – all seamed stockings, furs, the cloche, jewels, lips and lesbo sex when it was fun and not politics. A little silk pyjama, a long cigarette holder, a vast mansion of cream and gold filled with all the boys one wanted to buy and all the girls who had somehow managed to avoid suicide and were devoted to champagne.

Imagine lying in the middle of one of those round beds with some dashing superhero. Imagine being in a Chinese opium den with Clara Bow. Imagine going round to John Gilbert's house, where there were Cossack servants and a private orchestra. Imagine Gloria Swanson in her black marble bath.

You would have had one of those long 20s cars, all shiny walnut and leather seats, a black Packard touring sedan, perhaps, with a serious uniformed chauffeur, male or female, in skin-tight black jacket, jodhpurs, riding boots, gold buttons, gloves. Drivers by day, sexual bandits by night. Cruising from salon to mansion, from poolside to ocean lair, always being fabulous and looking good and getting fucked like crazy by people like, well, people like Errol Flynn and people like Marlene, ever cool in man drag.

And you? You are in long silk evening dress, tiny silk camis, a rope of pearls, buttoned shoes, a tiny suspender. Lying on the back seat there will be a fake leopardskin beneath you and some director on top.

It was a time to be bisexual and to be rich and to be without care for the future or romance or convention. The survivors then, and now, know how to handle the sleaze of Hollywood. They know not to bother to look for love and to avoid husbands at all costs. Husbands are always a disaster in Hollywood. It's not the place for them. It is the place for work and sex and driving. If you want a washing machine go to the Valley.

I wouldn't want to be Mae West: too vaudeville, too pantomine, too 'would someone like to come up from the audience and help me with my magic trick?' I wouldn't want to be one of the Maries – Astor or Pickford – too *Little Women* victims. I would be a cool sick bitch-goddess, a shimmying sociopath, rich and detached and ambivalent, dominating the girls, submitting to the boys, so no one knew where they were. But boy would those ideas spread till everyone had a chauffeur employed to screw and drive, and everyone would have hordes of whores with bizarre clothes travelling as an entourage of tinsel-decked pussy, looking as if they would do anything because they would do anything.

I, as the Queen Bee, would have had the best hat, the longest gloves, the thinnest waist, the best thighs, the highest shoes, the longest furs, the largest tiaras, the sharpest wit, the best money, the most power.

To do who one wishes, when one likes, wherever one pleases, these are the prizes of Hollywood, same in the 20s, same in the 30s, same in the 90s. There is much truth in phoneyness and the truth is still out there, among the implants and diets and buttocks and bellies.

No one bothers to lie about it.

They all want a pool and a car.

I shrugged off this comforting erotica of deluxe nostalgia and hauled myself into the present of Leon's pool and the ideas of Emmeline and whether I could be bothered, all motivations having long ago been sacrificed to the sybaritism made possible by my father's ill-gotten and well-hidden gains. These welcome funds currently poured forth as beautiful unearned dividends from a nameless account in Nassau.

I had fucked enough retards to know that I could act. I'm kind in that way, God knows why – some infirmity bestowed by genotype I suppose, but I could have a convincing orgasm (who can't and who hasn't?), and I could persuade a pencil dick that he was big prick in order to get him hardened up for one of those nights of quicksilver sex that one really should not bother with.

So I knew I could easily be Emmeline and indulge myself in the glamazon and pervery of it all; there were scenes in that script that could be fun.

The itch grew into a wet patch, almost uncomortable now. I slid three fingers sharply underneath my thong; their fumblings were obstructed by my clothes. Impatiently I leapt off the lounger and pulled my trousers down and off. I had access now. I closed my eyes and worked into the natural lubrication, pumped four fingers vigorously and wondered if it would be impolite to give myself a vaginal and a clitoral orgasm at the same time, here by Leon's pool. I was pretty sure that Leon wouldn't mind: abandoned sex was the stuff of his profession, after all, but who else was around?

These thoughts, like some biblical miracle, seemed to conjur up the shadow that now appeared before me. A Mexican appeared with a pair of secateurs. He was young, dark and muscular and when he smiled his face filled with rows of brilliant white teeth.

'I am Jesus,' he said.

My hand was halfway up my cunt and my legs were straddled so that my feet were on the floor on either side of the lounger. I still had the cat's-eye shades on (darling, never take them off! Look through the present darkly, that's my motto) so I was caught in the act, he standing over me, grinning, I looking up at him and wondering if he was real. Herein the son of the Lord, his miracles to perform.

There was nothing for it but to allow him in. Those wide-built South American men always have good dicks, they usually know what to do with them, and, because they tend to do labour that's very physical, they are possessed of a stamina which I can recommend. I have met a lot of them out bowling and I can tell you this, the man with the good right arm is the man who can push you up against a wall and pump you for at least half an hour. Believe me.

Jesus stared down at me, briefly at my face, then at my legs, presenting their glistening display of swollen lip and wanton clit, then at my fingers, moist with self-manipulation.

He leaned down, placed the secateurs carefully on the grass, removed his gardening gloves and his gardening hat, ambled over to the lounger on which I was splayed, like bargain merchandise in a July sale, kneeled at the end of the sunbed, pulled my legs down towards him by the ankles, split my thighs further apart, put his head between them and planted a strong, hard, determined tongue right on top of my clitoris with a force that nearly jolted me on to the ground.

I moaned out involuntarily, hardly knowing where I was for a second or two, and a second or two skydiving is a long time when you're not sure how you are going to land or where.

Two seconds increased to five or seven or ten or twenty and he would not stop. I was going to have to give it up to him. I knew that he was going to make me come before he rammed that hard cock into me, and come I did. Loudly, very enjoyably, and, as I did so, he put his finger into me to feel those little vibrations, and, before these pulses had ebbed away, he had removed his dick from his gardening jeans and slithered a condom on himself.

Yes, it was wide, and it was long enough too; a gift in fact, of the type for which the girl must show gratitude.

He let me stare at him for a few minutes, taking in what I was going to get.

'You want thees, *muchacha*?' he said

'*Si, señor!*'

Smiling with those great white teeth, he replaced himself, kneeling, at the bottom of the sunbed, so that his rock-hard dick was resting on the edge. He pulled my pelvis towards him, then eased me over his dick, so that my legs came to rest around his waist. Then he pumped into me, and that girth, that girth was wonderful, as he felt his way into all the right places, as if they were his own property and he had an inalienable macho right to explore them. My own fingers tickled the clitoris and, in a moment of extraordinary synchronicity, as I exploded underneath my stomach, so too did he, and he seemed to lose himself for minutes, hugging me tight, eyes closed, mind in some faraway place from which he could not return.

'Oh Jesus!' I cried. 'Jesus! Jesus! Jesus!'

His brown eyes opened. He stared into my face, removed my dark glasses, and kissed me.

'*Carina*,' he whispered. 'You make Jesus very very happy.' He smiled broadly. The sun caught his hair as he slowly stood up, pulled up his loose jeans, buckled himself back in, and collected up his gardening implements. Then, waving briefly, still smiling, he disappeared down a leafy lane and into a rhododendron bush.

I replaced the shades, put on my thong, and lay awhile enjoying the postcoital satisfaction, those fleeting moments of centred magnanimity that orgasm and a real man inevitably bring. I was still dozing in abstract detachment when Leon reappeared with a little Filipino girl bearing a tray of fresh drinks.

'Over there, Consuela . . .'

'So,' he said, 'what did you think?'

'Fantastic,' I automatically answered, thinking that he was referring to the holy experience of praising Jesus.

'Oh good! So you will be Emmeline, then?'

'Oh, yes . . . the script.'

I re-entered the real world slowly and with great difficulty.

The script. Emmeline.

'What did you think I meant, dopey?'

'Well it certainly seemed to do its job,' I said.

'Made you wet?'

'Made me wet, Leon. Made me want to get fucked.'

'Goodo. So are you in, then?'

'Yeah.'

Two hours later, driving down Sepulveda, I realised that Leon had been wearing a pair of binoculars around his neck and I began to wonder what he had been watching with them.

Enlivened by the idea of extra cash with which to buy unecessary luxury items, I smoothed the convertible down the twisting roads away from the canyons and spent the afternoon in a mall near Rodeo Drive.

I went for a massage in Big Bob's Pummel Lounge. The masseuse was new but I was accustomed to this. Nobody seemed to stay at Big Bob's for long. Nobody in LA stayed anywhere for long. They had fame to chase and authorities to avoid.

In the past I had been pummelled by a warlock from Crescent Heights and by a person who claimed that he was possessed by the spirit of the late Latino disco queen, Selena, though my fondest memory was of a large leather dyke, trained in the arts of osteopathy and psychosexual fantasy, who would cover one with delicious musky smells, crick out the knots, vibe up the muscles with her brutish man-hands, mend the spine, calm the spirit, and then finish it all off with any scene one wished to enact.

The woman could do anything: whipping, wax, anal,

fist, all as smooth as a caress and all in a ripped black T-shirt that said 'Fuck Art. Let's Dance'.

I can remember her motherly breasts, her manly biceps, her strong hands, the fabulous calm kinkiness of her presence, but I can't remember what she was called. She was well worth the $45. I should have married her.

Now, though, the cubicle was filled with the presence of an Irish man with long black and grey hair that drooped as strings down his face and on to his shoulders, where some of the tails had been plaited into arrangements of small glass beads.

His body – lean, brown and sinewy – looked as if it had just been charmed out of a wicker basket in Delhi. I could imagine his legs plaited together in some impossible yogic contortion. I could imagine him living on top of a mountain in Tibet. I could see him in some Zen priestly pastime, with a wooden bowl and sandals, but I could not guess his age. He could have dated back to the Turin shroud; he could have been 28. Only the grey told of maturity, and grey is no aid to an accurate estimate.

'My name is Anton,' he said. 'But you can call me Conlan.'

He had palms the size of frying pans and fingers that were so long and thin and whose joints were so bulbous, the digits looked as if they had been tied into knots. He flexed them carefully. All his metacarpals and phalanges, wrist bones and palm bones were visible underneath the tight brown skin of forefingers, ring fingers and thumbs – the bones grinding against each other. Then he wriggled all ten digits as if he was preparing to sit down and play the piano.

'I got these from me mutthur,' he said, indicating that his hands were his inheritance. 'Mrs Pat O'Connor. She also left me a commode, lovely thing, but I gave it to my sister in Donegal.'

I allowed the pink towel to drop from my body and

stared at myself for a few seconds in the long mirror set up underneath a sign saying: SILENCE PLEASE.

I am not tall, but I have round breasts, hard nipples, a thin waist and a firm schoolgirl's arse that likes attention. I am lithe and brown and neat. A boyish body for the buggers, a girlish chest for the straight het, a strict black Louise Brooks bob for anyone who likes a mistress, and an easy pout for those who like to push a girl's head down on to their shoes and make her lick the night away. Ah, yes. I can be all things to all men and to all women. I am eminently versatile, amorally adaptable, and I have imagination – that deadly sin and useful vice.

Naked, except for a tiny mauve cotton thong, I lowered myself slowly on to the warm towel that had been laid over his massage table. He covered me with another pink towel, which barely covered my arse, and, though I was face down, I sensed that he was surveying the length of my brown back, the curve of the white bum, the smooth brown thighs; even the painted silver toenails and the tiny gold chain on my ankle.

He was naked except for a knotted leather lace around his neck, a miniskirt made out of chamois leather, and a generous application of juniper. He gently pulled the towel a little way down my arse so that more of the flesh was exposed to him and he could see the indelible letters, RESPECT, tattooed black into my white cheek by the order of Jim, the great fuck and serious sadist I was dating at the time.

I wondered what Conlan made of the letters, but he said nothing. He worked in LA, of course; body modification in all its extremes must have passed before his eyes. Many dramas of skin pictures, implants, uplifts and sutures must have spread themselves before him, nude, submissive, vulnerable and surgically enhanced.

'I will do my Lomi Lomi transformational Tantric technique,' he said. 'It gives psychostructural balancing.

I tink you will foind it very relaxing, very relaxing indeed.'

'OK,' I said.

I looked up at the clock. It was 2.10 p.m. When I looked up again it was 3.03. I was still face down and Conlan was pushing the fingers that he had inherited from his mother in Donegal into places that are all too often overlooked by massage disciplines. This was followed by the use of the part of his body more closely related to his father than his mother. Penetrating me slowly from the back, he smoothed his dick up and down inside me, up and down, minute on minute, a stroke rather than a thrust, an easy insinuation rather than rough vigour, on and on as the clock ticked.

The hands went slowly around, and I wondered if he would ever or could ever stop, hard as he was for so much time, unhurried in his skill and determined in his unbeatable sexual strength. I let him do as he wished, as I knew it was the only way to be with him, to appreciate the full length of the dick slinking its way in and out of my cunt, his fingers slowly teasing my clit until, of course, the breath came with pleasure and there were mutual gasps as he bought us both to a series of Tantric multi-orgasms. As waves of pure pleasure ripped up and down my body I wondered briefly if I was about to see the light of which so many spoke.

'Thank you,' I said as everything finally shuddered to a halt and he withdrew.

'Very relaxing.'

He stared down at me.

'You are a lovely colleeen,' he said. 'You are a Rose of Trelee, one of the finest I have ever seen and I can assure you I have seen many in this land of loose angels. I have seen the Mother Mary herself. She came to me as a vision in the middle of the night, skin as soft as silken pyjamas, eyes as green as the sea that carries you to the islands of Galway, but she was not as fine as you.'

I pushed a tip into his knotted fingers as, carried away by throes of Tantric ecstasis, he began to recite the verses of the famous Irish poet Declan O'Hanlon.

I closed the door behind me. Lomi Lomi was all very well, but there was shopping to do.

I scored a lo-fat iced Frappucino laced with Tia Maria and, feeling euphoric with postcoital caffeine delight, I skipped in and out of shoe shops, through a maze of candy emporiums, through Pretzelmania and, finally, to Busts of Beverly Hills.

I did not need to buy any underwear but need is not the currency of the mall. Busts of Beverly Hills was known to be the 'Nation's Number One Outlet for Intimate Apparel'. They prided themselves on a high staff-to-client ratio which was 'guaranteed to enhance the shopping experience'.

Their ranges were comprehensive. The 'apparel' stretched from the outrageous cheapo glam sported by the feather-trimmed lap dancing girls of the Strip, to the tiny panties of the platinum calendar tarts, to the unashamed fantasy costumes of the high-class hooker (schoolgirl, nurse, baby, puppy – you name it) to the designer-labelled silks worn by serious Stars of the night.

I swept through 'lovely buns' power-stretch spandex 'briefers', and 'starlet black' girdles with super-firm curve control. I fingered things that were wispy and things that swore to create swelling where none naturally existed. I ambled past thong-panties to a department devoted to bras: plunging, moulded, seamless, foam lined, underwired and convertible. The shop sold support for all types. Chest could be pushed up by lace, pumped up with water, described by translucent mesh and controlled with good old-fashioned bone.

I saw a helpful-looking woman hovering over a rack of terry-towel bathrobes.

'Do you know how much these are?' I enquired, shaking an item that described itself as a sheer bralette.

'I don't work here,' the woman replied. 'I'm Michelle Pfeiffer.'

I fingered the panties. Racks dripped with the widest selection of gussets, lace and sateen in the world. No panty style was left out of the options offered by Busts of Beverly Hills: no side tie G-string ('full palette of bold colours!'), no animal print thong, no diamanté pussy-pusher or hi-cut butt brief were excluded from display in the pink-carpeted 'panty boutique'.

This stretched over the entire second floor and was provided with a bar at one end. Pink leather sofas were provided where the paying men could sit and scrutinise the goods they were about to purchase on the girls they had already bought.

I felt a panty-lust come upon me – that retail greed that can visit any shopper at any time and extinguish discrimination with wild words of madness that say, *'I want them, I will have them, and I do not care!'* It is an urge and a compulsion and a wonderful fulfilment to the modern girl who knows where to find true happiness. Look not to romance, look not to a career, look in the bottom of the bargain bin of Busts of Beverly Hills.

My tastes are eclectic in this area. I have no loyalty to brand or style, although I prefer underwear that is made to be seen, appreciated and pulled off. I had little ivory silk bikini briefs for everyday life, sateen thongs for buttock-hugging evening dresses and latex knickers to go under very short skirts so that when I bent over, to mend the car, say, the fortunate onlooker was comforted by the picture of my arse encased in that shiny, shiny wetlook black. Then there were rompers for the Lolita lust, beautiful embroidered taupe high-waisters with satin control panels in which to be forcibly taken by somebody who looked like the Croatian doctor in *ER*, some schoolgirl cotton gym pants (navy blue, always in demand) and a white latex and lace crotchless number, very tight, high on the leg, that looked innocent enough until you spread your legs to reveal a slit that allowed access to all entries.

This was particularly effective when teamed with a gold and white sharkskin 'bullet' bra (moulded to press the breasts into Barbarella points) worn underneath a white lace catsuit with a pair of open-toe two-inch platform mules made, by and large, out of perspex and silver leather and graced with heels made out of real nails.

My favourite panties, though, are from a line made of closely woven, completely sheer nylon with a white panel covering the pussy. They give the appearance of semi-nudity. Observed from the back the sight is firm bum; from the front, pervy puss. The whole is perfected by a simple, white pull-on suspender belt with elastane panels and silver clips.

Stockings? Shear, seamed, French heel; old-fashioned, plain, (no diamante, no Viv Westwood print, no silly patterns). These endow a smell of 40s *femme mechant*, and the modern man a good day if he manages to catch those legs struggling to get out of a convertible, or walking up the stairs, or engaged in any of those mundane urban activities that can all be sexualised with enough thought.

This I know. The magic is simple. It is a shoe, it is an ankle, it is the curve of the bum or the crevice of the unembarrassed cleavage placed in places where they are least expected and thus most effective. And so, through the 'Leg Salon', to the place selling what the French call the *porte-jarretelle* and what we call – with so much less erotic finesse – a suspender belt.

It is a tricky item – trickier than some people would imagine. Designed, for the most, to be worn by strippers, hookers and ambitious transvestites, suspender belts are costume, and costume is not always the mood that one is in. We are not here to do the cancan. We who are inspired by Anita Ekberg rather than by Benny Hill must argue against endless baby-blue lace and ruffled nylon effects that itch the skin and ruin the line of any clothes smoothed over the top of them.

Most garter belts are exaggerated in their creation and made to be worn only by lingerie models who have nothing to do except lean against wardrobes. Their job is to encourage unsuspecting onlookers to get married purely so that they can wear some frilly thing on the so-called first night of married bliss, a night, by the way, which is all too often the only night of satisfactory coitus.

I do not like the commerce of the garter belt, the manipulation of its rites, the gaudy expectation of *Brides* magazine and the unspoken dictate that says only one night is allowed.

My own affections are for plain lines where function advertises everyday use and everyday use is the sign of true kink. Things that can be worn only in the bedroom or on the stage are less erotic than those of more practical design that can be worn all over the place. The world should be the bedroom. Then fantasy can escape from confinement and play all over the place. Though only a select few will have the privilege of recognising the true dynamics of this subtle language of lechery.

My collection of garter belts is simple, wearable and effective. Black and white only, comfortable cottons or glam satin-sheen, the girdles are moulded close to the hips and pelvis, the suspenders are plain and made of metal. They are not the stuff of the second date (when you have shaved the legs, you know you're going to shag him, and you want to impress the sap out of him with incredible fuck-wear snatched from the racks that same day), but the stuff of an everyday reality that can cater for any adventure or surprise.

One day I expect I will end up in hospital and, in the event of this, as my poor broken body lies attractively in blood-spattered white Jacquard garter belt and the shearest stockings, an unconscious model of lawless provocation, I expect to accommodate the best possible care from that Croatian doctor on *ER*.

'Christ,' he will think, as he stitches up various places. 'I wish more people looked like that when they are wheeled in on the trolley.'

The fourth floor was the 'Foundation Forum' and all the Spandex powernet secrets of the long-legged panty girdle, the split-crotch body shaper and the corselette. This was manned by a trio of '*corsetieres*' comprising one femme-gent and two middle-aged women, all trim, all wearing black, and all knowing what they were about when it came to figure regulation.

The man patently wore his products himself, moving as he did with stiff-backed, wasp-waisted precision.

Two full-breasted, wide-bottomed, silk-skinned South American chicks were being poured into traditional corsets made out of bone and equipped with twenty or so eyelets that, after some pulling by the attendants who stood behind them, hands on threads, rendered the louche-looking customers with a structured confinement that pushed their breasts over the lace and gave them hourglass figures that exaggerated their arses.

They were as sleazy as hell and fabulous with it. The sluts. I wanted to suck their tits there and then, but I pulled myself away from this spell of spiral lacing and nostalgic brocade, swept past a blonde supernubile with tattooed tits, to the place of my penchant – the foundation garment.

Busts of Beverly Hills supplied a comprehensive range of girdles, body shapers, waist cinchers and full-control elastane all-in-ones. The last of these was my predilection. They combined a bra, panty girdle (sometimes), suspenders and reinforced nylon fibre that flattened the stomach, enhanced the arse to a perfect mound of smooth orbs and lifted the breasts into a cheesecake pantomime of nostalgic wantonness.

These tight-lace shapers advertised mature madams

with a lot of flesh to spill over the cups and straps. They were created for those fuller-figured Mrs Robinson matrons who needed a pinch and a winch and to lose half an inch.

They imbued the confinee with instant kink, whose charisma has never failed me. They are the undies spotted on the mother by the inevitable seven-year-old who has conducted searches and knows that she has drawers full of scented suspenders and limp seamed stockings. He will never ever lose the memory of the secret sights of her comforting pink flesh spilling over lace with her derrière forced into a satisfying Oedipal mind-fuck encased in a panel of unforgiving nylon.

The all-in-one is very difficult to peel off the body. Even with modern zippers and snap crotches, they are garments that confine the flesh and prohibit entrance to all but the most determined sexual predator. An effort has to be made; a hard-on has to be sustained. I like the idea of that. The foundation garment is a good test for stamina.

I sifted through 'Madame' (black, four garters, split-crotch, lace cuff at the leg); 'Goddess' (triple front inner panel, sheer lace bra-cups, easi-split crotch); 'Diva' (boned and underwired), but the 'Starlet' seemed to have it all. Made of lightweight nylon for comfort, the label said it offered total control of stomach, hips and thighs. Built from black lace, it was constructed with a panel at the centre of the pelvis that pinched the waist and gave shape to hips and arse. There were decorative firming panels at the front and back, underwired cups, comfortable bra straps, and a darling little hook-and-eye crotch. A snip at $40.

A tiny lesbo-crow with tape measure, strict mouth, crew cut and sharp red nails, slowly hooked me in, checking that it was the right size by pushing her fingers between the black lace and my skin. Reaching down into the middle of my breasts to see that they were snugly restricted, she stroked my nipples as she did so. Running her hands over the black nylon lace that lifted the buttocks, she eased the red nail between my legs to slowly fasten the hooks that lined the seam there.

I looked in the mirror. There I was, all breast, arse, thighs, encased in black lace and elastane, not an inch of flesh out of place, a smooth model of bottom-drawer sluthood.

Pervery wafted around the lesbo-crow like vapour. I know a dedicated voyeur when I see one. They are unashamed in their staring, and this one had taken a career that gave her a God-given right to peruse all the facets of all ages of flesh for eight hours everyday. She indulged herself in full-time sexual speculation with an hour off for lunch and the occasional detour to make checks in the stockroom.

She must have seen it all, this little mistress with pursed lips and tape measure; she must have fondled every breast in town in the name of comfort and poise. I suspected she enjoyed training and restraint and thus she enjoyed her job. Lord knows where her mind went with the zipper-front closures and sheer net and tiny lace flowers; she must have floated in a dream world made of soft cup designs and hourglass silhouettes.

'I think that's about right,' she said.

'Yes,' I said.

'It's fuckin' fabulous,' said another voice.

I looked around to see a six-foot-tall glamazon with raven-black hair, black fringe and a black ponytail surging out of the middle of the back of her head. She was bare-legged, legs splayed, feet in high black court shoes, like some dream drawing come to life with her stick ankles, toned thighs, huge arse, tiny waist. And her tits? Round and white and firm and large, large, large. All this divine provocation had been poured into a black-lace *Guepiere*.

Modelled on the original Dior version of 1947, the

undergarment was a tight lacework sheath with black satin/latex panel control and suspenders. A girdle and a bra all in one, it had been popularised in a Diana Dors pin-up, updated by various hip designers, and, on this fabulous stranger, took on an atmosphere of dominant decadence as it controlled her generous proportions and gave her an hourglass figure.

Her jaw was firm, her pitch-black brows plucked into strict lines, her eyeliner was thick and black, her skin was white and blotched with the occasional unfathomable mark – a tiny bruise on her upper arm, a mole at the top of her cleavage. These allowed me to imagine strange stranglings in the middle of the night. She had divine cynicism and hard-rock sensuality. My favourite.

Her clothes had been dropped into a pool on the floor, all manly, and I bet she emptied her pockets of change and left it on the dresser at night. Subtly I scrutinised the discarded garments. Black stretch Levi's lay with a black scoop-neck T-shirt. A Chanel handbag was open and revealed the full story as surely as guts thrown over sand could be read by any pagan shaman. There was a gold compact, expensive tart lipsticks in heavy metal cases, a shiny black plastic wallet, a tiny New Orleans voodoo poppet doll and a handgun.

'I'm Kit,' she said. 'And I can assure you it is not short for Kitten.'

'That's a shame,' I said. 'I could have done with some pussy.'

She leaned down, picked up the gun, and pushed its barrel into the side of my head. Then she placed her face close to mine and whispered into my ear.

'Perhaps you'll get lucky.'

She smelled of musk and motorbikes and I could feel the heat wafting from her body. We looked at each other in the mirror, expressions exchanged in the reflection so that these two women seemed to be others, strangers who had arrived in a sort of parallel sex-world in order to be soulless doppelgängers who could do as they pleased.

I stared at us both, seeing my own unafraid expression, and her angry brown-black eyes. The cold butt of the gun pressed into my skull, her breath warmed on my face, her unashamed hussy breasts rose up and down in the confines of their black lace.

I did not fear for my life, thought there were three seconds when I wondered if she was a psycho, some changing-room killer loaded up with resentment who had finally snapped and was out to do a department-store spree-killing, but I quickly relapsed into an irrational trust. I knew she was not going to kill me. She wanted to excite me. She wanted to direct five seconds when I would have to address the basic essence of survival.

She seemed to know, wise bitch that she was, that dramas like these serve to make a person surrender their complacency. As one realises that one is not to die, so adrenaline becomes the fuel of lust. There is no fight so there must be a fuck. It was a chemical thing, the great foreplay of mind game. I recognised it immediately, as she knew I would.

Thus an eternal dynamic was born – a dance that would not die and was to form the basis of us. Kit and I. Me and Kit. Not short for Kitten.

I was in love.

Chapter Four

So. Me and Kit. Kit and I. She drove a 1967 Chevrolet Impala, two-door hardtop, six-cylinder V-8 engine, sprayed black and splattered with bullet holes. She had once nearly died in New Orleans. She knew the names of obscure drummers. She had a record. She was everything you could possibly want. She lived in Echo Park on a street of Victorian mansions, some restored, some rotting, but all lingering in the rumble of the thundering freeway. There was a garden at the back, unkempt and wild. She said she had once found a human arm under a shrub.

The house was possessed of classy beauty. It was a 20s classic built by starlets whose money had purchased it when the Hollywood meritocracy settled around Angelino Heights and the Elysian Field. It was 'historical', an Echo Park original with clapperboard face, antebellum verandah, latticework porch and a multi-tiered roof which sprang into an asymmetrical gathering of gables. The late-afternoon sun would shower the palm trees, light up the Mediterranean pinks and blues in the street, then flicker over the front of Kit's house. The lamps would begin to glow as the sunset street echoed with children's games and we would lounge on the verandah – Kit drinking beer from the bottle, I with a white wine and ice.

'Why don't you move in?' She said.

She was very difficult to know as tall women often are, especially tall kinky bitches with scant experience of convention. I let her have the sexual control as it turned us both on and, anyway, I couldn't be bothered to fight for something that I didn't really want. I hate having the power: there is too much responsibility; I would rather be led and thus entertained, though there are limits, of course, and these became the tensions between us.

Kit, for all her gun-smoking braggadocio, sensed that I was a relentless nomad, as independent as she was. I could and would go any time I felt like it. I might return. I might not. I don't think she had experienced this before and it made her wild. She had always gone for young girl-boy slaves. They polished her car and spread their legs and did as they were told, but they did not challenge her or frighten her or make her think about things. I prevented her from stagnating, from turning into a bully, and, most importantly, from being bored.

The thing is it wasn't just the sex. We had a laugh. She was a revolutionary. I liked that. She did not cook. That was OK. She was big and, as Eric Stanton once said, 'A woman has to be strong; the bigger the better.' A butch with a femme façade, she could mend any car, as she had once worked as a mechanic. Her father had been from Minneapolis, a gay fist-fuck clone who had died of AIDS. Her mother was a straight in suburbia. So Kit had an inheritance and hatred and no intention of doing a job, though she was a heartbreaking illustrator and could play the piano. I swear she could bang out everything from boogie to Brahms, but she said it took all her energy being herself and I knew what she meant.

She didn't own anything except the Chevy, a range of handguns, serious underwear, fifty pairs of shoes, and some old noise-band albums. The first night I made her wear a white lace negligée and thigh-high boots. Then the Bride of Frankenstein lay on me and licked me with her tough tongue until I was begging for penetration and she forced her dildo into me, staring down at my face as she did so, pinning me down, black fingernails splayed out, refusing to let me close my eyes, or escape into myself, forcing me to stay in the present, staring at the tough adventuress that lurked behind the brown irises, to do as I was told, fucking me in one of those great dyke-fucks that make one wonder why God bothered to make men.

Kit did not like men much. This was a source of disagreement, as I always wanted threesomes (two women, one man; two men, one woman, whatever), but she did not like group activity, control queen that she was. Neither did she want me to work for Leon, and, though I was not fussed either way, I came down on his side partly out of loyalty to him, partly because I had signed a very lucrative contract, but mostly to make sure that she knew she had no real influence over me.

She hated this and tied me up, saying she would leave me like that until I died of dehydration, saying that she would lock me up and never let me go, but of course she could not – only in her mind could I ever be her total dolly. I could go some of the way for her, but I was not going to surrender to sickness. It could not be done, and it should not have been. But Kit did not understand that everybody must have their own life. She wanted to rule.

We looked great together, I can tell you that. Heads turned wherever we went: black-clad girl-chicks with fetish 40s handbags and firearms and no concern at all. She bought me a pair of those jeans that hang down the arse, so that she could see the cleave of my buttocks and the RESPECT tattooed on to them. She liked that. She didn't seem to mind that it was the symbol of another love, and a love for a man at that. As far as she was concerned I was hers and these letters were now her motto because my body belonged to her. The respect was now for her and her alone, a sign that I did as she bade and all was her volition. She was quite mad and very wonderful.

I liked her style, I liked her fantasies, and I loved it when she wore a uniform. Once, dressed as a policeman, she dragged me out of my car, handcuffed me to the chrome grille of the Pontiac, ripped off my clothes, and, in silence, spread my legs and raped me with the dildo harnessed under the policeman trousers. Then she walked away, leaving me for nearly twenty minutes, semi-naked, fucked, mangled in the dirt, an ache in my cunt that was for her, longing for her to return, unlock the manacles, kiss me, love me, assure me.

I knew the relationship was doomed to be short and intense rather than long and married. The sexual stakes were high, and Kit was very unrelenting; a personality that would not change, could not change, and had to be accepted for what it was. She was going to have to work hard to keep me interested, though her arrogance did not allow her to deduce this. Not at the beginning of the affair, anyway. At the beginning she did not have to try. She was enough with her strangeness and breasts and whip and aloof authority.

I loved lying back and letting her rule my world but I knew that she would hate me if I withdrew the privileges that I had bestowed; and they were privileges. She was special in that I had chosen her for intimacy, to carry the secrets that no one else knew, share the trust that I so rarely surrendered.

She would try to take over, I knew that, and would be destructive if thwarted – I knew that also because I had seen it all before. Men and women – they want it all, especially when they sense that they are not going to get it.

But we did not have many rows because we loved each other and I, for once, was on my best behavior. This is not always very good, but at least I tried, considering her feelings before I did what I chose. It was bad luck for her that I had the heart of a submissive and the soul of a sadist. She could whip my arse for me, fuck me till I died, smother me with her bouts of warm bosomy maternal affection, carry me to the bed, push me on to the floor, chain my ankles to the steering wheel, but I would never ever be imprisoned by her.

Leon rang me five times a day on the mobile, ordering me about now that was on his payroll. Preproduction for *The Ordeals of Emmeline* got under way. I had costume fittings and make-up tests, then wig meetings and script edits. I attended various casting sessions where porno men and women traipsed around with their portfolios and bodies.

'You will have to have sex with some of them,' Leon said. 'So you should make sure that you want to and that there is some chemistry.'

So I studied the chemistry, among other things, and was fascinated by the black men about whom everything they say is true, though once cranked up the blood seems to leave their heads in order to rush down to the groin and sustain the enormous hard-on. That third limb between their legs consumed all their energy, so that they could neither think nor speak – they were their dicks.

The girls were tanned and ambitious and real porno starlets with tits that had been cosmetically enhanced when it was fashionable, then reduced when it was not. And, as the men were their dicks, so the chicks were their tits. Their personalities were devoted to the support of the equipment promoted by the thorax. They spoke with their tits, they walked in a way designed to show them off, and they used them as leverage in pay negotiations. They were very frosted and cosmetic, the girls, all highlights, extensions, Brazilian wax, toned muscles, Botox lips, fake lashes, platform shoes, panty-shorts, belly-chains, and make-up, make-up, make-up.

Leon and I spent days sitting in directors' chairs while a secretary with a clipboard recorded the casting sessions. Leon in a pair of Arthur Miller specs, looked north London Jewish intelligentsia (which is what he was) rather than stateside sleaze-mogul (a role thrust on him by a default of laughing fate). I would rule from the throne in skin-tight leopardskin Capri pants, dark green Manolo kittens and sleeveless white cotton T-shirt. How did I look? Well, I was going for Bunny Yeager, as always.

Kit had tried to make me wear a yuppie Joseph suit and Prada handbag. She said I should look like a businesswoman rather than a Billy Wilder bit part, and, anyway, she liked the idea of me in a very tight grey skirt with no panties because my cunt would be forced to feel everything but access to it would be difficult. Yes. She liked this because she wanted to have private ownership of that access herself. That was why she bought me these chastity garments: she wanted to hold the key. She was like some medieval knight, that way. A king without a crown. And a mad king at that.

'I don't want your arse reddened by someone else,' she said. 'And I don't want your cunt all wet for some stud from the Valley . . .'

'I'll be thinking of you all the time,' I said diplomatically.

Leon treated everyone with professional respect and I liked that. He did not try to fuck everything that moved. As a depressive his libido was always down and his cynicism was always up. The porno babes who had made *Panty Party III* or *Oil Orgy II* would sit in his lap, wiggle their thighs into his groin and try to turn him on in order to get an edge on the pumped-up competition.

They got nowhere, these relentless soubrettes. No emotion would flicker down in the dark of Leon's pants. He did not want them.

Givenchy, a successful she-male starlet from Salt Lake City, once asked him if he was gay and he replied that he couldn't remember. He occasionally availed himself of a blow job from some mouth or another but, in general, the present was of very little interest to him. There were too many thugs and thickos to suit his tastes. They bored him.

'The only point of porn,' he said, 'is to scare the straights.'

'You're so 60s, Leon,' I replied.

He did not even care about the money, except where he could use it to annoy people. He had made himself for life; he did not need to do anything any more. Sometimes he would specifically study the laws of a state and assess whether he could break them. He was provocative like that. The politics of porn excited him, the porn itself did not. As a good ol' liberal, he liked the idea of selling renegade lifestyles to a redneck world and illuminating the uncountable oddities that ruled human life.

'Bestiality is legal in Denmark,' he would say. 'We should do a series.'

'I don't want to date an aardvark,' I said.

'What about mud wrestling with a crocodile?'

'No.'

'The publicity would be fabulous.'

'No.'

He would not let the idea drop. He kept saying that snakes would be cheap because they didn't have a union and you wouldn't have to pay overtime. Later I heard that he signed Givenchy up for a series of sex-with-racehorse flicks. I never found out what happened, exactly, as the event was shrouded in rumour, but I managed to gather that the stallion had bolted and

Givenchy had declared that she would never work with animals again.

Leon allowed Kit to be my chauffeur because it saved money on the transport budget. So we drove about in the Pontiac, me in the back, shades on, true starlet style, her in leather and dark glasses, armed, biceps swollen from all the martial arts and Lord knows what else she could do. The woman would probably mow down an entire army of Ninjas given half a chance.

I liked this dynamic and this understanding of fantasy. It hurt her to play but she knew that her presence on the set would give her more control. She would know where I was every minute of the day. It would be difficult, if not impossible, to enjoy any dressing-room debauchery without her knowledge.

Kit was less sexually verstaile than I, and more male in her emotional make-up. She did not fully comprehend that by playing with me on a porno set she provided bisexual interest, glamorised my image, and enhanced my appeal. More and more people, men and women, wanted to fuck me as they observed the dom activities of my leather woman, all peaked hat and knee-high riding boots. The crew bought the fantasy, and lived it, and enjoyed it, and, of course, wanted to join in with it.

Kit was interested in some of the women on the set while I was interested in anyone who would join us in the boat and row out further than we had ever been before, so far out that there was a very real risk that we might drown. I was always more bored than Kit and, consequently, I was more likely to cause trouble.

We shot the *The Ordeals of Emmeline* on a lot in the Valley and on an estate in Santa Barbara. Leon did not direct, of course, as he was too important for such a mundane duty. He had selected an employee – Kent Rodlick – to fulfil this appointment. Kent Rodlick was 26 and had already directed fifteen porn movies, including the much-heralded *Filth*, a police series starring

Clint Manly as a bisexual constable. Kent drove a new BMW and wanted to be Hugh Hefner but this was an ambitious dream for someone as ordinary as Kent. He was of the baseball hat and long shorts variety. The (shortish) legs ended in the newest Nikes, the T-shirt said 'PORN TO ROCK.'

He lived alone in New Jersey with a million dollars' worth of electronic equipment. He was a geek made good, not a stud in a silk dressing gown. Some of the other girls insisted that Kent was cute, but I knew that his new money formed an important part of this judgement. Cash and cash alone was the only thing that mattered to this milieu. Money made taste and directed all personal decisions. These girls got hot cunts when they saw new cars; they went down on wallets. They knew what they were about and understood the simplicity of the American Dream. Fucks were bucks and a rich schmooze could get you a freezer and a pool. So much for the 'chemistry' of which Leon so sweetly spoke.

'I think Kent's kinda great,' said Pussy Willow, a teen-cheerleader type who had starred in *Teddy Bare*, a naughty nubile feature where baby-doll pyjamas had been ripped off in order to enjoy a 'sleep-over' orgy.

'Veronica has had him,' said Toyota.

'No!'

'Yes. They got it together in his backyard.'

'Really?'

'Yeah.'

'And?'

'Average dick. Very vanilla. Didn't take the socks off . . .'

'Same as most people, then.'

'Yeah.'

I formed no relationship with Kent, of either a professional or friendly nature. On the set, when I was not 'working', I hung about with Kit and fancied Dave, who was playing the gardener. He was about 30, wore jeans and a stud machismo that one can't help wanting to test. I was going to have him, I knew that, he knew that; it was a kind of hypnosis, an endless interplay of mind control created by his superman self-esteem and the fact that he was known to have one of the most reliable dicks in the industry. Pussy Willow told me that Dave got up, stayed up, and could come on command.

'Kent wants him to star in his next movie,' she said. 'And, girl, I wanna be in it!'

I fucked him in an alley outside the lot. He had rough hands which scaled the skin around the arse and thighs and shoved themselves into my cunt, digging straight into the G-spot without a so much as a by-your-leave. He made me come immediately and understood the sheer bullying force that was required to push me over the limit and lose control. I don't know how he knew. He was a stud, that's all. He would watch me on the set getting the life spanked out of me, then, hardened by the sight of my red bum, the make-up smeared all over my face, the smell of the sweat made by hot lights, he would shove himself into me when Kit was away running some errand.

'I've got enough for the both of you,' he once said. 'Why don't we have a threesome?'

'I don't think so . . . Kit's quite conservative.'

'That dyke-biker? She sure doesn't look conservative to me.'

She wasn't, of course, but I knew that Dave would not be her scene. If there was to be a threesome she would have preferred to make it with Toyota, a beautiful Japanese girl who had started in the slutty Asian housewife genre, then levered herself up the porno career ladder via a series of forced insertions and pussy exams.

She flirted with Kit so blatantly that I wondered if they had developed the idea together as a way to make me jealous. Kit hated my lack of jealousy but I had disciplined that emotion a long time ago. I can't remember when I last cared about monogamy. There is no freedom when there is jealousy. It is a cut-throat emotion and it should never ever be confused with love.

One weekend we went over to Toyota's apartment in Koreatown, drank Kir Royales and listened to Dean Martin. Music to watch the girls go by. There were shelves full of books by Sartre and video racks full of latex gyno-hardcore. I looked at the jacket covers. There was nothing Toyota had not performed. The sleeves featured her in innocent enough poses – picnics on the lawn and so on – while the inside jackets were lurid galleries of colour photographs showing her close-up cunt receiving everything from cucumbers to bottles of champagne.

Toyota was wearing a micro-kilt and white cotton panties and she sat on Kit's lap so that they were face to face and groin to groin, Toyota's manic little pussy rubbing itself up and down on her, white thighs pushing against black leather. Later we all collapsed in each other's arms on Toyota's king-size bed. I took Kit's boots off for her. Toyota talked about the sexual wonders of danger. Then we slept.

Wolf Nicholson had been cast as Sir Grafton Rafton – typecast, it might be said. He had made his name playing German military officials in audience pleasers such as *Nasty Nazis*, *Berlin Blow-Jobs*, *The Night the Führer Went Down on Me*, and *Girls Just Want to Have Hun*. He turned to the role of Sir Grafton as a man inspired by the image of Erich Von Stroheim, deranged director of the 30s whose bordello orgies were legendary and who, both on and off the set, goose-stepped about in uniforms, medals and jackboots as a fetishman *par excellence*.

So Wolf bought his own boots to the shoot and was supplied with monocle and jodhpurs. He would have been absurd if it had not been for the fact that he was six foot three and wielded the whip with the skill of a man who had spent some time working in a circus. He had ascended from the big top to subcultural success in New York, where he had worked as a 'dungeon performance artist'.

He was not a cartoon, this Wolf: he was a little scary. Well, *I* was scared of him. Kit machoed him out with steely glares that would have felled an ox at a distance of thirty yards. This powerful *froideur* had no effect on Wolf. He was not a sensitive person, he was an alpha personality and he did not like other alpha personalities. No world was big enough for the both of them. Their egos could only clash like Titans.

His job (as an actor) was to discipline me and fuck me. Off the set, however, he was oblivious to my charms and refused to pay any attention to me unless the script and the shoot dictated it. There were no real-life scenarios with Wolf, no lupine lewdness. I had to be content with what I received in character, which was enough, I suppose, and more than enough for Kit, who hovered like an eagle when we were working together. At the end of the sessions she would drive me away as fast as the Firebird could go, which was pretty fast at 3 a.m., down the freeway out of the Valley.

Leon would occasionally visit the set to ensure that his money was not being wasted by scoundrels and to bully the cameraman, who, in fact, knew what he was doing, having made some creditable cult films, one of which was about a giant tongue that leapt out of a bowl of soup and terrorised the state of Wisconsin.

'Giant tongue, eh?' Kent Rodlick said when he heard this. 'It's sure got possibilities for porno.'

Did I enjoy spreading my legs for the camera? Yes. I liked the idea of the lens taking in my rich wet genitalia, the eye at the other end staring at the juicy lips of my vulva, penetrating me with microscopic sight. I liked it when, during the scenes, I became carried away and *during* the rushes I saw it all again. And I liked the fact that sex became another thing altogether; that there was little semblance of the intimate love-based coupling, enjoyed (sometimes, only sometimes) by the straight world.

Here in the land of demented divas and shameless shoguns, sex was something to be looked at, lit, set up, transferred to DVD, and judged with the detachment of technical know-how. Sex was a bunch of oddballs involved in the art of erotic stimulation, not a married coupling performed in the ashamed secrecy of some low-down shack in Sun Valley. I enjoyed being around people who knew no inhibition and who had taken it upon themselves to merchandise the very thing that is still guaranteed to unnerve a world blighted with fear. You. I. Them. The Lord. No one really knows what goes on when human animals decide to play for purposes of recreation rather than procreation. Everybody is tied up with sociocultural restrictions when they should be tied up on the bed. I particularly enjoyed flogging the Duke of Orleans' smooth brown back because he deserved it.

The Duke was played by Joaquin Esposa, a Latin American beauty, tall and thin, with long black hair that trailed down his back. Joaquin was quite famous, though not nearly as famous as he thought he was. He had crossed over from making B-movie porno schlock (such as Dint Love-Bug's *The Monster from the Bog*, which featured Joaquin being anally raped by a dolphin), to a couple of mainstream movies in which he played Cuban drug dealers and was damned to snarl such stereo-thug lines as, 'Did you bring the stuff?' and 'Less gedoudofhere.'

He had reaped some cult attention on the Net, partly for his lithe gypsy beauty (he was tall and dark with black eyes and a firm jaw), partly because he was the first to post up a digitally enhanced colour photograph of his anal sphincter (fully open), a rendition which, when subject to such detailed photography, looks not like a sphincter at all, but more like a geological marvel. Anyway, America being what it is, Joaquin got 1,000 hits a day from people willing to pay $20 a pop.

So he was big on babe-net and he had a seven-and-a-half-inch dick that stood up from those narrow hips as a strict tool worthy of worship, and worshipped it was by all the little nympho-nymphettes hanging around, all the Mitizis and Trixies and Kazzaras, the extras who wanted to get on, and who knew one of the best ways to do this was to grace Joaquin's ever-taut knob with their ever-loving tongues and lips.

He always seemed to be down some girl's throat, did Joaquin. And these girls had mouths. They had developed the muscles around the neck and face and they knew what they were doing. They were able to gobble for hours on end without so much as twinge on the jaw muscles, though they did sometimes complain of 'fluffers' knees' because they were on them for so long. I did not perform any services of this nature on Joaquin. He was a macho egomaniac, and though I sometimes like to fuck this type, if only to find out where they are coming from, I resented the fact that he thought he was the star of this show. Actually, as far as Joaquin was concerned, he was star of the universe.

Kit insisted that he had 'issues' around his sexuality – that anybody who swaggered about like that must be gay, full stop, and why couldn't he accept it? Kit thought this about most men, unsurprisingly, since her father had been the Queen of the Meat-Packing district. Certainly he was great-looking, with his long brown legs, smooth brown chest, and androgyne presence. He was very sexy, particularly from the back, because his proportions were perfect and he had a great arse. And to look good from the back was, of course, the main part of his role as the Duke of Orleans. He had to stand as a submissive, face to the wall, in nearly every frame of the movie. A beautiful slave still-life, he was an unexplained bottom waiting to be punished.

I always enjoyed watching the prop department tie his wrists behind his back everyday and I relished the fact that he could not escape from those knotted restraints unless somebody decided that it should be so. Sometimes the crew left him there like that, tied up in the corner of the set, while they went off to have long unionised tea breaks. They would pretend that they had forgotten him, but I sensed that they were enjoying teasing him, that they perceived his arrogance and knew that he should be penalised for it, like any bloke in any playground in the world.

Breasty Bigger, a fab Jamaican woman, told me that she had once had him but now he refused to talk to her or even acknowledge her presence.

'I remember when that man was glad of a job organising the sun loungers in a motel in Miami,' she said. ''S only 'cos he fucked all the old widows that he got hisself outta there.'

So when I whipped his arse for him on the last day, I did it for her. And she watched, horny as hell, standing next to the script girl, enjoying every lascivious moment as the stinging tails lashed that smooth skin. I gave him a good striping, I know that. Kit had taught me this skill. We had practised in the backyard with her whip. Aiming at tin cans. She was the best. She had the arms, the height, the strength and the muscles for it, deftly flicking a circus animal-training whip with balletic skill, round her head, out and in, like some demented rodeo queen.

I was better with a small whip, twenty inches or so long with a leather handle and one long black tail. I knew how to handle it to maximum effect, ensuring that the movement of arm and wrist co-ordinated with whistle and snap and that the end of that whip hit a different area of flesh every time. Most effective. And painful. Poor little foe.

Even Kit was impressed that day.

I was strict and cold in micro-mini wedding dress, lace stay-ups and a pair of neat white leather stiletto ankle boots. Then, when Kent said 'action', action there was. I went at him as he was tied face down against the bed, his immaculate brown buttocks exposed to my cruelty, wriggling and shaking as the whip hissed and cracked its target. By the tenth lash or so Joaquin's back and buttocks were criss-crossed with livid red weals and he was starting to gasp. His body fell forward in total submission as he surrendered to the pain over which he had no control. He would have howled if he had not been a proud son of a bitch.

He spent the rest of the day gingerly stroking his hot flesh and glaring at me coldly, as if it was my fault! I didn't write the script – I just did what I was told. It wasn't my fault that Latino testosterone failed to protect his arse, that he could be flayed and humiliated as easily as anyone, certainly as much as I had been on this shameless shoot. In the end, though, it has to be admitted that I did enjoy 'the ordeals'. Kit had to bang me with her dildo; I was that hot after filming punishment scenes with Wolf. And I had to bang her with mine the day that we shot the wrestling scene.

Two muscular young women spent that afternoon slamming each other on the kitchen table. Lena Leadbelly, with her man-killer legs, played Dee Dee in a skintight, smooth, fur catsuit or, more accurately, dogsuit, as that is what she was playing. Mistress Wilde was the servant girl, short, fleshy but strong and possessed of an ability to perform vicious scissor-holds. Both of these fighting women had been the bare-breasted barbarian babes of many a muscle-dom vid. Often oiled, sometimes wearing only pantyhose, always locked in combat, they were trained in the Turkish art of Yagli Gures, as well as feminine freestyle. They were both competitive, vicious and skilled.

Mistress 'Bone-Crusher' Wilde, an Iron Maiden from Tucson, Arizona, had straddled and smothered her way to the top. Now she sat on her opponent's face and squeezed her neck with her thighs until Lena went purple, lost her temper, threw her off, and slapped her very hard in the face. A true catfight ensued, an unseemly tussle that brooked none of the rules laid down by the International Wildcat Federation, the organisation that was supposed to adjudicate these things.

There was a brief hold up as the red mark of five fingers began to glow on Mistress Wilde's face, then a fascinated silence as both girls lost control. Screaming and hissing and grabbing at each other's crotch, they rolled over and over on top of each other, then off the table and slap on to the floor of the set. Hardly noticing, they continued to shriek and struggle, spitting and shouting obscenities.

As Leon rang his insurance company on his mobile phone ('Have these girls got medical or what?' he snapped), the wardrobe mistress worried that the women would shred each other's outfit to pieces.

Kit stared at the scene in silence, her dark eyes glistening with excitement. This was her kind of intimacy – a competiton of strength where foreplay was a muscular knee in the groin of a femme foe and a backhold was an expression of affection. No one was hurt. The two wrestling amazons merely continued the struggle on the floor, rolling round and round, sometimes one on top of the other, sometimes with one straddled on the other, moist cunt against suffocated mouth. The cameraman simply continued filming the scene, recording every valuable unrehearsed minute.

The rushes were hot. Everyone was pleased. Later that night I made Kit crawl on all fours around the apartment, naked except for leather knee boots, belly chain and tattoos. I knelt behind her, massaging her wet cunt from the back, until she was begging for it. And she got it. With a numero-uno, ever-hard, deluxe leather dong.

Chapter Five

The *Ordeals of Emmeline* was launched in a tirade of publicity. The marketing department spared no expense. Public relations people worked a ten-hour day. There was a screening party for 350 people, complete with red carpet, B-movie stars, and dim sum. I wore a sheath-tight red rubber evening gown cut into a fish tail at the back. The front, slightly shorter, lifted to reveal a pair of red satin sling-backs. Kit walked in front of me dragging 'Dee Dee' (who was in her fur costume and crawling on all fours) on a lead. The crowds behind the barriers went wild and there was a blinding wall of flashing bulbs.

'Over here, Stella, over here, smile, let's see your breasts.'

'Certainly not,' I said primly.

Later Leon's 'Pussy Force' and I went on a pink bus around America in order to promote both the film and Leon's company – Pleasure Dome Inc. Twelve of us spent a month crisscrossing from Oregon and Idaho to Indiana and Ohio. We wore pink, we had to be nice. It was exhausting. In Hawaii I was the 'celebrity' judge at a nude surfing competition and in Chicago I launched

Leon's new DVD 'virtual sex' line, which had been developed by one of his tech design companies. This range of innovative products used state-of-the art technology to accomplish a 'satisfying interactive experience'. The client manipulated a keypad to navigate a virtual environment over which he had sole command. He could ask the girl out on a date and then watch her make out in a variety of positions in a variety of scenes. He directed the 'heat' of an environment – that is, he controlled foreplay, orgasm, and multi-orgasm.

My section appeared on *Pussy Power 1*. The voyeur (as play manager) could decide what I wore, which club I attended, how I danced or stripped, which clothes came off, how fast I went, how slow, which of three different soundtracks was to be used, and so on.

Pussy Power 2, more hardcore, featured Goo Lightly doing oral, missionary, doggy and anal, with angles that went up her arse, on her face, or zoomed close in on the cute little purple merkin (pubic wig) that was her trademark. The technology even aided the 'manager' to decide when she came, which, as Goo said, was something of an improvement on real life.

The problem was that these virtual-sex scenes were so real that those who had experienced them felt as if they knew the subject and that her life was in their control. All the geeks suddenly became doms. It was a nightmare. We all had to fend off the armies of anoraks who thought that they had slept with us, that they could do so again, that the scene would be their choice. All they had to do was issue a command. Cyberspace relations were not healthy. I am not an interactive experience. But the hackers and phreaks did not know kissing: they knew love-bytes. It was distorted.

I complained about this to Leon and he said he would mention it to one of his presidents but I suspect that he never did. He was too concerned with the various organisations that had begun to protest against his wares.

There was an election coming up, never a good time for porno people, and at least two Christian candidates were planning to brandish the anti-filth ticket. Retailers were getting nervous, as were some distributors. The rumour went round that the Republicans were looking for a high-profile scapegoat. Leon's reply was to release three of the filthiest pissing videos he could muster. It was not a wise move, but it was a move that boosted the industry's morale and earned him much respect.

Leon (and his lawyers) put it around that they were not afraid. Pleasure Dome products could easily be described as 'art', which was, after all, the main criterion for most stateside zoning laws. As far as they were concerned 'obscenity' diktats were obsolete – discarded relics of an old world.

I knew that Leon had never bothered to play golf with the right people and that the old 60s rebel in him wanted a fight, particularly a fight about the freedom of speech. This was a man who had marched in Grosvenor Square, after all. A man who had financed the Weathermen and still wrote to one of his Yippie friends at Ford open prison. He was bolshy and anti-authority and he cared not a jot for the outraged sensibilities of fringe fascists.

His enemies were gathering like a storm cloud. Plagues of protests were beginning to rain down on his Land of Sodom. Everywhere he went there was a nun with a placard, or a group of shrieking mothers, or some uniformed official inspecting his person for depravity, and it did not help that everywhere he went he was followed by his pink pussy posse, all his starlets looking like the edible candy that they were, big breasted, big lipped and as lewd as you wanted them to be.

In November I went to Harvard and gave a lecture on feminism which made the cover of the *New York Times*. Leon was ecstatic. He was so pleased with himself that I thought he might have a heart attack.

'Babe,' he yelled down my mobile telephone. 'I'm in love with you.'

He was in New York and there was the sound of a loud party going on.

'Gotta go, babe – the German ambassador has just arrived . . . Boy, is he fat!'

The reviews were unanimous in their acclaim and many said that *The Ordeals of Emmeline* was destined to become a classic, like *Emmanuelle* or *I am Curious Yellow*.

'An erudite sex project,' said a critic writing for *Mature Man* magazine. 'The black and white camera work is reminiscent of Anatole Litvak. This is destined to set the way for a new genre – intelligent porn with spectacular production values.'

Others were just as enthusiastic, talking about 'fine performances', 'ensemble acting' and 'marvellous mish'.

Multigasm said, 'Stella Black is hotter than Hiroshima. I had to stand back for fear of being burned,' while *Crude Privates* described it as 'the ultimate quality in sexcellence'. *Peechicks* called it, 'refreshing,' whatever that means in those golden-shower circles. *Eager Beaver*, who had cornered the ethnic fem-on-fem minge-munching niche, gave it ten out of ten for the best pussy-splitting since little Toy Rogers had appeared in Brillo Brillstein's 1973 classic *Tight and Tingly*.

We won various adult-entertainment awards, including the most prestigious Dirty Dish de Jour. The rumor went round the industry that *The Ordeals of Emmeline* had broken all records and outsold everything. They could not move it out of the warehouse fast enough. I began to receive lucrative offers from other film makers. One director wanted me to star in the sequel to *Samurai Toilet Voyeur*, while another asked me to consider playing an amputee in *In Bed with Stumpy*. My website received 20,000 hits a day (well it did feature a live video feed of Kit shaving my cunt) and I was on the cover of seven magazines.

Finally *Details* and *Rolling Stone* came after me. They wanted it all – profile, pic, hair, make up, journalist following me around for the day, tape recordings of inner secrets, revealing lunches, my life as a who's who, what's what. *Details* sent a young man, *Rolling Stone* sent an old one. The young one had seen the first ever Stone Roses gig, the old one had seen the Stones at Altamont. They both looked at my breasts a lot. It was as if they did not know what to do with them, so I turned the mirror round and made them reveal all their little secrets, the shaming things that they could not and would not do with their girlfriend and wife respectively. I told the young one how to perform oral sex for maximum pleasure and I gave tips on retaining an erection to the old one. They loved me and hated me for it. But the press was good. The *Rolling Stone* cover went up in bus-stop shelters all over America.

And so your Stella became a star. I was the hot totty that everyone wanted to meet. And fuck. Every time I walked into a room I was bathed with the sure knowledge that every single person in it wanted to sleep with me. This is a responsibility my friends, a girl has to keep her Jimmy Choos on the ground and wield her power with care. I teased them, aroused them, dizzied them with the tension of holding in their own demented orgasms, then I would leave them. I was not going to shag every twit with a hard-on, I can tell you that.

I did all the usual things. I put on Versace clothes and hosted A-list parties in nightclubs. I went on Howard Stern. I began to date rock stars. I know it's a cliché, but who wouldn't shag the average guitar god given half a chance? Well maybe not Andrea Dworkin. But everybody else would. I dated singers who looked like Iggy Pop and guitarists with more funk-elegance than the whole of Sly and the Family Stone put together. I dated bassists from heavy-metal bands and deejays from rap bands. And soon I was the star-chick with sex-cred and a reputation that served to allure the best. And the best, in my opinion, were androgyne types with eyeliner, narrow hips, long legs, leather trousers and a sulky look of exhumation which mixed with arrogance and a Jim Morrison swagger.

The rock gypsies were always on the road so they could never be caught, even if one wished to. They had hotel rooms and rented apartments and chaotic unpacked suitases spilling their contents all over the floor. There would always be tapes and CDs and mini-studios and an answering service full of the voices of keen groupies calling in. They were entertainment, not friends. I fucked them as one would fuck any cool stranger, taking in their hard-on, liking the fact that it was attached to a rock god and that a hundred thousand women would be jealous.

I allowed the lead singer of the Assassins to rape me. That was fun. His name was Glen. He had the face of a devil and a dick from hell. (That's a compliment, by the way: he was so big I could feel him inside me two days later.) His influences were *Sisters of Mercy, Siouxie Soo* and *Throbbing Gristle,* so you can imagine what he was like. A dark antihero with savage grace and long fingers, his press cuttings told him he was the new Nick Cave.

I went to see him play at the Whiskey – he and his gang of four gaunt beauties, all black-haired, all in tight black trousers, slamming out loud sinister guitar chords, singing songs about necrophilia and distant women and despair. They encored with 'I hate Naomi Wolf' (which had been an indie hit), then he lit a cigarette, kicked over an amp, and ambled off the stage as he would have ambled out of a bookshop.

'No no no,' I cried when he dragged me away from the backstage party.

'No no no,' I still protested when he pushed me over in the back of the limo.

'No no no,' I cried as he slammed me up against the wall of the lift, pushed my dress up to my waist. No no no as he edged his hand into the black silk camiknickers, and slowly, lightly, teasingly tickled my clit with the gentle tip of one long finger . . . just dabbing, pressing the button as it were, to turn me on.

'Babe,' he whispered. 'How can you be so bad and look so good?'

Then he slid three fingers mercilessly into my cunt, kissed me hard on the lips and forced my hand down on the front of the leather trousers, where his cock bulged out against the material. Beautiful and hard. I couldn't wait to get it, but he wasn't going to get it easy. No pop star should. I wanted to confuse him, make him fight for me, cause a bit of tension in that adored sex-god head. I snatched my hand away from that dick, left it alone in its place, hard and straining against the leather, unloved by me.

He pinned my arms behind my back in order to kiss me. He smelled of cigarettes and whiskey and the post – show musk of ego-driven sexuality that had left him wanting it, wanting more, for he was driven by the adrenaline of performance and the euphoria of adulation.

'No no!' I cried.

I wanted to be taken by him. And he complied in that unfathomable mystery of complex instincts that is the stuff of final consent. He forced me down on the carpet of the corridor outside his hotel room, ripped my knickers in two, pushed my black silk shift up to my neck, twisted my nipples underneath the black half-cup bra, and suckered his lips down on to mine so that I could not speak and had to struggle for breath. Then he brutally flung my thighs apart so that all I was aware of was my exposure, a gaping wet hole that could have been seen by anyone walking down that corridor.

A passer-by would have seen a woman struggling to fight a man off and a man forcing himself down on her, forcing her to submit. They would have thought that a sex crime was in progress and would undoubtedly have called the police. I did not know what the law said about allowing men to rape you in public places, but I suspected that it was not allowed. It would have been the end for both of us. Or the beginning. We were the same in that we did not care. He was a cool nomad, that Glen.

'You want this,' he said, staring down into my face with inscrutable black eyes. 'You know you do.'

I didn't want it. I did. I didn't.

'Take me then. Force yourself into me. No no No! 'Yes, yes. Fuck me. Make me feel you, make me feel that big cock.'

'Yeah? Well you're gonna get it babe. You're gonna get it like you've never had it before.'

He forced himself down on my body and slammed his rod into me with one hard thrust that took me by surprise. My pelvis jolted up to meet his groin, take him all in, and love him for this danger and for this dick that could fill me up.

He was right. I did want it.

Glen sometimes lead me into the LA night, where his friends were Goths and vampires, eccentric deviants of the neck-sucking faith who wore Hammer Horror costumes and devoted themselves to a fetishistic existence where everyone dressed up and everything was ritualised. They turned Silverlake nightclubs into caverns, all shadow and candlelight and cobwebs and crucifixes.

They would gather together and celebrate necromantic anniversaries – Aleister Crowley's birthday, for instance, or the date of Edgar Allan Poe's death, or some significant full moon. Then they would dance slowly, the immortal denizens of the night, bodies entwined, arms round each other, groin on groin, to music by the Evil Dead or the Lovecraft Experience.

They drank from silver goblets full of red wine, spilling it down their mouths so that it looked like blood. They were tattooed and self-scarred and white-faced and lipsticked. The women, deranged Rossettis, had long pre-Raphaelite hair, often died a dark crimson, that was tied with ivy and fell down to the middle of their backs. They wore floor-length velvet medieval gowns, cut low in the front to show heaving white breasts, often corseted at the back. Nails were long and curled and black. Shoes were vintage fetish *objets* found in thrift stores.

The men had long black hair, Edwardian shirts, frilly lace sleeves, strange jewellery, patent-leather winkle-pickers, and long velvet coats or black cloaks. They were into everything, the vampires, they were into everything and they did everything and they never appeared during the daylight hours.

Once, at 3 a.m., Glen took me to a deconsecrated church in downtown LA. It was a proper church, with a prayer board outside, a spire, a wooden door and stained-glass windows. Inside there were pews and pointed arches and cold stone floors covered with rugs and straw. Dry ice wafted around the place and long white candles splattered the scene in flickering shadow.

The creatures of the night had made themselves fantastic. There were dyke girls dressed as Gothic heroines, pointed teeth, bloodstained ball gowns, green nails, hands clenched in hands, eyes only for each other. Tall heavy-metal types prowled with whips hanging from studded leather belts. Juddering suburban mutoids had Day-Glo orange buzz-cuts and black contact lenses. Their gaunt bodies were wrapped in woollen cobwebs. Tramps and tarts wore only panties and nipple tassles and fetish heels, necks blemished by hard kissing. Some boys had dark-blue hair. They were called Vlad and Dr Death.

A bloodsucking nymph from Nantucket carried a dwarf on her back. Here they were in this self-made model of distorted reality where myth was truth and truth was a thing to be played with, and weak thing a that, easily manipulated and teased as a cat teases a bird. They were California's shadow, the collective anima that avenged itself against a lifestyle of wholesome youth and sun-searching fun. They too were shoppers and stylists, this black-magic breed, they too were fans, but they had collected in a separate corner from the rest of the west-coast world – a corner where there were no stair-masters or aerobics classes or roller skates, only the nostalgic paraphernalia of long-gone shockmasters.

One inhabitant of this necropolis had been tied to a black cross. His white lace shirt had been slit to the waist, and he was wearing tight black leather trousers. There were tattoos on his arms and on his neck. He had long black hair and high cheekbones and a mouth that, reposed, set in an expression of arrogance and cruelty that I have always enjoyed. His name was Michael, after the archangel of Kabbalistic ritual. He was Glen's best friend.

'This is Michael,' said Glen.

I couldn't shake his hand as it was tied above his head to the cross. Michael looked down at me and stared straight into my eyes with his own deep-blue irises. He did not say anything, but his entire godforsaken crucified mien offered challenge. Go on he seemed to say, go on, sleaze-sister, play with me as you wish. Please your boyfriend. Impress me. And, hey, babe, I'm not easily impressed.

I gently pulled down the zip of his trousers and took his cock out. It was tumescent – enlivened by the excitement of immortal fantasy and by receiving attention from the coolest chicks in town. I teased him with the tip of my tongue and, good as gold, it sprang up. I teased him some more, then took the tip into my mouth and began to rub my tongue and lips up and down his shaft, so now he was as hard as it was possible to be.

Almost uncomfortable. Moaning, he strained against the shackles that bound him to the cross, arched his body, so that the chains began to rattle, moans became groans, so the night-time brood of zombies and succubi gathered around, watching the decadent pleasure of their most favored kindred.

A couple of the girls kissed each other, crimson lips on crimson lips. Glen stood behind me kissing me hard on the back of neck, teasing my hard nipples with determined fingers. Michael's archangel pelvis pushed itself hard towards my mouth, dick at my mercy now. I moved my face and there was white stuff everywhere. His denizen friends stared in silence. I laughed, turned around, and retreated gracefully into the dark mystery of the crowd.

An hour or so later I was sitting at the bar enjoying a cocktail faux-blood fusion served in a silver goblet. A woman wearing a full-length black veil sat opposite me; by her side was a skeletal freak in a top hat. Glen had disappeared, to find a cigarette he said, though I suspected he had deserted me to chat up Morticia van Dancing, a dominatrix songstress who had graced the place with her presence that night. Glen was impressed because she had gone on a prime-time chat show and displayed the piercings on her labia. It had been a live-cast so there had been a nationwide rumpus followed by satisfying sales for Ms van Dancing's album, *Malice*.

So off he went, lascivious popstar-boy egomaniac that he was. I didn't resent Morticia so much (Glen and I were free after all, and, indeed, we had signed a paper in blood to say as much, one night, after I had been disorientated by dick and wine) so much as the disrespect. A lady should be treated as a lady, I feel. We were on a date. There were protocols.

I was thinking these and other dark thoughts when a man introduced himself as Satan. He had seen *The Ordeals of Emmeline* five times and he said he was in love with me. Said he would do anything for me, that I was the icon of his life, and his virgin bride.

'Hardly,' I said, flashing him a glare from underneath the black fringe. Glen, some one hundred yards away in the crowd, was beginning to receive exotic minstrations from *la femme* van Dancing. And it was not subtle. He was sitting at a table and she was gyrating her hips in front of his face; hips that would soon turn into those televised lower lips as she slowly parted the folds of her skirt and her minge swayed slowly towards his mouth. I rolled my eyes and turned back to Satan.

'Well.' I said coolly. 'You can buy me a drink.'

'I will do anything you want,' he said.

'Anything?'

'Anything.'

'What kind of car have you got?'

'A 1979 hearse.'

'Well, of course you have.'

So I left with the Prince of Darkness because I liked the idea of messing with the Devil's head. He was deathly pale, as was *de rigueur* in that milieu of cavorting exhumation. He was glamorous in a deep-green crushed-velvet coat, tailored at the waist, with wide lapels, that swept along the floor as he walked. A silver Catholic crucifix hung around his neck, his nails were short and painted black and there was a goat's head tattooed on one hand.

This is what I made the Devil do. First he tied my wrists and ankles with soft white rope, then he carried me out of the club, fireman style, my arse over his shoulders, casually waving as he strode past a surprised Glen. Strong, he carried me through candle-lit cloisters and down into the catacombs, which were cold and wet and dark and full of the night breed, ravaging each other, biting one another's neck, and kissing each other with blind abandon. Then out into the car park where he put me in the back of his hearse.

The hearse had been customised. The back was covered with black carpet, the windows had purple and gold velvet curtains, and there were soft dark cushions scattered around. Still tied, I lay face down over the cushions. Satan eased my dress over my waist to give himself a full few of a pair of tiny cream-silk briefs, a white suspender belt with sheer cream stockings and blood red stilettoes. Gently he pulled the knickers down so that my cheeks were bare, framed by the lace of the suspenders. And he left me like that, face in pillows, bum in air, sprawled in the back of his death-mobile as he drove into the night, a fifteen-minute or so ride.

I was a little nervous by now, having placed my trust in a man named Satan who I did not even know and who had, after all, gained something of a bad reputation over the years. He might have gleaned better press since being played by Al Pacino and Jack Nicholson, but who knew? Anything could lurk out there in the LA night.

The puss did not listen. It never did. It reacted with unworried intuition, wettening up as the cold air brushed around my bare flesh, and the various excited orifices loosened in expectation. The body knew it was going to get fucked. The body wanted to get fucked. All the nerves were waiting.

His apartment, in Los Feliz, was painted dark blue, purple and gold. There were drapes and candles and, over the top of one door, the words 'ABANDON HOPE'. At one end there was an altar/table with gold candlesticks, rocks, flowers and strange idols of mythical creatures. And it was to this that he tied me, face up, legs spread, pudendum naked.

A Catholic nubile lurked within me, and now, surrounded by the paraphernalia of religion's artefacts, my mind eased back to the days when Mel and I had encouraged the nuns to tan our backsides with their flails and whips, make them red for all of our mutual pleasure and punish us with pain in the name of the

Lord. This residual of untrammelled kinkiness could still be triggered by anything from the sight of the Holy Mother (tits out, babe on lap) to a confession box, to a gold cross, to a pew.

He placed some church music on the tape deck, a Gregorian chant I think, lit candles and waved heavy incense around the place so that the acrid smoke of heavy musk stung my nostrils. I must have been a sight for him, the virgin bride, all in white, long crimson nails, spread waiting for him in his pervy place of solitary fantasy.

There was something about those intelligent brown eyes and the knowing grin that made me want him. I couldn't tell if he was passive or active, top or bottom, male or female. A switch probably. He seemed to be everything to everyone – a vamp tramp who would do anything to perform the devil's work.

Satan liked to look. He was all eyes. I had seen them before, the men who like to have sex by sight. It's an old-fashioned thing, the erotic interplay of hypnosis and fixation. I suspected that he could have spent the night simply staring at my tits and thighs, subsumed in a voyeur's trance, though occasionally leaning down to brush soft lips against perky clit.

I was in smooth beautiful nick, pussy shaved, legs immaculate, toenails blood red, body swathed in glitter, smelling of Joy. My long white Miss Havisham bridal gown spread as a pool around me, trailing its folds on the floor. I was shackled to the alter, waiting for him to act, waiting for him to ease my thighs a little further apart and insert himself into the heart of the virgin bride.

'So, Satan . . .' I said as he walked around the altar to inspect my every sprawled angle, 'are you the Devil?'

He did not answer. Instead he turned out all the lights so that the place was pitch black except for two candles flickering on Celtic sconces on the wall. I could see nothing, only sense him, sense his hands stroking my inner thighs, over my belly, over my breasts, on to my neck, which he now kissed with a full biting force of the vampiric state that he emulated. He bit deep and hard, as if to really suck the blood.

I went up to meet him, and I was in his grasp and in his power. I had put myself there, in this strange man's place. I had to go with it or have a mean time. So I went with it and he knew what he was doing, burning candle wax so that it dripped slowly and hotly on to my sensitive thighs, then inserting a vibrator into my fanny, letting it go, warming me up, pushing it harder and harder into me so that everything was relaxed and tingling and ready for that final thrust of manhood.

Which is what I got. Firm. Wide. Large. Slow. Very very slow. He was in control, and with full control he eased the dick in and out of me until he knew that I had arrived in another place and could not come back, would not come back, hardly knew who I was, merely travelling around in some other sphere not giving a damn. It was a minute or so before I fully realised that not only had he withdrawn but he had left my body and the room. He had abandoned me to private postcoital pleasure, having provided the service for which he was required.

Later I found out that his name was Roy and he owned a shop on Melrose.

Kit could only sneer when I offered various inane excuses for behaving like a total tart. It was business. Leon told me to. The marketing people were pressurising me to get my face into magazines. All that. This was a waste of breath, really, as both she and I knew very well that I was playing the field because I wanted to. We would fight and make up, fight again, then fuck. She would haul me over her lap and spank me with a leather paddle until I burst into tears and made promises that I meant at the time, there in the moment of frenzy and pain, when my cunt was wet and I wanted it with her. But, as I deserted her to fling myself to the throes of fame, she became more and more withdrawn.

Angry and sulky, she would spend hours poring over her collection of guns. This had been left to her by her leather-clone father, who had bought them to accessorise the various uniforms in which he liked to play. Kit's father had had a rich fantasy life with a particular predilection for cops and cowboys. So, like any good ol' gay American boy, he had indulged the full range of his penile dementia and spent a fortune acquiring the finest firearms money could buy.

He had left Kit several Ruger single-action revolvers, a Ruger Rimfire pistol, a Colt 'cowboy' western style revolver, a Glock 23, a series 92 Beretta, a Wilson automatic pistol designed for close quarters combat and a .38 'special' Smith and Wesson double-action revolver, the heavyweight man stopper used by both the army and the police.

For Kit each gun was a character, a person almost, with a set of qualities that made them unique. She would talk in detail about tactical sighting systems, low-light aiming, tritium inserts, and Parkerised finishes. She could tell you the magazine capacity of any Beretta and how to modify an AR-15. She would spend hours at the kitchen table surrounded by chamber-cleaning tools, bushing wrenches, silicone cloths, universal lubricants, magazines and boxes of ammo. Gently dismantling her weapons by prising the various components apart, she would slowly put them together again, oiling, lubricating, polishing, rubbing the tips of her fingers tenderly up and down the cold steel barrels and touching cold blue carbon with erotic tenderness.

She still turned me on. I found myself wanting to know more about this inner land in which she now chose to travel, with a Glock in her sock and a Ruger by her side. It seemed that she had found a personal escape route where the only pleasure was the prizes to be won from sharp-shooting the symbols of her father's unashamed decadence. Her father had worn them just for show, had not even loaded them. He had enjoyed the shopping and he had liked the reaction that they stimulated, but he had not been interested in the full potential of their lethality. Kit was. Kit shot them. She knew which was the most effective ammo. She knew the specifics of each weapon and could tell you its weight, its barrel length and, most importantly, its range.

Then she started to build her own weapons. I did not notice at first, as I was out most of the day and night, being lipsticked and pictured, pampered and posed in the name of Pleasure Dome's decree. Then I saw new books lying around the house. She left some of them face down, pages splayed. They had titles like *Home Built Rocket Launchers* and *Flamethrowing for Beginners*.

'I can make a fully operational hand-cannon out of a piece of drainpipe and some lighter fluid,' she once boasted to me.

'Good for you,' I said. 'I can make a Dougal out of a detergent bottle and some wool, but it doesn't mean to say that I am going to.'

She got up, left the room and slammed the door.

Relations, as I say, were tricky.

Chapter Six

One day, about three months after the release of *The Ordeals of Emmeline*, Kit dressed rather more carefully than usual. Out came the T-shirt saying, 'FEARED BY MEN, DESIRED BY WOMEN'. Out came the skin-tight Levi's and biker jacket. On went the black cowboy boots and spurs. On went the black stetson. Then she packed her Ruger into a concealed holster underneath the jacket, sorted out some Leadbelly CDs and disappeared in her Chevy without saying anything.

This would have been strange under any circumstances. Kit always told me where she was going. But it was rendered more mysterious by the fact that I had my first day off for four weeks and we had planned to spend the day together, mooching and lounging and having sex. I had even been looking forward to it, despite all the recent sulks and tempers. I did not really want to lose her after all: I simply wanted to have my cake and eat it. I wanted no boundaries, she wanted monogamy. It was as simple and as complicated as that. She was intelligent enough to know that to constrain me would be to lose me, while I enjoyed pulling as far away from her as possible, and then snapping back to the true warmth of a sincere relationship. I wanted to do as I wished but I did not want to leave her. We were both beset with conundrums and control issues and love and hate. Neither of us really knew what to do.

We had attended some sessions with a Couples Counsellor in Santa Monica but we had all ended up in bed together, so it had not really worked. After a couple of passionate threesomes the Couples Counsellor became jealous and possessive, so then I had had piranha women snapping at my tail. After that little fiasco I suggested we go to a man for advice. Kit laughed out loud for about thirty minutes, slapping her thighs like some cowboy in a saloon, genuinely amused at the idea that a man would either know anything or be of help.

'Don't be so silly,' I said. 'They're not that bad.'

But she just snorted and shook her head.

I spent the day alone dealing with the business of porno fame. Signing filthy pictures for the fans. Recording a phone sex line. ('Baby, baby, I'm beggin' you to come in my face, oh yes') and so on. Talking business. Choosing some pervy vintage girdles for a calendar that I had been scheduled to shoot. I rang Leon but he did not return my call. I rang Glen. He was in Tokyo with the band.

'We're huge here,' he shouted down the line. 'Massive security! I got women throwing themselves at me. Dunno what to do with them all. Did you shag Satan?'

'Yeah.'

'Fuckin' tart. I'll ring you when you get back; keep that pussy shaved for me . . . You know how I love it.'

Kit returned later that evening with a smug expression on her face and I knew that something had happened. She leaned back on her chair in the kitchen, put her boots on the table and aimed the Ruger at a picture of Britney Spears that was hanging over the cooker. Pow. The bullet blasted Britney's nose and lodged into the wall.

'Leon wants me to star in his next film,' she said carefully.

'What!'

'Leon wants me to be the star of his new film. *Biker Bitches from Hell*.'

'But he can't! I'm his star! I made *The Ordeals of Emmeline* It was his biggest hit *ever*! I went on the bloody bus round the country. I've done the work. I'm his only contract girl!'

Kit lit a long, thin cigarillo, blew a couple of rings through dark-red lipstick and said calmly, 'He says he can't cast you as the lead – you're not tall enough.'

'I could wear heels!'

'You're his bisexual ingénue, my dear. His evil nymph. He wants a glamazon type, you know, bigger titties, strong thighs, that kind of thing. Says I won't even have to change outfits. And I can take a gun. He wants you to play the second lead.'

'Second! Second!'

I could hardly find the words to describe my disgust. Second indeed. Leon must be mad. Since when did anyone want to be second? They had both gone behind my back, wheeling and dealing and elbowing me out. I felt betrayed and revolted and very disorientated. Leon and Kit were pivotal figures in my life – if I could not trust them then I might as well jump into the Firebird and get right out of there right now.

'Fuck you both! I'm not going to be in it at all then,' I said

'Oh, baby. Don't be like that . . . don't be jealous. It's not that bad. It means we can be together.'

'I don't want to be with you you fucking bitch.'

Silently, drama queenly, genuinely hurt, I went to the bedroom and started to pack my things. There wasn't much. Most of my professional costumes were owned by and kept at Pleasure Dome. Here there were shoes, a hundred pairs or so, from A to Blahnik and back again, some fabulous pearls that I had wheedled out of Leon for the Paris premiere of *Emmeline*, and various shades of true gang-bang lippie, which had found its way to some odd places over the last few months; on the end of the devils dick for a start, and around Kit's nipples. She had tough tits. Liked to have them whipped.

The old scenes rewound slowly over my inner screen. I was furious. She came into the room and leaned against the wall, like a man, looking at me. I was flushed and I knew that I was pouting. I also knew that I did not really want to leave. I wanted to be told what to do. I wanted her to take the initiative, sort this out and make me feel better, as she had done so often in the past, all knowing voodoo queen that she was.

She knew, as I did, that these moments of love frenzy and hysteria were the moment when definition was our strength and our sex. She was the top. And she had to stay the top if I was to stay interested. I might have some control, but I did not want it all. I wanted to know who was the boss. I always wanted to know who was the boss. It gave me a feeling of security that I had never had. Nobody had ever known what to do with me, nobody had ever been able to tell me what to do, and so I had run in all directions, doing as I pleased. This was good. I was free. But sometimes . . . well, sometimes it was sexy to have the wings clipped. Then one wouldn't bash against the light so much. Kit knew this, the delinquent witch.

She watched me flouncing around the room, packing, very Harlow harlot, in a black and white huff deserting a chisel-jawed gangster. I threw silk undies here and there, wound seamed stockings in balls, scrabbled about in the boxes of shoes. I was red in the face and I hardly knew what I was doing. I could feel her staring at me, with total calm, and I could feel her taking back the control with every Zen breath.

'Don't go, baby,' she said. 'You know I love you. I

only went behind your back because I wanted to make sure that I was with you. It's the perfect answer to our problems. We can be together . . .'

'But you won't let me do what I want! You're always trying to imprison me!'

She ambled up to me and enveloped me with her presence. I was wearing a lilac summer shift and a pair of matching kitten heels in lilac suede. They were embroidered with seed-pearls. They were perfect. I had been thinking early Bardot in the South of France and it was working.

She ran her fingers through my hair and looked down at me, dark eyes flashing underneath dark fringe, bosoms heaving. So big, the woman. Then she sat down on the edge of the bed.

'Honey, sometimes I don't know whether to whip you or kiss you.'

I stared at her, mouth turned down, sulky pout, waiting to have my mood forcibly changed.

'Come to Mama.'

I didn't move.

'I said, come here!'

She snapped this order out, for she was firm now, and frightening. She could still make me nervous, and, for me, anxiety and precoital mortification were as good as any foreplay. She was taking back the reins. I was going to get my arse whipped if I didn't watch it, and I didn't feel like it right then or there. I didn't to feel that springy riding crop lashing my thighs or the skin of my butt.

The threat of punishment is often as good as punishment. The knowledge of authority can instil pure passion. Sometimes the pain itself is not required, just an arrogant tilt of the head, the clank of car keys falling on a sideboard, the stomp of a boot walking with determined clump across the floor. Height and muscle. Kit had all that. I just wanted to know that I was not allowed to go. I wanted her to make that decision for me.

'Take your panties off before I rip them off you.'

Staring unblinking into her eyes I hoisted up the summer dress so that she was granted a full view of my underwear – they were white, high-waisted, beautifully made so that they shaped my hips and accentuated the curves. Still looking at her with ever-ebbing defiance, I slowly pulled them down and stepped out of them. Then, with the dress still above my waist, I walked towards where she was sitting on the end of the bed and sat on her lap, face towards her face, legs on either side of her legs.

She kissed me on the lips, very lightly.

'We can make it, you know,' she said and twisted my nipple so that the dart of pain sent a jolt straight to my clit. I moaned and surrendered. Reaching down the back of the dress, she slowly pulled down the zip, eased the garment above my head and cast it aside. Pushing my body down so that my ankles were above her ears, she planted her tongue deep into my wet minge, where it made itself at home, thrusting and tickling until I nearly went mad.

She licked me until I came and I was hers again. Then she threw me down on the bed and pulled down her jeans. She was wearing a strap-on and she fell down on top of me, a demented missionary miss, thrusting her pelvis with sharp thrusts, digging that dong into me until she had my cunt and my psyche.

'You're not leaving,' she whispered into my ear. 'And you're going to learn to do what you're told.'

So I forgave Kit, that night. I even fell in love with her again, but these developments did not prevent me from giving Leon a hard time.

'Why the fuck did you go behind my back?'

'I'm sorry, babe, but I had to test the ground with Kit.

Please don't be upset, my lovely, my Own, my Divinity. I'm paying you more than her, though, for Chrissake don't tell her that. And the second lead is a fabbo part. It's a fab script. The writer's won awards, you know . . . we're breaking taboos here. There are several very hot scenes. In one, Toyota gets a gun stuck up her arse . . .'

'The Moral Majority will be pleased,' I said.

'Who cares what the God squad think?' He replied coldly.

'Why can't I be the lead and wear high shoes?'

'Wouldn't work, honey. You simply don't have the weight. You're too femmy. Trust me on this – the second part is much better for you.'

'What is it then?'

'Well. Her name is Date Bait.'

I had to admit that this sounded promising.

Kit and I drove the Firebird to the California–Mexico border where *Biker Bitches from Hell* was shooting in a village named Los Santos. Los Santos's misfortune was to be east of the coast so that it had never reaped any of the advantages to be gleaned from the business of the sea, which snaked, blue and glittering to the west and invited the usual scores of jet-board speedsters and disco maniacs.

Los Santos's business was difficult to discern: the suburbs were trailer parks, and the centre was an old Spanish church surrounded by tumble down clapboard shops. The surrounding landscape was jagged – an arrid expanse of sharp rocks and dry shrubs lurking underneath pyrotechnic evening skies. The recreations were cable, casino and rattlesnakes, in that order. The town looked like the set of a spaghtti western and film makers had long used it as a cheap location near Los Angeles. The inhabitants, mainly grinning Mexicans, had learned to be polite for a price and were surprised at nothing. They knew that the Hollywood *banditos* kept them in tamales, so they did not ask for much – just the usual location fees and to have their photographs taken with the stars.

Everywhere you looked there were black and white pictures of Botox-lipped hybrids and hunk-jawed lug-heads; all the B-movie hopefuls of Hollywood under-culture, that odd place of Samurai shenanigans, lagoon monsters, lady-freaks, jockstraps and jism. The people of Los Santos had seen it all and were proud to have done so, remembering these cinematic successes in municipal commemoration.

The local cinema was called the Mamie van Doren and the diner was Kung Fu Cookie, after the legendary double DD martial artiste Lezzy 'Lips' Chong Tong. The muscle hulk Fergix had given the town his loincloth as a memento. The council had framed it and it was now hanging over a fireplace in the town hall alongside a signed picture and a cutting from *Variety*.

The Mayor, a septuagenarian cineaste, sat in a rocking chair on his porch reading film magazines and regaling any listener unfortunate enough to float into his vicinity. He did not know which was a movie plot and which was his real life. He had seen so many films and known so many actors that the boundaries between illusion and delusion had mingled in his ageing memory banks and produced a confusion which imbued his anecdotes with a bizarre effect of surreal abnormality. He told Kit, for instance, that Andrea Savage (the platinum-blonde goddess of the Mondo Bimbo movies) had once stayed at his house but that he had had to throw her out of the window because she kept demanding vegetarian meals.

We holed up in the aptly named Los Locos Motel, which is where many of the scenes were to take place. Los Locos was managed not, as you would imagine, by some Central Casting Latino type, all desert grime and poncho, but by Mr and Mrs Patel, two super-bright Pakistanis who lived in a palatial Airstream caravan in the backyard and had already sent two of their children to Yale. Their third child did not seem to be destined for this achievement. He seemed content to slouch around the place, smoking joints, playing Gameboy and watching us girls undress.

He would watch with round brown eyes, secretly staring through the windows, hiding in the shadows. Givenchy insisted that he was in love with her, and there was no need to disagree, though the delights of Givenchy were destined to please only those with sophisticated tastes, blessed as she was with jiggling breast implants and a seven-and-a-half-inch dick.

The plot was very much as the title would indicate. Six chicks on choppers ride into town and play nasty with the locals. Kit, in a long army coat, polished black boots and SS-style officers hat, was Queen, the leader. I was her glowering sidekick in a tiny leather miniskirt, suspenders, and needle thin four-inch-high stilettos. My pleasure was the art of tactical knife throwing, my predilection was troublemaking and my past was a humdrum mall of malevolence and mating.

Givenchy, she-male divine, was playing Heaven, while the rest of the line-up was Pussy Willow as Play Thing, Goo Lightly as Apache, and Toyota as Kamikaze. Leon had hired Jed Blacksnake to direct. He had not done much. A film entitled *Beautiful Mutoid* had been a success on the festival circuit. His reputation rested, by and large, on the fact that he was the son of the late Jack Blacksnake, who had been a legendary horror-movie director until he died in a mysterious fire after a gambling binge in Reno.

Leon unreasonably reasoned that where father went, son must surely go too. He believed that talent ran in genes and he thought that Jed would give *Biker Bitches from Hell* a deranged overtone that would ensure its success in both the porno and weirdo markets. Jed Blacksnake was 32, which is a good age for a man. They have learned to fuck, they are often single, and they still know how to have a good time. Bereft of the melodramatic pessimism of callow youth, they can enjoy themselves because they are free of responsibilities, free of wives, and incognisant of the dreadful gloom that is middle age – those inescapable years when the dick goes, the waistline goes, the hair goes, and, (if she is sensible) the wife goes.

Blacksnake was half Cherokee, half Japanese. This gave him slanted black eyes, high cheekbones and a smooth brown skin. He looked fantastic. Six foot high, stick thin, his black hair snaked down his back in an evil coil. The clothes, always the same, were black Levi's, black shirt, black Stetson, snakeskin belt, and the occasional item of Indian jewellery. He lolloped slowly along, long-limbed, with a knife in his belt and an ace up his sleeve.

Cool as a bloody cucumber, cooler, he hunkered down in the location van, watching rushes, looking at scripts, working. He spoke only when it was absolutely necessary, which meant that no one ever knew what he was thinking and everybody acted out just to get a reaction. But when he smiled, when he smiled you felt it; there were rows of slightly crooked teeth and a light that seemed to emanate from him.

Blacksnake's smile was worth working for. It made you fall in love with him. We had heard that he was hung, that blacksnake was an appropriate name, though I never believe those rumours until I see the gear-stick straight up and ready to go. My poor young eyes have seen so many useless parts and I have been at many showdowns where there has been no shooting.

The legendary cocks are so often smaller than their reputations, particularly in the porno business, where it is the owner's advantage to spread his own rumours. It is cheaper than paying a PR. And girls will talk. Talk is cheap and before you know it the hussies have made a hard-on that does not exist.

The first night some of the actresses started a pool – $25 to the one who got Jed to give it up. Oral sex was not counted: the prize money only went to she who achieved full penetration, either anal or vaginal. Pussy Willow, delicately tonguing a strawberry daquiri, was all blonde know-how and supreme self-confidence. She had, after all, got herself out of Michigan via various beauty-queen titles and a mouth that would have impressed a plumber. She was pert and perky and beginning to lie about her age now that she was too old to work in the upwardly nubile 'Barely Legal' genre.

She had suckered her way to a stardom, of sorts, by a performance trick that entailed the ability to give herself oral sex and bring herself off with her own tongue – a trick that drove men wild and that had appeared in every one of the *Wet Pussy* videos that she had made over the last five years. Anyway. Miss Pussy insisted that she was not only going to fuck Jed Blacksnake, but she was going to marry him. She was tired of the dance circuit. She wanted out of porno. It was about time she retired to the traditions so aptly performed by her mother, who made the best pies in Detroit, even if they did come out of the freezer at Freez-o-Mart.

Kit, of course, was not interested in Jed Blacksnake, so I had to pretend that I wasn't. Privately I resolved to make my own plans with regard to this particular trophy. If he thought he was too cool to submit to the charms of Miss Stella, he was very very much mistaken.

'You keep your sleazy hands off that dipstick,' Kit said, 'or you'll get it, girl.'

'Of course,' I lied demurely. 'Not my type at all.'

Little did Jed Blacksnake know. The eyes of the severest porno hussies were upon him, sizing him up, scrutinising his every move and reading his body language for clues about his predilections. These clues were well hidden. Givenchy said that he preferred men, but I wasn't so sure.

'Bet he likes it up the ass,' she insisted. 'Never met a man who didn't.'

Jed Blacksnake turned out to be more difficult to seduce than any of us had imagined. He was so inscrutable, with his unflickering black eyes and oriental protocols. Pussy Willow pressed her breasts up against him all day, Givenchy did her best but she didn't have a hope. Toyota would have done anything, the crazy bint, but I deduced that she was not his type. Kit (to my intense irritation) got on very well with him, probably because she was the only one who was genuinely uninterested. She cozied up to him for the very purpose of annoying me. They would have laughing little chats together, sitting in corners with beers. He would smile as she winked at him and performed little comedy routines for his amusement. She knew what she was playing at, the meddling whore. She was excluding me on purpose and diminishing me by cutting me out. It drove me wild. Kit knew how to push me. I don't know why or how. I don't know why she was the only one who could. I just knew that she stimulated wild savagery as easily as she breathed. She was the queen of chaos.

As the sun beat down and all the tiny paradoxes became more intense, the energies began to unleash and the shoot slowly evolved into a bizarre sequence of subtle and sexual events that forced themselves forward as if they had a life of their own. No screenwriter could have imagined the subtext, no movie plot could have communicated the complexities, and no audience could have fully understood the full dimensions of all the erotic interplaying.

I would catch Jed Blacksnake staring at me secretly, flicking his eyes away when I noticed, and I would glare at him coldly, sensing that repulsion was his attraction. To hate him was to lure him and to challenge him was to turn him on. I suspected that in that psyche somewhere fantasies lurked, that he was a weird son of a gun with a dark side of unimaginable deviance. It was waiting to be unleashed by little me. Perhaps he had been put on this Earth for that very purpose.

'I wanna fuck that Blacksnake,' I said to the Director of Photography, an old existentialist named Len.

'So does everyone,' he replied coolly.

'Does he put out or what?'

'Sometimes, yeah. Not so much when he is working. I don't think he's lookin' for a relationship.'

'That's fine with me. I want to fuck him, I don't want to breed with him.'

'Who do you wanna fuck?' said Kit coming up behind me.

'You, my love,' I said, putting my hands around her waist. 'You, my love.'

'Yeah yeah yeah.'

Jed was knowing and amused and he didn't miss a trick. He had been raised in Beverly Hills, after all. The sidewalks were lined with pussy and any man could get laid, especially any man with a name and director's credit. He ruled as the king of this empire of film and floozie. He was the mogul in charge of everyone and to whom everyone had to answer.

He began to obsess me.

King of the Road, Indian chief, enigmatic warrior. I began to wake up thinking about him. I performed the day's tasks in order to gain his attention. I just wanted him to fuck me, then smile at me, smile at me and fuck me. I wanted to hear that calm voice speak to me alone. I wanted to know how he was so cool and how he was managing to resist me.

I suspected (and hoped) that he was a warm person who had learned to protect himself from the rigorous debaucheries of Hollywood. That town demands too much, provides too many distractions and never ever speaks the truth. One could lose oneself in the swamp of inanity. Any man could be strangled by the coils of flattery and asphyxiated by superfice, that is any innocent traveller who does not know the game.

His father had been brought up on a reservation in Utah. There was a mystical element about him that kept him at a distance from the frantic erotica that played out in front of him, both on and off the set. He had charisma, that unfathomable atmosphere that sweeps around some individuals like a scent without a smell, attracting, alluring and impossible to explain.

He could have been a sphinx without a secret, though I hoped not. He could have been stupid, but I thought not. He could have been very closed down, damaged by his own protection, perhaps a bit of a bore. I hoped not. But I wanted to find out. Almost against my own will I began to study his every movement for clues that would illuminate the secrets of the mystique. I scrutinised with subtle animal observation, the predator watching the prey. I was as subtle as a snake, as I did not want to incur the wrath of Kit, who had eyes like a hawk, a gun and a twitchy right hand.

So, the plot? What happens is this: six howling hellcats ride into town, humping hot hogs, dressed like gang girls, all bad attitude and bad breaks. Their lives? Drinking, fighting and fist-fucking. Their pleasure? Death, sport and speed. They all pack heat, they all have form, and the only thing they care about are the bikes and the sisterhood. They descend on unsuspecting Hicksville in order to liberate Heaven (played by Givenchy), who has been imprisoned in the local county jail following an incident where a bully humiliated her and forced her to crawl on the bar-room floor on all fours. Although Heaven was not averse to this under some circumstances, this particular evening she was wearing a pure-white jersey catsuit and had just had her nails done, both of which were ruined by this abject scene.

She rises up in fury, punches the man very hard (closed fist) in the face, overcomes him and rapes him. The scene is she-male cock out, melon breasts heaving, then and there, over the table, in the bar, in front of everyone. It is at this point that she is arrested by the sheriff, who, inevitably, turns out to be the brother of the bully.

Heaven is in trouble so the hellcats pile in, butch gone mad, nymphos of the night, determined to break the friend out and show everyone a thing or two. Apache and Play Thing flirt with the drooping male wimp behind the bar, a short man whose eye view is lined directly into the middle of their cleavages.

Frank, with geek glasses and snivelling mien, is destined for comic relief rather than hand relief. The big bitch women dance with him in between them, crushing him with their breasts and bellies, laughing all the while as they have got themselves a sissy sandwich and they're not planning on letting him go. The end of the scene sees Frank lose consciousness. Drowned by the breasts, asphyxiated, he slumps to the ground, where, from a low-angle camera shot, the scene ends with various pairs of high heels walking over his lifeless form, puncturing his body with cruel stiletto thrusts as Tippi Hedren was cut to ribbons by the sharp beaks of the birds.

I, as Date Bait, tarnished with amorality and bearing scars (both external and internal), amuse myself by throwing a knife at Kamikaze, who I have tied to a tree. This performance is rendered more dangerous by the fact that Date Bait does not remove her shades. Kamikaze does not flinch. She does not care. She left her soul in a bordello in Chinatown three years ago, according to her flashbacks.

Kit was in her element as Queen. I should have seen it coming. She had been a closet exhibitionist all along. She loved performing and she loved the attention, though she pretended that she did not care and shrugged with macho insouciance if anyone praised her or patted her on the back.

'You're just a bloody show-off,' I said.

'Speak for yourself, kid.'

Her role was an extension of her own character. As Queen she was togged up with a rifle and a leather officer's hat. She had a tattoo ruler mark on her arm to mark the level for fist-fucking and, as Queen, she could mend her own bike and make her own bombs.

She blows the back of the jail out with gelignite, rides her chopper into the cell, grabs Heaven, and high-speeds it out of town followed in a screeching shoal by the rest of the gang. They hole up in a downtown Motel schmotel where they subject each other to various deviant kink scenes while the police scour the border towns looking for them.

The gang girls get filthy in Room 27. They are all at it, stripped and oiled in an orgy scene, intertwined in a jacuzzi in states of frenzy and posture, licking each other's clit, nuzzling nipples, moaning and groaning. Pussy Willow gets her arse whipped by Apache (played by Goo Lightly wearing her dark hair in plaits and a minute fringed suede miniskirt), a light flogging that leaves a tapestry of streaks on her buttocks and upper thighs.

Queen, meanwhile, cuts my clothes off me with my own knife so that I am only in black bra, black 50s panty girdle with suspenders and black stilettos. Then she drags me to the bathroom, handcuffs me to the taps, pisses on me and leaves me there. The last scene, one of ultimate modern romance, sees Kit and me making out in our hotel room. My dialogue indicates that I am impressed by her firearms, which she answers by tying me to a chair and bringing in 'Kamikaze' for some 'fun'.

This sequence was performed for real after a lot of champagne. Toyota was up for anything and she could take anything, having worked for some years as a needle-bottom to a piercing Mistress in San Francisco. She was as mad as a snake that Toyota. We should have skinned her and made her into belts.

So I am handcuffed to a chair, legs apart, breasts falling out of a little leather waistcoat, hair back-brushed into an evil looking mess, black eyeliner smudged into bruises around the eyes, sulky, while Kit controls the speed of the vibrator that she has forced in between my legs.

This is what I see.

Toyota, seized with lust, throws herself on to the floor in front of Kit's motorcycle boots and licks them in an uncontrolled fit of frenzied supplication. Kit hauls her up and throws her face down on the bed. She looks over to me to see how I am enoying the girl scene, then she looks at the inch rule tattooed on to her lower arm as if speculating how many inches were going to disappear up Toyota's overexcited fanny.

'If you move,' she says to me, 'I'll flog the hide off you.'

She pulls down Toyota's black lace knickers leaving them halfway down her legs, then she slathers her white buttocks with K-Y jelly.

'Get up on all fours!' she commands.

Toyota obeys. Now her arse is right out there, anus puckered for us both to see. Kit greases it, oiling it with slow erotic strokes, and pushes one or two fingers into her to ensure that the back passage is good and relaxed. If Toyota was going to get a gun up her, there should be no holding out. But Toyota's back door was accustomed to swinging open, it had been well used and had, after all, paid for the Porsche Boxter that she so proudly drove around LA.

So Toyota is semi-naked and greased up and her butt is juggling in excitement. Kit removes the Ruger from a leather holster she wears around her waist, and comes up to me. Holding the barrel in front of my mouth, she says, 'If you ever betray me, I will kill you.' Then she pushes the vibrator further into me and turns back to Toyota. Slowly, with menace, she holds the gun under the girls nose.

'This what you want?'

'Yes . . . Yes.'

'This is what you're gonna get . . .'

Kit strokes K-Y up and down the five-and-a-half-inch barrel of the gun, only five and a half inches, I laughed to myself, but five and a half inches of death nonetheless, every inch an inch of double-action fire power – the Mark II semi-automatic pistol, one of the most popular weapons in America. And one of the most beautiful. A thin elegant streak of silver, it looks like a ballet dancer next to the snub-nosed Smith and Wesson LadySmith or some clumping Colt .45. I did not know if there were any bullets in it or not. Neither did Toyota, so though I was fascinated by Kit's abnormal decadence, I also hoped that she knew what she was doing.

Toyota didn't know what anyone was doing. She was in another world now, a world in which she, a strange girl, wondered unaccompanied. She knew how to transcend scenes and how to use the excitement to achieve her own ends. This was as much about fancying Kit as escaping from her own sun. Kit pressed the stainless-steel brushed satin butt on to Toyota's mouth and made her kiss it so that black smudges of lipstick smeared the polished steel. Then slowly, oh so slowly, she inserted the tip into Toyota's pervy little sphincter, further and further in, cold and hard and dangerous, until all that could be seen was the black handgrip.

So there she was, Toyota, on all fours on the bed, buttocks in the air, pants down, a gun up her arse. And Jed Blacksnake filmed it all. We were all hot after this. Girls, guys, crew, no one knew what to do with themselves. Fannies glistened, cocks wavered around, everyone wanted finishing off, not least the director, whose dignified politesse had subtly changed to an electric nerviness which was, I assumed, his version of erotic excitement.

His hands did not shake, he did not lose a beat, but I knew there was a big dick hardening nicely in those black pants, a dick that wanted to be brought off. And so naughty Stella, with the instincts of anything found on the Discovery Channel, naughty Stella homed in on the weak prey.

'Let's go into town and get pizza,' I said as brightly and as innocently as any pert maid of any TV advertisment. Butter wouldn't melt, honeys, not in the mouth anyway.

'OK,' he said. 'We'll take one of the bikes.'

Of course he rode a bike; he lived in Beverly Hills. He was a Hollywood kid. They all had bikes. He selected the Enfield, a beautifully customised 1969 Interceptor – 736cc, four-stroke parallel twin, cast-iron barrel, alloy head, – a model with serious bike cred and a top speed of 110 m.p.h. He eased himself on to the bike as if he was about to fuck it. As some are at ease on horses, others know their way around a department store, he sat on top of that machine as if he had been sitting on top of it all his life. We were going to be safe.

I eased myself as provocatively as possible on to the seat behind him, grasped his waist with tight arms and pushed the bone of my crotch into the small of his back so that he could feel it like a female hard-on, so that he could think about it all the time while he was revving the engine and negotiating the bends. I hoped the man could think about driving and fucking at the same time and I hoped his hard-on wasn't going to be a liability out there on the slick dark open road.

He took perfect control. There was nothing this man could not do. We zigzagged out of the motel car park with poise and accelerated towards the desert road that led to the back of the town. No street lights, just black sky, stars, headlamp, and us. The warm wind blew past, fumes of petrol blew in our noses, leather, Him. Me. He zapped into the ever loving distance, wrist working the handlebars. Slowly, as slowly as the serpent that conned Eve, my hand slithered down the front of his trousers. He continued riding the bike as if nothing was happening. I closed my fingers around his naked cock, which, of course, was as hard as it could be – not even a little excited, but full up and ready to go.

He rolled into the fast-food joint, in and out, we picked the box up from the girl in the front and tied it down on to the metal holder on the back of the bike. Neither of us was wearing a helmet so both of us looked wild and messed, with windswept hair and the light of excitement flickering in our eyes. I was breathing quite hard and hot in my leather jacket. He was silent. Without saying a word he put his finger under my chin and lifted my mouth to his.

'Get on the front of the bike facing me,' he said.

I hesitated. Lord knows why – I was half-mad with lust.

'Go on. It will be OK. Only take your panties off.'

'I'm not wearing any.'

'Good.'

I was still wearing the micro leather skirt, which rode up to nothing as I got on the bike and straddled my legs over his. He revved the engine and eased the front wheel out and on to the road. I hugged on to him, smooth puss riding on top of his groin.

'Get it out,' he barked as he zapped the bike up another ten miles an hour.

I unzipped his trousers and pulled out the stiff dick and then, as the wind whistled past my ears, the landscape disappeared into the distance in front of me, I eased my wet minge slowly down on top of it, as if kissing it, wet and slow.

He shouted out to the wind. I felt him inside me, hard

and hot. I closed my internal muscles around him, kissing him with the inside of my cunt, making him know that I was his love hussy, and I could please him in many, many ways. Even he, leather-bound ice king, even he could not imagine them all. I tied my thighs tightly around his groin, sat on his cock and continued to slowly move myself up and down on him. He accelerated. Sixty, seventy, eighty. Speed. Road. Dick. Danger. Then, with my tail still pistoning on top of him, my face looking over his shoulder into the dark distance, he slowed down, bought the bike to a halt, hauled me off it, threw me down on the ground, and finished the whole thing off there in the dirt of the desert.

Filthy tart, relentless man, banging each other's insides out until my screams of delight echoed to the distant stars and around the desolate rocks, heard by no one except the strange chief that I had wanted for so long.

'Better get goin',' he said, zipping up his zip and adjusting his belt. 'Pizza'll get cold.'

Kit was waiting for me when I got back. Her face looked as if she had just been asked to eat a stew made out of road-kill. I was covered in innocence. Covered in the dirt of the desert road and the oil of the bike, as well, but enacting perfect virginity nonetheless. She rubbed the grime off my face with a hard wet finger and looked down at me.

'What's been happening?'

'Nothing. We went to get the pizza.'

Silently she put her hand underneath my skirt and up into my cunt, which was, of course, still seeping with the love juice of exuberant coition – an illegal passion fuck on the bike and in the road. I wanted more of that man. One was not going to be enough. He was pure hard unavailibilty, and that always makes me go crazy with love or lust or whatever you choose to call it; I want them because I know I will never be able to have them. I'm just an old-fashioned girl like that.

Kit pulled her fingers out of me and rubbed my own salty juices over my face.

'I can still feel him in there!' she snapped.

Then she slapped me on the cheek, the crack resounding into the quiet air. Tears immediately sprang into my eyes. I dissolved immediately into submission. I knew there was very little I could do when Kit was like this. I just hoped that she was not going to be too cruel to me. I had my limits. I was guilty and I needed to receive the ministrations of her all knowing authority.

I had no control of my own. I had not really done my best. I had flouted the safety of any real love that she might have for me. She was genuinely furious and knew that now was not the time to flog me. An angry whip is a dangerous whip: it slashes to wound and knows nothing of the erotica of deviant love. Punishment should be passion, passion should be love. Kit knew this. I knew this. We played. We did not want to destroy, or maim or alienate. These things sprang from affection. She knew now that she must stand back or the killer compulsion would subsume her. She was swept away with jealousy and the need to keep me, but she knew too that she must take care.

She dragged me into our motel room and pulled all my clothes off with furious speed. Then, still silent, she slapped my thighs once or twice, very hard, so that the skin stained red.

'Put your hands above your head.'

I obeyed. Taking a pair of handcuffs she locked them around my wrists. Attaching them to the hook at the top of the door of the room, she hung me on it.

'You can stay there,' she said, 'and think about what is going to happen to you.'

Chapter Seven

I hung on the door. My arms were pulled above my head and they ached. My wrists were attached to the hook with the handcuffs and the metal jagged uncomfortably on my skin. I was naked except for an ankle chain. The night was hot, close even, and humid. It closed around my body as an invisible wrap, silky and warm. I could smell my own scent and sweat as Paloma Picasso mixed with bodily need. I wondered, vaguely, if Kit was making my submission public and what she had planned. She was capable of anything. This I knew. She had once been arrested for lewd behaviour in a bar and she had a long record of speeding convictions that were mysteriously cleared from the computer after an affair with a (female) cop. Then there were the guns. Always the guns with Kit. I could not imagine what she was planning and my body began to quicken with the erotic distortions of angst. I regarded them with detachment. Sexual anxiety was familiar to me and I knew that apprehension preceded the euphoria of theatrical foreplay.

Forced to let go, I was in the power of decisions that were not my own. This was always exciting, always a turn-on, but the possibilities were wide-ranging; all I could do was trust. As I let her have the power, so the mind and nerves collaborated, the warmth tingled as sexual energy, and I began to become excited, to want to see her and to do as she wanted.

After an hour or so I heard whispering outside the door, then footsteps, and Kit reappeared. She looked like some Hadeian concept. She wore a black officer's hat, a white shirt whose buttons were forced open by her breasts, which – swollen and beautiful – flowed shamelessly over a half-cup bra. The Ruger rested in a holster on a leather belt; her black Levi's cut into the slit of her mound; the stiletto ankle boots were made of black PVC.

Her black hair was piled into the hat, leaving only dark tendrils to curl around her face; she wore blood-red lipstick and thick black 50s eyeliner. I had never seen her look so good. Mistress mine. A tricky whore but a beautiful one.

'Jed says we're to shoot a scene tonight,' she said.

She stood close in front of me, her cleavage in line with my eyes, and unlocked the handcuffs. I fell into her. She lifted me up, like a child, and carried me to the bed, where I sat on the edge. Sulky.

'Are you hungry, baby?' she said.

'Yes.'

'Would you like some of this?'

She brandished a take-out box that smelled of pizza – a delicious smell to the hungry person, as I am sure most people will agree.

'Yes.'

'Yes what?'

'Yes, please.'

She opened the box and fed me some.

'Good?'

'Yes.'

'Yes what?'

'Yes, thank you.'

'Jesus, you've got a long way to go.'

But she was benign, fed me some more, then wiped my face for me, a secret smile on her mouth and the serene expression of someone who knows exactly what is going to happen next. She was the scariest teacher, and the weirdest leather dyke – a shifting personality disorder of ever-moving psychosexual roles. I realised that I had not met all the fantastic renegades that lurked at the centre of this wild woman from New Orleans. I still knew nothing about her.

I had pressed some triggers to my own advantage, but they were only triggers. I did not know the characters that peopled her old soul. They were an alien cast. A party of pretenders hosted by one strange leader. I could not guess who was planning to come out and play tonight, though the uniform indicated that she was in theatrical mode.

'What are you going to do to me?' I said. 'I want to know.'

'Be quiet Stella, and put this on.'

She sprinkled talcum powder over my naked body, rubbed it in slowly, and sucked for a minute on each of my nipples so that they stirred and contracted. Slowly she eased me into a shiny shiny rubber dress. A sleeveless black shift, it was cut to the knee. The back, at the bottom, had been cut into a circle which revealed both buttocks and pushed the cheeks through a rubber frame. It was a dress in which to receive punishment. Pure and simple. It was a dress that could not be worn in public despite the fact that it was designed to expose the portions of the body that a goodly number of the population would like to see more often.

I twisted around to look in the mirror. The fabric was sheath tight. The orbs of my arse sprouted through the tight rubber as a portrait of provocation.

'And these,' she said, pointing to a pair of black slingback sandals made of smooth-haired fur. Strappy at the toe (to reveal magenta nails) they crisscrossed at the heel and fastened with a tiny gold buckle.

'Jesus, those are cute,' she said. 'If you weren't such a bitch I'd go down on all fours and kiss them.'

She didn't, of course. She made up my face while I sat silently on the edge of the bed looking at myself in a tall mirror that leaned against the wall. The dress constrained me. It was a size too small. I could hardly move into any position of comfort. I had to sit with my knees together, the dress taut across my thighs so that any old tom could inspect the dark shadow that led to my labia.

She brushed my hair fiercely with the round Mason and Pearson hairbrush that she kept by the bedside, always at hand. Then, silently, she took my hand and led me outside. Hobbling on the high heels, I followed her carefully to a clearing at the back of the motel where the crew had set up lights. The cameramen were all in position, and it was evident that a set had been made to the decree of the director.

The girl gang stood silently around a 1970 Harley Davidson Sportster. This is a bike with history and attitude. A relation of the 1957 classic, it is a lean street machine, all low end torque and high end speed. They were waiting for me with expressions as cold as sci-fi replicants and they were dressed in the uniform of all the biker bitches of pandemonium. Leather jackets, skin-tight black Levi's, spiked heels, white T-shirts, gum, cigarettes, belts, attitude. And they were all wearing shades.

'Lie face down on the bike Stella,' Kit said. 'Put your fanny on the seat and your face on the fuel tank.'

The girls stood around, towering, glamazon, silent. Jed Blacksnake, eyes glittering beneath the rim of his black stetson, smoked a thin cheroot.

Kit tied me down on to the bike. My wrists were

manacled to the chrome bars of the front forks, my ankles to the exhaust pipe. My arse, then, was the picture. Forced up the seat of the bike, the cheeks protruded through the slit rubber as an easy target for any punishment that Kit chose to implement. I rested my face on the cold black metal of the fuel tank and submitted.

The effect of the dress, and of the raised pelvis, was to focus my attention entirely on my backside. It was as if it was the only part of the body that I possessed. And she beat it, slowly and fiercely, with a black leather paddle. She made it red, and slapped down on it, so that the need seeped between my legs and, soon, in a matter of four or five minutes, the ego had left me and I had joined in a bizarre melded fusion of metal, oil, rubber and the sting of sensual sensation.

She smacked me again and again and it was as if she was never going to stop. The pain eased from naughty foreplay to something stronger, something that was difficult to bear. It was the moment when I wanted her to to stop, but I knew that moment: it would pass, we would go through to another level – a level whose finale was a rush of pure pleasure as the endorphins kicked in, confused things that they are, manipulated shamelessly by sexual sophisticates and tarts of the worst order.

Kit, strong hand, silent dom, went on spanking my protruding cheeks with the leather paddle until my chest started to shake and tears ran down my face. Jed came in for a close-up. I tried to struggle, wrists clinking against chrome pipes, ankles hitting more metal, the smell now girl and leather and fuel.

And still she went on.

Yes, yes, yes. I repent. You bitch. I repent.

As all the old guilts left the dark shadow of my mind I released the old sins that I did not know that I had committed. These are the burden of men and women. True pain let me release past pains, those warped torments that are formed by youth and the lying memory. The other girls moved slowly closer to inspect the scene with all the close fascination of erotic fixation. They stared in silence, hands manly in pockets, nursing desires.

Kit suddenly stopped. Throwing the paddle down on the dust, she kicked it away with her stiletto, stared down at me, lit a cigarette, and ambled casually off the set.

'That woman's got rhythm,' I heard an electrician whisper to his mate.

I could hardly move. Cunt and cheeks and spirit were hot. The air, sharper now, began to bite the sensitive punished flesh of the reddened arse. I struggled with mobility. I struggled with sense. I was alone, but the happiness was there, unfathomable, unexplainable, and very, very satisfying.

'Your turn, Givenchy,' said Jed.

Givenchy stepped forward, hairsteric and she-male perve. Long and lean, as if everything had been purposely extended, here was a rangy man with tits made in Rio. Givenchy was a deviant diva with high cheekbones, sensual mouth, immaculate brow line, and glossy highlighters brushed with loving care for hours every morning. He read bike magazines, she wore the best jewellery; he used to play basketball, she read Angela Carter. He could pump hand-job jism with the best of them, she watched videos full of damaged love because she liked to know that she could cry. He wanted to fuck the trade down by the docks; she wanted to go on picnics in the woods.

Givenchy. Her real name was Max and her mother had never damned her.

I knew my arse was up there ready for this gender-travelling babe. The drag girl unzipped her Levi's, talon red nails clicking against the zipper, and eased the tip of her hard man's cock slowly between the soft wet lips of my labia. She smoothed her way in, dick good and hard, further in until she was leaning over me. Then our bodies were on top of each other, symbiotic, scent, flesh, heat, bike, all as one. I could feel her breathe on the back of my neck, feel her dick deep inside pushing towards my womb and all the other places of erotic mystery. My head went completely.

'Stay with it, Stella,' Jed snapped. 'Don't leave us.'

I yanked myself back into the present. Her husky male voice asked if I liked it. He pushed his dick in, pumping on and on until the shudder of orgasms wavered from her groin to her back to her throat and she groaned like a man.

'Kit,' said Jed.

Kit walked back on the set. She, praying mantis woman and harpy of the underworld, slowly untied me and eased me up so that I was sitting on the bike, arse against leather, face towards her. She kissed me on the lips, tongue on tongue, and I wanted her very badly indeed. Standing in front of me, Kit undid her flies, released the dildo, and as my ankles clung around her waist, thighs squeezing her body, she pushed it hard into my cunt and I came immediately.

'Jed's got a hard-on,' I whispered into her ear.

'Let him have one, baby. You're not having him again. You know that, I know that, your no good motherfuckin' tart ass knows that. You are not having him again!'

'No,' I said meekly, for the butt was painful now, the dull ache of punishment was setting in. The bruises would be there for a week, testament to my slavering slavery. I was her girl again.

Later Jed Blacksnake told me that he had arranged the scene with Kit after she had threatened to kill him if he ever came near me again.

'Givenchy taking you on that Harley was one of the

hottest things I have ever filmed,' he said. 'Babe, this is one great movie.'

There were five more days to go. Five more days of recreational deviance enacted for the benefit of Jed Blacksnake's cameraman and for the great wide unseen crowd of eyes who would anonymously inspect our intimate parts and enjoy our unrepentant emissions. The audience, the fans, the press, the people – they were the paying procterscope and we performed. Porn was play and play was sometimes life, there in the land of the *vaqueros* and light-up virgins. We were the Biker Bitches from Hell and we did as we pleased. We all had scenes, some with each other, some with the various studs posing as gas-station attendants, barmen, cops and creeps.

Kit placed the butt of her Ruger against a man's forehead while Toyota grabbed his dick out of his trousers, sucked him stiff, and then left him there, hard as hell and with no place to go. She stalked off, hips swaying, leaving him to Givenchy, who tied the guy down and inserted her fabulous hefty white-trash dick into his virgin arse.

Vince 'Dong' Stanton was a virgin in the film; in life he was a master of anal trickery and known, in particular, for an unusual line-dancing routine in which a row of men linked with each other anally while stepping out to a dirty hoedown barn-stompin' track by the *Tennessee Good Old Boys*. Givenchy told her mother most things, but she had never confessed this. Velma thought her only son did Whitney Houston impersonations in a burlesque club off Broadway.

Pussy Willow and Goo tended to work together, known (in porn parlance), for their 'interracial double bj act'. They were sinful hardcore bitches with tight pussies and wet lips and they knew how to do it. These two liked sex so much it was fascinating. There were no dark Catholic secrets for Pussy and Goo, no small-town repression or rape by relations. Pussy had been a wholesome homecoming queen. Goo was a graduate from Vasser. They were lewd tarts who liked getting it. It was as simple as that. Pussy Willow was playful, perky and perverted. Curvy rather than a stick ass, she had a good round bum and large breasts that fought to escape from the cotton confines of ever-tight T-shirts. She was a a curvaceous burlesque of rotating mammary that mesmerised anyone who stared at her for more than three seconds.

The crew lost the power of speech when Pussy was around. She was blonde and she was stereo and, boy, was it working for her. It was hard-ons all round. She could make the simple act look like foreplay – a cigarette, a crudité, a postage stamp. Pussy played with her lips and men gawped, dogs in a pack, fixed by the presentation. Pussy had no off button. She was always on. Sometimes she sucked her thumb and no man would say no. She had once extorted $10,000 that way.

'Everyone wants pussy,' she said, and she was right. Everyone did. She was cheeky and she was disgusting.

Goo's predilection was to smother every hairy motherfucker she could lay her arse on. And what an arse. The Director of Photography was in love with it. He could never drag his paralysed eyeballs away from Goo's beautiful cheeks.

'Those black women,' he would say. 'The Lord sure knew how to build 'em.'

A tear would well in his eye as he shook his head, muttered, and knew that Goo was way out of his league. Goo shook her booty like a disco queen of sluterama. She was Superfly, ripping 70s vintage to her own decree. This meant skintight orange loon pants stroking her thighs like a second skin, Day-Glo bikini tops, Afro wigs (all colours), hooped earrings, bangles and an attitude that would have made Shaft run for cover. The girl had sex and soul and she moved like a long-limbed warrior queen loping to her own private James Brown soundtrack. She came from Alabama and had once spent Sundays reading the Bible to Grandma. She knew more about Exodus than anyone I have ever met, but the funk queen knew how to fuck.

Goo's scene? Wearing a silver leather bikini top (down the front of which she kept a stiletto knife) and silver knee boots with six-inch platforms, she manhandled a Hell's Angel to the ground, pinned him there with her thighs, sat on his face and taught him how a pussy should be licked. She instructed him so slow she tortured him. She sat on his face and made him lick her brazen lower lips slowly, gently, tickling at first. She taught him how to dip his tongue deep into her warm snatch and kiss her clit, then how to munch with concentrated care. She made sure that he knew that only her pleasure mattered. He, rough git, caveman defeated, received a lesson in losing macho delusion. His dick stood up hard and made a mound in his leather trousers but Goo would not let up. He had to work the jaw and every muscle of his face as she sat astride him, moaning and instructing. She slapped him in the chops if he stopped and ground her pubic bone up and down on his face so hard his skin was bruised for days after wards. Ha! Serve him right. He could not escape because he was trapped by Pussy Willow, who, in a determined sister act, placed her plump butt firm down on his calves, sat on them, then smoked a cigarette and flicked the ash on him.

Finally the Angel made Goo come with his tongue and, having satisfied herself with queenly arrogance,(the condescension of the woman was impeccable) she finally returned the compliment, jerking his stiff purple head out of his zip and sucking it up to a good size. She eased herself up and down on it, her arse to his face, so that all he saw was her long black back, those shameless cheeks, and a grinding groin playing with his soul and granting him emission. It took about five seconds. His cream oozed over her fingers. She wiped it off over his face, kicked him in the ribs with a silver toe, and left him to his ignominy.

Later the leather-clad Angel got rough and took it out on me. Jed staged a great rape scene. Always my favourite. Staggering into a saloon, knocking back the doors western style, he asks your poor little innocent Stella where her bitch friend is hiding. Stella, brave and ever, ever petulant, rips her attitude straight off James Dean, and spits in his face. She is wearing a micro-mini and looking good. But she is alone. Angel is out for revenge. His manhood has been stolen and he needs it back. He needs it back very badly. He is big and ugly and probably about 45. He has been on the road for 20 years. He can take a corner at 98. He has killed four men.

As far as he is concerned one girl gangster is the same as any other. They all needed to know who was boss. So the Angel twists my arm behind my back, pushes me flat over a bar-room table, and tears my little lace black panties to pieces with his bare hands. Sliding out the leather belt with one slick crack, he lashes my arse and thighs with it. I am silent. The cameras are behind me, getting the flesh-tingling punishment, the thighs, the stilettos and the belt coming down, striping the flesh.

Then (and I was very ready for it, wet like oozing) he fucked me. He had a big dick and he took me from the back, pumping into me hard and fast and with the stamina of a mad horse. Relentless. Savage. Semi-wild. I did not have to perform any pleasure, the pleasure was mine. The Angel was a fab fuck. His rough hands felt great on my clit, rubbing it with rude violence, as he blasted into me. Then the zip was pulled up and the camera followed him out of the door, walking tall, arrogant, heels banging against the wooden floorboards. I was left behind, slumped face down over the table, weak with exhaustion. My, what it is to be modern.

I was pleased to get the Angel. He could have done anything with me after that, but Kit was keeping me on a tight leash, literally sometimes, with the collar and all. I wasn't allowed to do anything. But Angel was in the script and we were all professionals, if that is the right word.

The rushes were good. Everyone was impressed. Even Kit (whose throat swelled up in an allergic reaction if she had to say sorry or emit compliments) admitted that Jed knew what he was doing. He was Russ Meyer and David Cronenberg – almost an exact mix. There were kitsch posturings and adulation of the female form; there was glossy fetishisation of deviant objects combined with the visceral reality of hard-core sex, all tricked out with an atmosphere of sinister gravity and an enhanced colour that was too bright and slightly unreal. This was the lucky result of the free use of a hi-tech but as yet untested camera – the SpectralVision 3000.

The emerging movie was horrifying and it was sexy. It was also cold and visually innovative. We observed the elements that made a Blacksnake film, but who knew where his mind lay? He never revealed. Black eyes were always unreadable, the cheroot in the mouth, polite and detached, supportive but unavailable. He was an enigma. I was beginning to think that he had been beamed down from another planet. He was not one of us, but some lizard type whose blood was cold and who preferred the night.

He and I went nowhere. Kit had successfully kicked over that particular fire. One of the grips told me that Jed hated trouble on sets and was not going to contribute to anything that risked damaging the film. He had to answer to Leon after all, and Leon had a two-million-dollar stake in this movie.

Jed kept his distance, repelling us all with immaculate manners. He was inpenetrable but this did not deter Ms Pussy Willow. She was insouciant in the face of impeccable discouragement and she refused to relinquish her ambition to marry him.

'He's mine,' she would say, sucking a rocket-shaped ice lolly with the porno professionalism that was second nature to her. She did not need any actors' studio. The icy phallus dipped down to the back of her throat and eased its way back through her lips while she retained a convincing innocence that was her particular (and only) acting skill.

'He's mine, he needs me. I want to bake cookies and have his babies.'

She was never off the mobile phone to her mother (who still lived in the trailer park), discussing the imminent engagement and whether Grandma would remain alive long enough to enjoy the wedding party.

'Does your mother know what you do?' I once asked her.

'Aw, yeah. She always wanted to be in show business herself but things got difficult after the trailer blew up. She's real proud of me.'

I could not see that a man as cool as Jed would want something as obvious as Pussy. She was so giggly and pert all the time, all jiggles and wobbles and endless ardour.

'Jed likes Pussy,' Kit said with irritating authority one night as we lay in bed.

'No he doesn't!'

'He does actually. He told me, in confidence.'

'Why?'

'Why did he tell me in confidence?'

'No! Why does he like her?'

'He didn't say. Opposites attract, I suppose. There's no reason why he shouldn't.'

'She always looks as if she has just won the lottery. It's so irritating, all that jiggling about and playing with her hair. If God had wanted us to play with our hair he would have welded tennis rackets on to our heads.'

'She's fun and she's cute.' Kit snarled. 'And she's got big titties. That's all men want. You must know that, Stella. He might have made the cover of *FilmFreak* magazine, but he is the same as the rest of them. A suede jacket with tassles doesn't change anything. There is a dick and a brain and they are in the same place, even if you are the hottest director since Lars von Trier. Anyway, you're only angry because he's ignoring you.'

'Don't be absurd.'

I wondered if it would be possible to kill her without incurring a prison sentence. God knows there were mitigating circumstances. I entertained an amusing scene in a witness box where I wore a little grey dress, sobbed into a hankie, and showed the jury the blemishes that scarred the tops of my innocent thighs. I would go for a prim secretarial look – early Miss Moneypenny perhaps, with seamed stockings, little hat, a pair of white gloves. I would weave tales of cruel provocation and they would sympathise. Nodding their heads in easy acquiesence, they would agree that any rational human being would have been carried away by the instincts of primal survival and forced to murder her.

She would go down in legal history as the biggest bitch in the free world. I opened my mouth to emit a verbal assault but she turned off the light and left me to lie staring at the ceiling, mystified, irritated and sleepless.

The last week of the shoot was enhanced by the presence of Leon who arrived in a white stretch limo. The car was so big the roof had been designed to double up as a helipad. The interior was the size of an average apartment in Tokyo and it was equipped with a crystal chandelier, antique gold sconces, a DVD television and video, a fax machine, a telephone, a photograph of Leon's mother Zelda, a washbasin, a fully equipped drinks cabinet and a small landscape by Vermeer.

The seats were so deep that it took Leon some five minutes to emerge from them, struggling as if to escape from the clutches of a giant clam. Finally the cream leather released him and he emerged in the sunlight. Blinking, he swore he had been blinded and struggled to find his Ray-Bans, which were hanging on a real gold chain around his neck, as usual. And, as usual they were teamed with a silk shirt emblazoned with a motif bright enough to cause an epileptic fit. He was also wearing a loose white linen suit (crumpled) deck shoes (brown) no socks and a badge that said, 'OBSCENITY IS IN THE EYE OF THE BEHOLDER.'

His face was deep red-brown from playing a celebrity golf tournament in Palm Springs and he was accompanied by a bodyguard built like Terminator 2. One of the younger gaffers, tired after three working nights, thought that the gigantic lug-head actually was Arnold Schwarzenegger and kept slapping him on his swollen biceps and calling him Arnie despite the fact that the man told him at least three times that his name was Dennis.

'Arnie!' said the poor young thing, blinded by exhaustion and delusional with sleep deprivation, 'you were so cool in *Kindergarten Cop*.'

'Yo, Arnie! Dude! Do you still drive the Hummer?'

'Arnie! Who builds your suits?'

'Arnie! Do you know Pamela Anderson?'

'Arnie!'

'Arnie!'

'My mom loves you.'

He wouldn't let up and he didn't know that he was playing with an individual armed with a Colt .45 and trained in every aspect of advanced 'executive protection'. The besuited behemoth had attended the Academy of Advanced Security Specialists in New Jersey, where he had learned the fine principles of defensive tactics (armed and unarmed) countersurveillance, bomb search and limousine procedure.

'I had to buy the borg,' Leon whispered to me. 'There have been death threats.'

The gaffer walked past waving his baseball hat.

'Arnie!' he yelled. 'Who loves ya, baby?'

Dennis was six foot five. He wore mirror shades (as instructed by the Academy) a navy-blue suit, white shirt, black tie and an expression of deep misery.

'He looks a bit depressed,' I said to Leon.

'He is,' said Leon. 'Clinical as it turns out – barely balanced by medication. He only stopped throwing up when I sent him to that bulimia clinic in Beverly Hills. You should see his CV, though: overachievement isn't in it. Collegiate wrestler, black-belt Foo Bang Do, applied-science degree, diploma with full honours in everything from Search Procedure and Tactical Assault to Micro-wave Radar Sensors and Kidnap Strategy. There's nothing that man doesn't know about motorcades . . .'

'Who else has he, er . . . guarded?' I asked.

'Well, he saved the life of that dog who starred in *Denise Goes East*. Do you remember? The Bichon-Frise? One of the best actors in Hollywood? She was was worth about three million dollars.'

'And?'

'And he used to work for the Artist Formerly Known as Lulu.' Leon paused to wave at Goo Lightly, of whom he was particularly fond. She waved back and blew a kiss. Her long white claw-nails had been painted with mini portraits of Martin Luther King and they tapped delicately against immaculately painted Day-Glo orange lips as she moued.

'My man!' She shrieked and disappeared to her trailer to change.

Leon turned back to me.

'Is he violent?' I enquired, staring at the Cro-Magnon

shoulders and immersing myself briefly in the pure weight of the man. He looked as if he could throw a girl about the place and I began to enjoy a refreshing wave of erotic interest.

'I hope not. I don't want another court case on my hands.'

We sat in the shade watching Jed shoot a close-up of Goo. She was wearing a chain-mail bikini and her shoes were perspex fantasy mules. The transparent heels were hollow and held a pair of live scorpions. Long, lean, dark, every muscle of every tendon toned to tight definition, she was draped over a classic Triumph motorbike as if she was about to make love to it. The camera, on wheels, edged closer to her breasts.

'Breathe, Goo,' said Jed. 'We need to see them rise and fall. Make-up! Where's the sweat?'

A girl rushed forward with a a bottle of massage oil and delicately smoothed it on to Goo's thorax. As she gently stroked the brown skin, the nipples hardened beneath the silver links of the bra top.

'Jeeze, Mamie, you can do that any time you like,' Goo groaned, as the visagiste continued stroking beads of lanolin into her cleavage and over the tops of her arms.

'Break it up, girls,' said the second assistant director. 'The light is going, let's get on. Position, Goo.'

Goo sat side-saddle on the bike, legs splayed, back straight, black bush pulsating underneath the chain-mail briefs. Slowly she eased one hand down and snaked it slowly towards her crotch. The strap of the chain-mail bra slipped off her shoulder and down her arm. She closed her eyes, funk queen on heat, ready to fly.

'Hold it,' said Jed. 'Where's the shadow?'

'Oh, man!' said Goo. 'Can't I just git my liddle fingers goin' down there?'

'Wait, honey,' said the second assistant director.

'I can come more than once, you know . . .'

'We know,' said a second second assistant director.

'Just hold it,' said an additional second assistant director.

Various adjustments were made. The older electricians were immune to working with hot pussy but the younger gaffers hardened underneath their shorts and twisted the peaks of their baseball caps in unconcealed excitement. Torpor floated down on to the set and settled with humid sensuality; aquiescence seeped slowly into the atmosphere. A small world made of many mens eyes focussed on the small dark space between Goo Lightly's legs. There was silence.

No man lit a cigarette. No man whispered.

Mr Patel's son trained his binoculars from a surveillance point in his motel room. Dennis stared through mirror shades. Goo slipped her fingers underneath the chain mail and manipulated her clit. Twisting her body around, back stretched over the seat of the motorbike, long brown legs now draped over the handlebars, pelvis up, finger in, she made love to herself. Now nobody existed for her. She was alone in solipsism as she fingered herself to a climax out there in the dying sun.

Perspex heels rattled against the chrome of the handlebars. The scorpions flicked and twitched as Goo's pelvis thrust itself up to receive the cock that was not there. On and on to juddering orgasm. And immediately again. Until, at the seventh time, she left herself alone and threw her head back on to the seat of the bike, eyes closed, enjoying the smug calm of onanistic bliss.

'Cut,' said Jed. 'That's a wrap.'

Leon stared at his actors with calm satisfaction. He had seen the rushes and he knew he had employed the right director. *Perfunctory Buggery* and *Lovely Newbie* magazines had already run some complimentary advance publicity. He seemed satisfied that his money was being well spent.

'How are things in general Leon?' I asked, sipping an

ice-cold vodka. I wasn't working that day, and I planned to make the most of it. He looked at me, took off his shades, and I saw that underneath the tan his eyes were tired and lined.

'Your lord and master is being persecuted, my lovely,' he said. 'I find I am forced to defend myself against agents of iniquity who want to pull me down and impoverish me. The women of America are oppressing me. The Catholic Mothers have risen up; they have decided to root out all evil and it is costing me a fortune in attorney fees. They might bankrupt me but I must pay for our cause – the cause of civil rights, Stella.'

Dennis the bodyguard stood silently behind the table, about three feet away from his employer. Three feet was apparently the designated personal space allowed by the Exectutive Protection Code of Protocol. He stared through mirrored shades into the middle distance, observing the scene with silent *froideur*.

Leon slapped his palm down on the table. The bang took Dennis by surprise. His head rotated mechanically around on his neck, surveying the terrain for an assailant. His hand dipped towards the holster under his arm like a trout diving under a rock.

'Put it away, Dennis,' Leon said wearily. 'There's no sniper.'

He had consumed three margeritas and was quite drunk now.

'I will fight the good fight!' he shouted.

As he lobbed taco 'dipsters' and globs of 'tangy salsetto' into his mouth, I managed to gather that he had been skirmishing with his old enemy Ms Rowena Brocklehurst, a Christian fundamendalist and Republican candidate who was harassing him on the antiporn ticket: a sure-fire vote winner in middle America.

Rowena had founded the Catholic Mothers and was their president. She was also a lawyer. Litigation was her weapon and she had begun to fire it. The Catholic Mothers were a well-organised, well-financed movement empowered by leading feminist dignitaries and publicised by certain Hollywood starlets. They had launched themselves in Abilene, the buckle of the Bible Belt in Texas, in 1967, and had emerged to prominence with a their now famous (Wo)Manifesto of Christian Change.

They were a powerful enemy with a network that infiltated into the most influential Senate committees and connected with selection of groups that ranged from the Moral Majorettes (a youth squad based in Maryland) to the Anti-Felatio Feminists in Utah. They were also rumoured to have recently befriended the Disgust Brigade, a militant squad of terrorists who organised operations from a secret headquarters thought to be based outside Phoenix. Their leader, a shadowy figure named Cowl, had achieved cult status thanks a talented graphic designer and a snowstorm of leaflets.

Leon and Rowena Brocklehurst had hated each other for years. Now they hated each other in the political realm as well. This forum had become their personal stadium, and they seemed intent to bring each other down with legal strangleholds and public crotch crunching.

Leon had not helped his cause by by announcing to a writer from Reuters that he was a religious man. He worshipped at the shrine of Elvis, which made him a devout Presleytarian. This sound bite had gone all over the world and was already a T-shirt on Venice Beach.

'There is a fight coming, Stella, I tell you that. We are about to have a fight. That woman is ambitious. She'll go all the way to the White House.' He shuddered melodramatically. 'She's inciting the Catholic Mothers and they're causing trouble all over the market. The distributors are shaky as hell. I've already had chains in Illinois and Idaho refuse to stock the fisting and pissing stuff. I mean what's wrong with fisting and pissing? If it sells it sells, right? I mean, it's not my thing, Stella, as you know, but it is somebody's thing ... and who are we to disagree?'

His mobile phone rang.

'Yeswhatisitforchrissake?'

I left him barking orders at one of the battalion of lawyers he employed on a retainer.

Relations with Kit deterioted further. She resented the fact that I had so obviously enjoyed the scene in which the Angel raped me over the bar-room table and engineered a strategy of covert manipulation to ensure my maximum discomfort. This did not work. I am not a jealous person. I gave that particular emotion up. It is a dangerous drug and it never worked for me. So Kit's attempts to flirt with Goo or Toyota or whoever failed to stimulate any passion. I would not have minded if she had enjoyed herself with these two. They were lovely. Why not? I knew that she was not in love with them and I did not feel threatened by them. I quickly outmanoeuvred her. As Kit spent more time with the other girls on the set, I used the release of her vigilance to my own advantage. I fucked Angel for a start – hard in his trailer. He had a great wide hard cock and I did not see why I should miss out on it. Sometimes a girl just wants a man to pin her down on the floor and spread her legs for her. I liked his rough-road sensuality, I liked his steel-blue eyes, I liked the fact that he was genuine gypsy, zigzagging about on his bike, taking jobs when he felt like it.

Angel was an old-fashioned American outlaw but it was not Angel that I really wanted. It was Jed. The more he withdrew the more frenzied I became. My coast was clearer now that Pussy had set her sights on Dennis, and Dennis, not a rocket scientist despite the training in all aspects of computerised technical surveillance, flattened himself as quickly as long grass is flattened by hard rain.

'Oh, honey,' she said. 'Dennis an' I are a lurv-match . . . You should go for Jed again.'

I tried every method of seduction available to a woman. I tried cool disinterest. I tried bursting into tears and having a 'creative' crisis. I tried sitting on the bar in a leather miniskirt and no panties. I tried talking about obscure Japanese movies and insinuating myself into his interests. Finally I lied.

I tapped on his motel room door.

'Our shower is broken,' I said. 'May I use yours?'

He should have laughed out loud, but he didn't. His mind was probably on the movie. He had little left over to assess the complex machinations of mating ritual.

But now it was the last day; for the first time in two months he could relax a little. The film had wrapped. Everyone was going home the next day. For the first time in two months Jed had nothing to do. Kit was safely out of the way and I was in Dorothy Lamour mode. That is, my friends, a long white robe, a turban, and delicious little white fur-trimmed mules with gold heels.

I was lucky.

I made sure that the door of the bathroom was open so that the mirror on the opposite wall allowed him the full privilege of ablution – an exercise in profligacy that I had scripted myself. The shower curtain was, of course, open. Standing underneath the frothing jet I massaged myself all over with suds, my fingers pleasing myself between my legs, waving my buttocks in his direction, as shameless as any jungle primate. I could see him in the mirror. He put down the paper on which he was working and started to look.

I made love to my own body. It was a fabulous performance. Then, as innocent as a newborn lamb, I tripped out of the bathroom, wet and naked underneath the bathrobe, letting it fall apart over my tits, allowing him glimpses. He did not bother with any lines. He simply walked slowly up to me, pushed me up against the bathroom door and kissed me.

I allowed the robe to fall slowly to the floor. I was trim and tan and smooth and ready for it. And he took it. There was no undignified scrambling. This was no Carry On film. No pause for mutual consideration of feelings, needs or desires. No foreplay.

Zip down, condom on, straight hard sex, legs around his waist, on the top of his bed.

He pumped himself into me, on and on until I began to lose myself to him. I looked at the ceiling and then over to the window of the room. The curtains were open. And, just at the moment that he came with the discreet pleasure of the self-contained man, I saw Kit walk past outside. She peered in, nose against the glass, saw what was happening and looked at me in the eye just as my own climax rose to meet his.

Her expression did not change. She merely looked at me with distaste and continued walking.

Oh Christ, I thought.

The next day we drove back to Los Angeles in silence.

Chapter Eight

'Girl, I've had enough of you.'

She reached under the bed and pulled out her leather suitcase, an old-fashioned thing with brass locks. It had been given to her by her father just before he died. It was where she kept her guns.

Oh Christ, I thought. The bitch is going to kill me.

But it was not the guns that came out of the suitcase. It was a black box bearing the name 'Kink-Lock'. A swirling mist of tissue paper revealed a stainless-steel device consisting of a metal belt and a silver 'pudendum' shield.

'This,' she said, 'is what you need.'

'What is it?'

'It is the finest chastity belt on the market – designed by Italians, crafted in Sheffield, sold in New York, polished by the tongues of an occult slave ring in Tokyo. The company employ career criminals to design them. There's no way anyone could break in unless they know something about explosives. There are two different locks and a hidden hinge. There's even the option to fit an anti-tamper device which sets off an alarm. It is fireproof, burglar-proof, shockproof and rape-resistant.

'The Cunt Trap Mark IV is the highest security pussy prison money can buy. It is totally inpenetrable! Honey, this body armour is gonna keep that clit under control. You're not gonna be able to move without Mama.'

She held up a tiny silver key.

'And, baby, I am the keyholder.'

I was not sure that I liked the idea of being incarcerated like this. The device looked like a man trap from some Dark Ages forest. It was made of stainless steel polished to a metal finish and it looked very uncomfortable. I would have struggled and complained but I was shackled to the door, my wrists pinned with the handcuffs. I could not move.

'I don't like this.'

'You haven't tried it.'

Kit scattered some talcum powder around my buttocks, pelvis and labia. Then she unlocked the waistband, turning the key anticlockwise in the lock at the front about five times until it was disengaged. She clicked open the belt and eased it around my waist, where it fitted perfectly. She ensured that there were no gaps between the neoprene rubber lining and my flesh. There weren't. The belt could have been made for me.

'I gave them your measurements,' she said.

'I'm very grateful,' I said snidely.

'You will be, you slutty little bitch.'

The crotch guard hung down at the back between the legs. Kit closed the waist band and eased the connections of the lock so that the spigots were engaged. It snapped shut with a metallic click.

'Spread your legs apart,' she directed.

I did as I was told. She swung the guard up between my legs in the front and engaged it with the spigots and guide pins. Aligning the joint carefully, she eased the lock into position and turned the key five times. She checked that the silver guard was seated correctly, around the front of my waist and under my pussy, to the anus, which was blocked by a thin strip of metal that curved between the crease of the buttocks.

The crotch guard was protected by a sliding shield and a vaginal slot through which my labia protruded, framed by the metal, but inaccessible and immobile, no matter what position I adopted.

'From now on,' she said, 'I will decide who you have sex with.'

So there I was. Trapped in a pelvic guard made from steel polished to a mirror shine. A radial lock sat on my belly, a neoprene-lined shield guarded my genitals. They both prevented preventing sexual intercourse or any attempt at self-gratification. I was imprisoned to the whims of Kit's pleasure.

'I'm not sure about this,' I said.

'Trust me,' she replied.

'I'm going to have to.'

Then she released me from where I was hanging on the door and laid me in a foetal position on the bed. Handcuffing my wrists behind my back, my pelvis was now locked up in a metal cell. Clit and anus were out of bounds, my bladder was under her control. A tickle began to flicker between my legs.

'How long am I going to wear this thing for?' I said plaintively.

'The brochure from the company says you could live in it for the rest of your life without any harm,' she said engimatically.

'How will I go to the loo?'

'You'll come and ask my permission and I will take you to the bathroom, unlock you and then lock you up again.'

'And bathing?'

'You can keep it on.'

She turned off the light, closed the door and went off to make supper. I smelled the food and I could hear voices. She was not alone. I strained to hear. I was sure she was with a man. Surely not? The metal chafed between my legs, but the device was a good fit, unforgiving but not painful. I thought about the Blacksnake dick that I could still feel inside me. I thought about Kit fisting me. I wondered what would happen if she lost the key. Why was I giving her this much control?

The sympathetic nervous system began to sense that the body was prohibited from pleasurable responses, which immediately set up a craving for those very responses. Imprisoned, my sexual core became a centre of tension where the whole body wanted to escape and where the mind could only think of hard penetrative acts – anus and cunt wanted stiff penile shapes because they could not have them.

Ah, the thrill and excitement; the filth and the dirt.

What more could a girl want?

So I was locked up. Stainless steel on flesh, rubber on labia, more security than any white-trash renegade slumping in a hell-hole Death Row. What had she done to me? What had I given her? What had I given up? I eased my fingers around my inner thighs, around the flesh of my cheeks and between my legs. The rods of this cage fitted well. Snug against the skin, they stayed in place and prevented any fingertips from pressing into forbidden zones. The pussy prison, unyielding to vibration on the pubis, disallowed even the tiniest stimulation. She had sent me away. A sentence without a trial; the judgement made from the cackling jury of her own mind – she had pronounced a sentence, and, for once, she had won the game.

She did not always win. I was slipping. I had given Kit far too much. I could only see days full of humiliation and begging and discomfort. She could do as she pleased. I would have to be grateful for everything because, as I soon realised, it would not take long before I became very, very desperate. Desperate for the bathroom, desperate for relief, desperate for affection, desperate to have my body back.

Kit returned to the room at 3 a.m. I was asleep, but not for long. I awoke to feel the chastity belt being removed and clicked open. Something animal-like groped and bit me. In dreams I thought it was a beast, but it was the Patel son. He had driven from Los Santos to penetrate me with his keen young dick, and not a big dick at that, a measly proportion that would leave a girl wanting more, wanting another dong, wanting the offender to get the hell out of the hole and the room. There was a rabbity shuddering and it was over. Son of Patel withdrew and handed twenty dollars to Kit.

'Not a virgin any longer,' she said.

'I think I am in love,' he said.

'I want the bathroom,' I said.

'Please may I go to the bathroom?' she corrected.

Silence.

She slapped me sharply on the right buttock, then the left, hard palm against flesh, the sting quickly seeping from the flesh.

'Please may I go to the bathroom?' I said sulkily.

'Can I watch?' said the son of Patel.

'You may,' said Kit.

So he did. Kit locked me up again afterwards, key in groove, clunk-click. Ritual dedication.

I felt uneasy after the unsatisfying Patel experience. There had been no orgasm for me, just a mild sensation of erotic frustration, wanting more but not getting it. It was 5 a.m. I wanted Kit. I wanted her rampant attention and the leather dong and her pelvis crushing into mine. And I wanted out of the made-to-measure iron maiden. But she was cold and she wouldn't touch me.

'I hate this thing,' I said.

'You'll get used to it,' she replied.

'I won't.'

'Go to sleep Stella.'

'I can't, not with this thing.'

'Go to sleep or I will gag you.'

So I had to stare at the ceiling listening to her breathe, sleeping with all the goddamn comfort of an innocence that she did not possess. The cold finish of steel was my underwear. Sexual angst flickered as throbbing heat and spread. Cunt hot, mind wandering, madness impending. It was a cell of sorts, a cell with a small window and a large view over a dark landscape where flesh must be oppressed and contained.

The next morning she lead me to the shower and washed me. Soaping me down with a sponge, spraying water from the shower head in and around the chastity belt, she inserted her fingers between flesh and metal to ensure that the thing had not shifted and was still fitting me.

I wanted her hand to force its way into me. She teased me. Rubbing soap slowly into my inner thighs, she massaged my buttocks, scratched the nerve endings on my back, stroked the top of my neck. She did everything except the one thing that I needed and wanted. I wanted to pull the belt off and throw it in her face. She was turning me on all over and ensuring that I stayed heightened rather than satisfied. She knew what she was doing. I wonder if she had co-opted other playmates to similar scenarios or whether she had read books. Later she told me that it was a simple pleasure: she enjoyed the comfort of knowing for certain that nobody could fuck me. It was as straightforward as that. Her insecurity and jealousy were assuaged and she could enjoy herself, calm and happy rather than bitter and suspicious.

'I like having control over your clit.'

'You like having control full stop.'

'Yes.'

I had to dress carefully, for the cunt trap was bulky. It showed through most things like a mangled car through a net curtain. Kit was unhelpful, saying that I could always stay in the room, but I wasn't going to give her that much power. I had to opt for a Lolita summer dress – upwardly nubile on the outside, medieval love object underneath.

Gradually I began to see the chastity belt as an instrument of erotic stimulation – a turn-on rather than irritating equipment. I moved into the same space that Kit occupied and lived in a realm of fantasy where daily life ebbed into a far-off continuum and there was only my trapped cunt and her control.

I began, slowly and inexorably, to let go and to submit. I began to trust her as I had never trusted anyone. I began to allow her to have it all. It was not as infuriating as I thought it would be, shifting the conscience to cater for the reality of immediacy, because she was kind enough, in the end.

She knew how far to go. She knew it was only foreplay. It was merely a matter of tricks and kicks. I allowed the confinement to entertain me rather than to oppress me. As the days rolled on, the ultimate symbol of historical repression became part of my life. I played with it, I tried to deconstruct it, I undermined its basic power. I wore it because I wanted to. Because I wanted to see what would happen in the end. Because I loved Kit and wanted to know more about her and myself.

I allowed her to confine me so that we could both know new things. We were worldly wise women dedicated to our own recreation and unafraid of any of the opinions of the common populace. The chastity belt might be a patriachal power tool but it was also a sign that she cared. It had cost $500, after all; it was an artwork in its own way, as polished as an Alessi kettle and as fine a postmodern design as any Starck collectable.

Oh, Mistress Mine, how did I let this happen?

Biker Bitches From Hell premiered at an art-house cinema in Silverlake. This was a first for porno and the movie reaped a lot main-stream press as a result. There was a party afterwards at Out There – the new bar designed by the Crimbo brothers, interior designers *du jour* who had cut their teeth on the famous Bob Dylan memorial at Universal Studios and graduated to Mr Trimberts and other New York restaurants.

The Crimbo brothers were known to have stimulated the movement known as the 'New Copyists'. This was wrapped up in much art jargon about the deconstruction of postmodern constriction, but, in reality, they had steered a revival for Charles Eames surfboard-shaped coffee tables, Heywood Wakefield chests and Harwell Harris airline sofas in various vinyls. Born in the early 70s, they were young enough to appreciate that the 50s designers knew what they were doing and that anything mid-century was an antique. The Crimbos drew much inspiration from Stanley Kubrick. Having already copied the milk bar in *A Clockwork Orange* to great success in a hotel on Sunset, they now made Out There into the space lounge in *2001: A Space Odyssey*.

The Crimbos plundered, they networked, and they both wore Comme, which probably would have been enough in itself. There we all were, LA's finest: porno stars, the hip Crimbo crowd, press and patrons, pussy and perves.

Kit and I rolled up in the Firebird.

Jed rode in on a classic BSA Goldstar.

Leon, bodyguards and the rest of the girls poured themselves smoothly out of his limo, and, as they did so, a giant laser spectogram flashed across the front of the theatre – 'PORNOGRAPHY FOR THE PEOPLE', it said.

We were immaculate that night. Toyota was entirely naked except for a black rubber G-string. Her body had been henna-painted from top to toe with a curling mehndi design. A kundalini snake wound down her spine, its two-pronged tongue disappearing into the cleavage of her neat white arse.

We united in a pure symbiosis of rampant sexuality and bizarre posture that caused one photographer to go down in the scrum. The paramedics arrived with a stretcher, ensuring maximum coverage on the mainstream network news stations that night. There were Hell's Angels, rock stars and Pussy Willow's mother, who wore a bleached white beehive and was mistaken for a member of the B52s. There were a lot of men who looked like Skeet Ulrich.

And there were a hundred screeching Catholic Mothers, who vibrated in a noisy protest on the street. *Pornography is oppression. Sex is violence. Take Back the Night. Rape. Repent.*

Kit was wearing a sleek silk top hat, a loose lace shirt with ruffles, skin-tight leather drainpipes and a pair of boots that pushed her up to nearly six foot. She was packing a snub-nose small-frame single-action revolver – a ladies' gun, but small and easy to conceal.

We walked in hand in hand and the photographers nearly went mad.

'Stella!'

'Over here Stella!'

'Who's the big sister?'

'Is it true about you and Michael Jackson?'

There was a slight fracas when Goldie Hawn arrived, realised she was at the wrong premiere, and left immediately in a wail of police sirens. Leon (who liked to eat) had sprung a budget of $100,000 for the food, so the buffet table was not so much a buffet table as a parade in honour of food as art, art as design, design as a cantilevered zucchini appetiser built in homage to Frank

Gehry. Here the postmodern *objet* became an uneasy dialectic between cubes of chocolate gelato and shards of gravity-defying spun sugar.

The superstar chef Josh de Lass had spent years redefining the parameters of international cuisine to produce a master synthesis known as the Unified Theory. Alluding to every known idiom, de Lass shamelessly blended Bombay with Boulogne, New York with Kyoto, Tex-Mex with Thailand. The result? Spreads of multicourse extravaganzas where Mediterranean pork balls floated on beds of Cajun basmati rice and pecan-crusted chicken nuggets deigned to live in lakes of Japanese ponzu sauce.

This evening de Lass had united with the conceptual artist Bear Goldmouth to produce a gallery where engineering melded skilfully with a free-ranging survey of dynamic structures. The crab cake became a cuboid and the chilly Borscht became a Miro motif; the ice sculpture was Henry Moore's reclining nude and two melons floated in a tank of water, as Jeff Koons' basket balls had once done. A three-tiered revolving structure covered in petits fours owed its idea to Rebecca Horn.

Walking slowly past anise-scented fried oysters and banana tempura, I came across Jed Blacksnake. He was skulking underneath a Calder-style mobile from which the superstar chef had hung caramel-coated plums. He had to dodge occasionally to avoid the fruit slapping him in the face, but he looked the best I have ever seen him.

He was wearing a traditional Indian hat, as seen in old John Ford movies, and his long black hair was tied into a loose braid with beads. Intelligent eyes darted above high cheekbones; he was silent and centred and amused. As always.

'Hullo,' I said, slightly shyly, as I did fancy him and I could not fathom him.

'Hullo.' He smiled invitingly but I was well and truly

shackled. Kit, the mistress keyholder, had locked me firmly into the Kink-Lock chastity belt. I wore it underneath a translucent evening dress. She wanted everyone to see it. He looked at the mechanism without registering any expression. I was ironclad, a prisoner in a transmundane stronghold, untouchable and unsanctified.

'Did Kit put you in this?' he said

'Yes.'

'Bitch.'

'Yes.'

'Where is she?' he asked.

I thought for a delightful moment that he might force her to give the key up and entertained an enjoyable vision where she submitted to his strength and I was violated by the compulsion of his love.

'Talking to Leon in the bar.'

She was miles away. There were at least thirty waiters, six eating disorders, a didgeridoo sound-therapist, a B-movie gangsta rapper, a man who looked like Rod Stewart but wasn't, ten mobile phones with email facilities and two MTV cameramen between us. He made no effort to go and find her. Instead he stood where he was, casually bit into a prawn ball and said, 'Would you like to give me a blow job?'

'OK.'

So I did. Under the table. Under the basmati rice and spinach salads, in the middle of the party, beneath the table cloth, hidden, but in public. I pushed my face between his legs, licked the tip of his dick, mouthed his hard-on, rubbed him hard and sucked him off.

'I've missed you,' he said afterwards.

I kissed him.

Fuck Kit. Fuck the pussy prison. Fuck the lock.

I could have fallen in love with that man.

The next day the premiere for *Biker Bitches from Hell* made the cover of the *LA Times*. The day after, we were all over the global press. The following week I was on the cover of three different weekly magazines and the Big Bongo soft drink company asked me to endorse their product.

'Speak to my manager,' I said.

Kit got me $2.5 million.

Rowena Brocklehurst dived into the mêlée with a strategy of fundamentalist activism that concealed the salient fact that she was using Leon to boost her run for the Republican candidacy. Now opinion was fact and fact was a matter of faith. She was a posturing prophetess but she was a prophetess with a publicity department. *New York View* devoted the cover story of its prestigious colour supplement to 'Sex and God – The New Controversy!' An illustrator portrayed Brocklehurst smashing a naked Leon over the head with a crucifix. I noted with alarm that Leon had been depicted as the loser in this rendition, but he was more concerned about the fact that the artist had drawn a walnut where his dick should have been.

'It doesn't look like me at all,' he said.

'It's not supposed to Leon, it's satire.'

'Satire schmatire, I've never had any complaints in the nut department, Stella, as you well know.'

'No, Leon,' I said soothingly.

The *New York View* article was balanced in that it offered both sides equal space to plight their opinions. Rowena Brocklehurst announced her intention to inspire all conservative women of faith to fight pornography in the name of God. The Catholic Mothers were ready to rise up to scourge all sins of the flesh and force out the filth that was contaminating the children of America and stealing their souls away. The Lord was on their side, and the Lord had told her that pornography was oppression.

Hallelujah.

She reminded the writer that the Catholic Mothers

had campaigned for some seven million of the votes that propelled Ronald Reagan to power.

'I am a virgin,' she said. 'And proud to be one.'

The writer (an Ivy League professor of sociopolitical religionist studies) concluded that Rowena Brocklehurst might be a virgin, but she was also an academic with distinguished qualifications as a scholar of law and a hundred percent following in a key demographic which consisted of white, middle-class, middle-aged, low-income conservatives. Furthermore she was 'blessed' with a beautiful head of hair and long-term experience as a charismatic evangelist. Both of these things could carry her to the top of the opinion polls and all the way to the White House.

'The Catholic Mothers are the most aggressive anti-porn movement in America,' he wrote. 'They employ no fewer than sixty full-time lawyers dedicated to intimidating supermarket chains, theatre owners and publishing houses. They were responsible, lest we forget, for the successful ban on the work of the arts photographer Ernest Mann whose "Leda" (which showed a woman having anal sex with a swan) was forcibly removed from a gallery in Kansas. The gallery owner then became embroiled in a legal suit whose costs forced her business into liquidation. Rowena Brocklehurst is a very serious opponent.'

Leon attempted to diffuse the situation with irony which is never a good idea in America. Irony is understood by only a tiny population of insomniacs who live on the east coast, and they already supported Leon's cause. He observed that if Rowena Brocklehurst was a virgin she was unlikely to be an expert on sex. If she wished to inform herself, however, the Bible would be a good place to start. He suggested that she study the life of Solomon, a man who chose to keep seven hundred wives and three hundred concubines, which, as far as

Leon was concerned, was a great deal more adventurous than anything he had witnessed in a porn film.

Arnold Brocklin, antenna attuned to ratings, invited both parties to his show for a bipartisan 'debate'. This turned into a predictable and unsightly punch-up encouraged by the network whose policy it was to hand out free beer to the audience in order to stimulate the violence required of good television. The studio was divided into two sides for supporters, both Leon and Rowena bringing their followers as any football team brings fans to a stadium.

Leon's 'disciples' included a row of naked white-collar workers from Ottumwa, Iowa, whose placard announced that they were 'Christian Naturists'. The row behind them was filled by a group from the Kentucky 'Big Breast Alliance' and a lone nun from the Order of St Elvis.

Kit and I sat in the back row with Givenchy, Goo and several Democrat Congressmen who had flown in from Washington to assess the political possibilities. The Catholic Mothers, meanwhile, sat on Rowena's side, their generally grim demeanour enhanced by the presence of the Hollywood starlet Belize von Belize, who sat demurely fingering the rosary that flowed over her 38DD chest.

A sinister group of people wearing black masks on their heads were thought, at first, to be the Continuity IRA but turned out to be the Disgust Brigade. Any hope that the words of Leon or Rowena would be disseminated in an arena devoted to sensible discourse vanished in the first three minutes when a Christian Naturist frisbee'd a pizza at a Catholic Mother and the entire audience dissolved immediately into the kind of brawl seen only in saloons in B-movie westerns.

The next day the tabloids reported that a Mr Murray Girardeau, watching the show while riding his excercise bicycle, had become so seized with fury that he had fallen off the machine and on to his head, dying immediately. His family were suing Arnold Brocklin for $300 million.

The result of all this was that *Biker Bitches from Hell* went into mass circulation, was shown in theatres all over America, and showed gross returns that propelled it to number ten in the box office charts.

I was a Star.

Two weeks or so after the Arnold Brocklin show Kit and I were lazing in the Jacuzzi in her garden. We were drinking champagne. She had kindly removed the chastity belt after I had condescended to spend 45 minutes working on her clit with my tongue, so I was enjoying the feeling of the warm suds throbbing against my sensitive cunt. It was a relief to be out of that thing, but, I had to admit, incarceration had heightened all my sexual senses. Kit only had to place a fingertip on my mons to send me into a seizure of greedy sensuality.

Her mobile telephone rang. She spoke briefly, snapped it shut and looked at me.

'Leon has been arrested,' she said.

Chapter Nine

Leon was arrested in Alspokane, an industrial town in Georgia where the Catholic Mothers had a stronghold, thanks to the fact that the local prosecutor, Minton Bismarck III, was married to Rowena Brocklehurst's sister. Minton Bismarck had long conducted a campaign to cleanse Georgia of sin and the smooth implementation of his diktats was assured in a place where the populace comprised impoverished blue-collar workers. Here the *National Enquirer* was the highest-selling newspaper and the Bible was the only book in the house.

Polls proved that the majority were pro-life and pro the death penalty, they believed in family values and firearms, while (according to one market survey) eating the highest per-capita ratio of Twinkies in the United States. The people of Alspokane did not play golf, they played with their chainsaws and they believed that the Lord was right when he murdered Onan for his sins.

Alspokane, then, was the site of Leon's arraignment. He had been picked up by the police outside a downtown cinema, where he was attending the opening of *Biker Bitches from Hell*. The marshal handcuffed his hands behind his back, to the delight of a local photographer, who syndicated the image around the world and used the proceeds to buy a new Winnebago.

Nationwide exposure was of little immediate aid to Leon. He had not, by any means, won the support of the press. Editors and proprietors still considered porn to be a hot potato, civil rights or no civil rights. Furthermore, he had been arrested in the South. The rules were different there.

His lawyers informed him that if he failed to beat the charges made (which included obscene pandering, lewd provocation, and incitement to illegal sexual practices as directed by Section 1(a) of the Law Governing the Basic Decency of the People of Georgia) he could face a prison sentence of fifteen years.

'You're lucky it's not the death sentence,' they said. 'It would probably be a public holiday down here.'

Minton Bismarck III was a dangerous man. He was rich, he was connected, and he was clever in a place where the demands of education had long ago surrendered to the demands of wage-paying employment. A fat fish in a pond full of struggling minnows, he had successfully removed Enid Blyton from all the public libraries in Georgia, on the grounds that stories about fairies encouraged homosexuality. He was known to privately believe in the coming of Armageddon. He was Christian with a capital KKK.

Those of a more balanced bent wondered why Minton Bismarck III had allowed *Biker Bitches from Hell* to be shown in Alspokane in the first place, if it flouted so many of the local laws. They naturally surmised that Minton Bismarck III must have purposely encouraged the premiere (or turned a blind eye at least) in order to lure Leon into a trap; once he was in the city, he could be arrested. His presence was required to make a point.

Rowena Brocklehurst, interviewed on CNN, announced

that, while she felt human pity for any soul descending towards hell, Leon had broken the law and law was there to govern everybody. In her opinion it would be a good thing if he did go to prison; an example at this point would do much to block the sewer of of unnatural eroticisation that was soiling the souls of Americans.

There was panic in the adult-entertainment industry. No case had been heard, no guilt confirmed, but all men knew the consequence of litigation. Thus the Catholic Mothers succeeded before they had even started, as nervous distributors started to turn down certain 'risky' products and apprehensive shopkeepers resorted to mainstream fare.

'There's to be no more fisting!' Toyota wailed. 'I'm only allowed to do squelching, tickling and sodomy!'

'That would be enough for some people,' I said.

Leon posted bail and was granted it on the condition that he did not leave the state. If he left the state he would be hounded as a fugitive and imprisoned.

'Bloody Hell Stella!' He shouted down the telephone. 'I'm holed up in some god-forsaken redneck backwater The attorneys are all here but no hotel will allow them to stay – we're all in trailers in an RV park – can you imagine! Sidney Ornstein has already gone native: he's listening to religious radio and driving an Olds 98. I keep reminding him that he's Jewish but he just stares blankly and hums hymns. I've had about as much of "Onward Christian Soldiers" as I can take. I think they put something in the water here, I really do. And God knows what the whole thing is going to cost me; the blood-sucking shysters have already put a bill in for two million bucks.'

'What are they saying about the situation?' I asked

'I've got a fifty-fifty chance.'

'Christ.'

The odds were dreadful.

I put the telephone down and walked into the kitchen. Kit was drinking a cold beer, feet up on the table, reading a manual entitled *A Practical Approach to Propellants*. The cover showed a picture of a man's head exploding.

'Leon needs our help,' I said.

'Good,' she said. 'I feel like a fight.'

'I love you,' I said.

She looked up at me.

'And so you should.'

I was wearing a pair of baby-doll pyjamas and the chastity belt.

'Jesus, you're cute.'

She stood up, looked down at me, staring into my eyes with some unblinking intention, and, without a word, lifted me up as if I was a child. My arms held her neck and my mouth brushed her cheek; I was small, loved and protected. It was a great place to be. All responsibility abnegated; all the inhibitions of adulthood routed by simple size and dominance. I could be three or five or eleven. I could let go.

She carried me to the bedroom.

'Daddy's gonna make you come.'

She lowered me gently down on to the bed, placed a teddy bear in my arms, slipped the frilly knickers down, and threw them on to the floor. Still silent, still staring straight into my eyes, she unlocked the metal waistband, drew the shield from my body, prised my legs apart and pushed her hand between my legs.

'You're my own little girl.'

She rubbed my smooth bare lips with her hand, making me feel it, knowing how I liked it. The pleasure rose. I disappeared down a tunnel of time. The years rolled back. Thirty, twenty, fifteen . . . Tears came into my eyes. I was hers. She was unafraid, she dared to go where no one had been before. She was strong enough to take on all the old mysteries and brave enough to unleash true emotion. She was my only authority and she knew everything.

Kit and I launched the Porn Star Liberation League thanks, by and large, to generous funding supplied by the adult-entertainment conglomerates XTC and Babe. This comforted Leon in his hour of despair, but I am afraid the philanthropy was not personal. Leon was liked and respected in the industry, but the decision of both moguls (Milton Lilbourne and Frankly G Moore Jr) was related purely to the advice of their executives. Both companies were multimedia corporations with billion-dollar turnovers. They employed hundreds of people and produced everything from Sex Instruction CD-ROMS to hard-core fisting magazines. XTC had recently gone public and the last thing the CEO needed was a legal defeat that would affect the industry, affect sales figures and profit margins, send stocks down, and make shareholders nervous. Best to give the ranters the money and stand well back, they thought.

We galvanised a freewheeling movement made of hussies, sex workers, adult entertainers and the most outrageous performance artists in the free world. Everyone from little Maisie (known for incurring the wrath of Disney when she cavorted in a pair of mouse ears and staged scenes where Mickey sodomised Minnie) to the hardest-core readers' wives collected as a gorgeous publicity machine to aid the plight of a man who was fighting for the freedom to make filth. And for the First Amendment, of course.

Maisie immediately caused a storm by stealing Rowena Brocklehurst's underwear (a surprisingly scant ensemble) from her washing line and then wearing it to a charity gala in Hollywood. Milton Lilbourne offered to buy it and auction it for charity if she took it off in front of him. Maisie complied.

Rowena Brocklehurst threatened to have everyone

arrested for breaking and entering, criminal damage, emotional upset. You name it. But her lawyers advised against it. The panties were provocative and made of lace. The bra was flimsy. These things should not be held up in court to be scrutinised as evidence; they could well turn against her. And, anyway, she had enough on her plate as it was.

We issued a mission statement:

> The Porn Star Liberation League is a direct-action group dedicated to upholding civil rights. Our purpose is to promote the understanding of human sexuality and to fight the demonisation of individuals who work in the adult-entertainment industry.

We received blanket coverage. Of course. It was an excuse for mainstream family newspapers to run pictures of big-breasted women in lamé outfits and call it a news story. We made great images: the supervixens against the Catholic Mothers, women taking up arms against each other in a symbol of the division between the sisters of the twenty-first century. We represented the schizophrenia that rent the *Zeitgeist*; the violent schism between those who had opted for God and family values and those who chose to have a life.

The Catholic Mothers appeared as uniform lines of grey cardigans and were photographed sitting in pews in churches. The Porn Star Liberation League appeared in suede miniskirts and were photographed lounging by swimming pools.

One was dark, one was light.

One was fun and one was not.

One sipped cool cocktails.

One ate grits.

Both were scary.

Several surveys proved that the Catholic Mothers were running scared. They had not envisaged the breadth of our power and they had no understanding of how to operate the media machine. We lived in it. We were made of beligerent marginalised majorities and we knew what we were doing. They lived in kitchens in Wichita.

'We are the vanguard of sexual situationism,' said Kit.

Then Rowena Brocklehurst employed a bright spark who had successfully promoted the (Christian) stadium band Legion of Rock. He persuaded the mothers that they were doing themselves no favors by projecting an image that made them look as if they had all just stepped off the boat in New England. The next thing we knew there were sunny pictures of jolly matrons playing with adorable children and tossing things over barbecues at bake-outs.

'Oh no!' I said, tossing *People* magazine down on the floor. 'They look almost human.'

'Well they're not,' Kit snapped.

Kit's passions were fervid in this arena. She was a woman possessed of as much motivation as any professional politician. Her father had died of AIDS at a time when this was to be both feared and ostracised. He had been forced to live most of his life in the misery of repression. They came from the South. Kit knew what it was like. This was personal.

We retaliated with the full force of our funding.

We held meetings in out-of-the-way hicksville places, gave out free food and everyone came. We printed 25,000 baby-pink flyers and distributed them.

This is what they said:

'Thou Shalt!'

We staged a series of Nude Take Overs where various porno stars, beautiful bodies butt naked, appeared in public places and acted normally (that is, they went about their business as if fully clothed) until they were arrested. These 'happenings' were a great success, empowered by the press, who were, of course, alerted as to the time and place of each naked appearance. Photographers, film crews and journalists lovingly documented the naked beauty being manacled by various sheriffs and filed stories that inevitably included pertinent quotes from the Liberation League manifesto and, usually, a mention of poor Leon, bastion of the American dream, penalised for his success and languishing sadly at the hands of the wrong right.

Pussy Willow ate a Big Mac and fries before the police arrived at the McDonald's in Portland, Oregon. Goo Lightly stood stark naked at a public telephone box in Fort Lauderdale talking to her mother for two hours before anyone hauled her in. Givenchy lasted two minutes in Bloomingdales.

Then everyone started doing it.

Tiny militant chapters sprang up in out-of-the-way places and bred exhibitionists as quickly as a guinea pig breeds with her brother. The world was suddenly full of naked liberators. They turned up at car-boot sales in Baton Rouge and followed Republican politicans around Washington. They walked into public libraries in Memphis and queued to buy stamps in Milwaukee. One brave 'ho from Montana even managed to bribe her way into a rodeo. Naked except for her cowboy boots, she bucked a bull into submission and received a standing ovation.

Everywhere you looked there were pussies and tits, shaking their booty and acting up. The *Wall Street Journal* observed that the economy must be very strong. In times of wealth hemlines go up; the more secure the shares the more you see of the supermodel. Applying this theory to the current fashion for public nudity must mean that America was enjoying an unprecedented period of prosperity.

'We're doing well,' said Kit, surveying the thick pile of press cuttings.

'Yes.'

'I have a good idea,' she said.

'You always do, my love.'

She rang the arts photographer Ernest Mann and persuaded him to surrender his usual $90,000 price tag in order to contribute to a worthy cause. The picture, she added (persuasively) would appear on billboards in every state in America from Indiana to Montana and it would be painted down the side of a five-storey building on the Strip in Los Angeles. It would be one of the most resonant images in the history of political activism.

Ernest Mann was not a person to avoid the main chance. He had often asserted that art sat at the top of the capitalist edifice. He agreed immediately.

'You have to go to his studio tomorrow,' she said. 'He wants to do you ... *nood.*'

'Naked?'

'Yes, Stella.'

'Aren't you coming?'

It was very unlike her to allow me to spend a day alone with a man, and a famously attractive man at that.

'No. He doesn't allow anyone in the studio while he is working. He doesn't even have assistants. Says he likes to have total control over his own focus.'

'You trust me then?'

'No,' she said. 'I do not. You will be wearing the chastity belt and you will come back to Mama immediately.'

'What about the bathroom? What if I have to go to the loo? What if he hates it and doesn't want to photograph it?'

'Tough.'

'I think you should come with me, with the key!'

'No.'

'You could sit outside in the car.'

'Forget it.'

I opened my mouth to complain again.

'And don't whine.'

'But . . .'

'I said don't!'

I submitted to silence and a three-tier fudge, almond and strawberry toffee cheesecake that lurked in the fridge. It squidged with senseless sludge in a Pie of Pies box.

'Give me some!' she said

'Fuck off.'

'Oh, for Christ's sake.'

She grabbed at the box. I snatched it away from her. She grabbed again. I pushed it in her face, cream and toffee everywhere and ran from the room. I could hear her coming after me. I hid behind a door.

'Come here!'

She found me, grabbed me, pushed the remains of the cake into my mouth, and kissed me violently, face on face, licking and biting.

'I hate you,' I gasped, pulling my mouth away from her.

Her eyes were charged with true passion and her groin heaved compulsively against me. She always wanted me.

'One day, little one,' she smiled, curling my hair behind my ear. 'One day you will go too far.'

'You hope,' I said.

Ernest Mann's studio was on the wrong side of Baldwin Hills, on the wrong side of La Brea and the wrong side of Jefferson. This territory was ruled by the El Savaje and the Todos Locos, feared Hispanic gangs who had been at war with each other for so long that no one, including them, could remember what it was they were fighting about.

El Savaje sold rock. Todos Locos sold guns. Together they owned more weapons than any other organisation in Los Angeles and there was a rumour that one of them had recently purchased a nuclear warhead. I sensed that I was driving into a volatile neighbourhood when the grass started growing longer and the dustbins started to throw up their content. Signs turned from English to Spanish, from Spanish to hand-painted and misspelled and finally from misspelled to boarded up and burned out.

Mann's studio was located in the middle of a network of allies made of corrugated iron and wood and crowded with the contents of the inhabitants's lives. Outside his door his neighbours had made a settlement out of a sofa, cactuses, a bicycle, an old television, a wall of *National Geographic* magazines and a six-foot-high Cheyenne totem pole covered with garlands of glinting fairy lights. A few yards away two naked male mannequins lay in a bath in the midst of a clutter of chicken wire, broken neon signs and an assemblage of shoes.

There was a smell of cooking (chilli) there was the sound of music (salsa) and the yawl of a baby – the first I had heard since I arrived in California. People don't have babies in LA. They have protein drinks and personal trainers.

Ernest Mann invited me in. He was wearing a white T-shirt and a pair of jeans, both of which were quite dirty. He was dark, aged about fifty, and looked like Serge Gainsborough.

I swear he did.

He had that louche, insouciant, wise, dominant mien that always makes me go mad. And bad. Those older men. They get you because they know they can. You let them because they have seen it all, know women, do what they like because they always have.

He drank red wine and did not look as if he had pursued much physical exercise, apart from sex, which I surmised he had enjoyed much and often and in every different degree. I knew immediately that his cock would be fabulous. I have an instinct about these things and I am very rarely wrong. He moved with a casual self-confidence that was not macho, but worldly. I knew that women had always wanted him from a young age and that they had always come back for more.

His eyes were amused, slightly lined, and he seemed to be constantly smiling about something. He probably had a lot to smile about, as he was patently a man who always got what he wanted.

I bet he had had fist fights.

I bet he had hung out with Charles Bukowski.

I bet he fucked everyone and made them believe they were the only one.

His 'art' was about the place. He photographed nudes. He had always photographed nudes. Morose prostration was his metier. He understood shadow and muscle and he was able to communicate autoerotic self-sufficiency. His trick was to combine sensuality with a lurking sadism and in this he had found a market with collectors who appreciated the female form when it was rendered as debauched and defective.

His *Ondine in Calipers* had recently fetched $73,000 on the open market and his *Nymph with her Eye Being Pecked out by a Bald Eagle* had achieved acclaim at the Venice Biennale.

I was made for him.

I stepped out of my short, white, summer dress and lay naked on his long, black, velvet sofa. Naked, that is, except for the chastity belt locked securely between my thighs and around my waist. At first Ernest Mann did not say anything. He sat in a chair in front of me, legs apart, staring at me as if waiting for an idea to arrive from the heavens and inspire his impeccable commercial instincts.

It was as if he had not even see the polished stainless-steel shield that imprisoned my pussy. I rotated my pelvis towards him to ensure that he received the full view.

'I wanted to do you as Pasiphae,' he said in low gravel that was the whiskey voice of smoking and many other sins. 'I wanted to do you as Pasiphae but I couldn't get the bull.'

I looked at him calmly.

'She was the mother of the Minotaur, you know; he lived in the labyrinth and ate Athenians.'

'I wish I could eat an Athenian,' I said. 'I'm starving.'

He laughed, husky, and genuinely amused.

'Baby. You shoulda said something.'

He gave me a banana and watched me eat it.

'You look as though you are very supple, honey,' he said. 'Do you do Pilates?'

'No. It's probably the sex. I have had to do hundreds of different positions.' He seemed impressed.

'How does that thing work?' he said, indicating the chastity belt.

'Kit locks it and keeps the key,' I said simply.

'Stand up and come here.'

I stood with the Kink-Lock five inches in front of his face. He stroked the metal waistband with his fingers, testing it for give, and looked deep into the ridges that held the shield in place.

'So you like being her prisoner?'

'Kind of, yeah. It pleases her, and she's a lot of trouble if she's not pleased.'

'It's not uncomfortable?'

'No.'

'Lie down again.'

I did as I was told. He set up white parasols, tested the lights, set up more lights, fiddled around with batteries and cables. I went to sleep to the soundtrack of *Betty Blue* and dreamed of Pasiphae and all the weird goddesses inclined to radical lifestyles.

I was Ameratsu, Japanese goddess of the sun, who locked herself in a cave so that the whole world went dark. I was Athena, who sprang from the brain of her father and had no fear. Warrior, champion, fighter of giants. 'In all things I lean towards men,' she said. 'Except in the matter of marriage.' And I was one of the Erinnyes, winged spirits with snaky hair who carried whips and torches and chased their victims, relishing their torture and driving them mad.

I awoke to feel a rough brown finger stroking my nipple.

'Just getting the shadow right,' he claimed.

'Make yourself at home.'

He did. Heaving himself on top of me he dedicated himself to stroking the eurogenous zones that were not placed under Kit's lock and key. He knew my inner thigh as if it was his own home. Sometimes the leg is all you need. Big hands stroked me – throat, thighs, buttocks. He slapped my backside a couple of times. The stings ran hot; I wanted to fuck him so much I might have died for it. The ultimate sex martyr. A good way for the Directrice of the Porn Star Liberation League to go.

'We gadda get that thing off, honey,' he said. 'I want you.'

'You'll never do it.'

'Don't be so sure – I did metalwork at art college.'

'Kit will freak if you damage it.'

He got up and rang a number on his telephone. After speaking in fast fluent Spanish, he put it down again.

'Lucky for us I got friends in low places.'

Three young Mexican men arrived within seven minutes and swaggered into the studio as if they owned it, which they may have done.

'These are my friends from the Todos Locos,' he smiled, waving his hand to indicate that they could take anything they wanted. 'They have been breaking into cars since they were ten.'

They were tough and young and wore macho as if it was a very expensive shirt. They also wore very expensive shirts. I hoped that Ernest Mann knew what he was doing. They all had guns pushed down the back of their low-slung trousers.

'Don't worry,' he whispered, seeing my nervousness. 'I've known them all since they were bambinos. They trust me.'

He looked at one of them.

'I think I might be related to Manolo, if you know what I mean . . .'

I looked at Manolo. He was Latino, but there was something about the way he carried himself that was reminiscent of the older man.

'Ah Maria . . . lovely woman,' he said nostalgically.

The smallest member of the gang, a slight dark youth with gold teeth and a bandana, stepped forward with a wide grin and held up a tiny pick.

'Pedro could break into the Vatican if he wanted.'

'*Si*, Ernesto! I godda new Lexus last week.'

I lay on the sofa while Pedro sat astride me and poked about in the lock with his little wire skeleton key. I was not optimistic. The Kink-Lock came from top-of-the range 'spouse security' hardware. But Pedro was confident, he clicked and picked with patient precision while his friends swaggered around the studio, punching their fists in the air, chugging beers, putting salsa on the tape deck.

Ernest Mann sat in his chair and watched, amused and entertained. I lay back while Pedro's fingers inserted themselves around the belt. I allowed him to enjoy my hard nipples, but I was more aware of Ernest Mann. I was hot in that rubber and metal; the juices were seeping into the prison.

'Jesus!' I said. 'How much longer?'

'*Cinco minutos, señorita!*'

Suddenly the lock snapped back. I was free. I couldn't believe it. The Cunt Trap Mark IV had two different locks and a hidden hinge. It was fireproof, burglarproof, shockproof and rape-resistant. It was supposed to be totally inpenetrable but it had snapped open to a teenager armed with a hairgrip.

Pedro grinned, wildly pleased with himself, he held up his wire and kissed it dramatically.

'You can have her now, *señor*. We watch?'

He looked at me. I nodded and shrugged.

'It's OK with me.'

The photographer sat on the edge of the sofa. I knelt in front of him, back to the gang audience. He was as hard as a rock. I pushed my face into his groin and sucked his cock. It inflated, hard and forceful. He began to lose himself, eyes closed, breath slow and heavy. Allowing the mositure to glisten on the tip, I took over and he let me. I pushed him down on to the sofa and sat astride him, like a cowgirl, riding up and down on top of him, wet, excited, controlling him deep inside me, expert porno muscles tightening at the whim of my mind, toned by professional sex and controlled by the expertise of long lascivious experience.

He closed his eyes, jolted his pelvis up and thrust himself deep into me. Then, taking back the control, he pushed me back on to the sofa, pulled my legs around his waist and let me have it hard. Tears sprang into the corners of my eyes. The three Mexican boys cheered and clapped.

'Ees better than late-night cable.' They said.

After they had left, Ernest Mann padded around the studio in bare feet. I was aware that he wanted to say something important but was having diffculty saying it. I knew the signs. I had seen them before in men who had lived in LA for a long time. They had encountered some very single-minded women and knew that the processes of romantic expectations are subtle and complicated. Hollywood men are forced to learn (sometimes the hard way) that clarity averts misunderstandings and dispels the risks of the dramas that arise as a result of unspoken notions turning into dangerous misconceptions.

He trod as carefully as a person walking over terrain in which land – mines were buried.

Finally, out it came.

'I cannot enter a relationship,' he warned. 'I can give you nothing, so . . . so don't get your hopes up . . . and er . . .'

'Oh, don't worry, I interrupted him. 'I don't want to marry you. And I don't expect I'll want to have sex with you again, either.'

Kit suspected nothing. Pedro relocked the lock with his wire. There was no evidence, except for the satisfied expression on my face, which I managed to conceal in a frenzy of desperation to go to the loo.

'Please, Kit!' I said, 'Kind Kit.'

The picture? A black and white full-length portrait of your Stella naked except for the kink-lock chastity belt. It was simple, it was stark, and it was mesmerising.

The feminists hated it. We told them to go back to the seventies where they belonged. The press did not understand it. We issued a helpful release explaining in words of few syllables that the gesture was symbolic. The chastity belt was as an icon of traditional sexual repression, and repression is exactly what the Christian right wanted to bring back to cultural mores. We had disempowered it and thrown it back into their faces. The Catholic Mothers said that I was a lewd prostitute and disgusting bisexual cavorting myself for immoral purposes. I pointed out that I was 30 years old, a graduate of Oxford university, and worth $5 million.

Albania Doe, a powerful essayist and thinker, syndicated a ten-thousand-word thesis in our defence. Entitled 'Jesus Loves Spatialization', it was quite a boring thing that attempted to update Foucault's thoughts about the 'multiplicity of force relations', but it won her a Pultizer and provided a positive effect on our cause.

The image became the subject of dissertations at Santa Cruz University. We negotiated a lucrative licensing deal with a merchandising company in Fresno. The Porn Star Liberation League became posters, mouse mats, tee-shirts and mugs.

Chastity belts were everywhere. A TV crew turned up to make a documentary. An indie band from Seattle released a record called 'Shag the Hate State' and used the Ernest Mann picture on the CD cover. Leon was interviewed by *Time*. The *Washington Post* concluded that at last women had recognised the truth of the nature of their own power and were utilising it to their own advantage.

We were winning.

Leon's lawyers warned Kit and me to be wary of the Disgust Brigade. It was easy to dismiss them as a fringe gang of lunatic bigots, but they were feared in many areas of the South, thanks to the success of sophisticated strategies achieved in total secrecy and with psychopathic violence. No one knew how many there were, but they were known to have strong alliances with a network of hate groups, among whom they had achieved mytholgocial status thanks to their dedication, extremism and faultless knowledge of the biblical references relevant to their cause. They were known to have organised the bombing of several abortion clinics and they were thought to have assassinated a clinician in Maine.

The leader, Cowl, imbued the group with a ghastly charisma and a relentless efficiency. He (or she) was proficient in the art of covert tactics and military espionage because he (or she) had served as a sergeant in several revolutionary councils and then as a global mercenary, selling out to the highest bidder. This, in most cases, was the Righteous Path, one of the most dangerous Christian terrorist organisations in the world.

There were many theories and rumours about the identity of Cowl. Some said that she was an ex-prostitute enflamed by religious zealotry but nobody even knew which religion. The Disgust Brigade seemed to be Islamic Nazis with socialists leanings. The visions by which he (or she) was known to be motivated were seen as prophetic messages by the supporters and the long-term side effects of unmedicated mental illness by detractors. Some said visionary, some said delusionary. It's an old story. It's an Old Testament. The truth had been lost in time.

'It's like the Jackal,' said Givenchy. 'Or like the Che poster. They've got a great art director, I know that. The graphics of that organisation are beyond beliefs. Did you see the logo? Apparently *Vogue* are desperate for a photograph, balaclava and all. They've heard Cowl wears Versace . . .'

'The wanker deserves to be caught then,' Kit snapped.

'Cowl might not even exist! This all might be the figment of the imagination of some Net-Head. You never know! Though I personally think that it is a woman. There's a reference in a Janis Joplin song . . .'

'I expect she killed Jim Morrison,' I said.

'Don't stir it, Stella,' said Kit. 'There's quite enough rubbish out there already.'

Kit and I refused to be intimidated until the afternoon that two men arrived in a new Mercedes and announced that they were the tactical assault division of a special regiment, working within covert counterterrorist operations on behalf of a peacetime Hate Watch squadron. They had received 'intelligence' via government agents operating within Christian identity groups that the Disgust Brigade were united in a move to extinguish the Porn Star Liberation League by any means possible. They had mobilised their 'Intolerance' operatives and these people were known to be well funded, well armed and fanatic.

'They are murderers who will obey any directive issued by high command,' said one.

'They will do anything that Cowl tells them,' said the other.

They both looked like extras from a popcorn movie, so we assumed that they were some kind of joke telegram.

'Intelligence?' Kit sniffed as they drove away. 'God knows where they got that from. They sure looked very dumb.'

We forgot about them until the evening that I was taking a jacuzzi in the garden. I was enjoying the bubbles tickling all the various intimate regions and had slipped into a relaxed state of bliss. Kit was inside the house ordering take-out buffalo wings when I looked up to see a figure in combat trousers staring down at me. A pair of black boots were about three feet away from my head. The intruder was wearing a balaclava and carrying a rifle.

I screamed. The figure ran into the hedge, climbed over a fence and escaped into the darkness.

Kit dashed out.

'Oh Jesus, Kit,' I said clinging to her, wet and trembling. 'He was armed.'

'He, he? Are you sure it wasn't a woman?'

'I don't know!'

She carried me into the house, wrapped me in a white towelling bathrobe, laid me on the sofa, and managed to calm me down with a cup of tea and all the stern words of calm common sense.

'Now, baby, we are not going to panic. We've seen peeping Toms before, after all. They usually turn out to be fans, as you well know.'

She cradled me into her chest and I felt her warmth. Then she lead me by the hand to the bedroom, tucked me into bed, and sat on it. I calmed down. I even began to believe that nothing could happen to me while she was there.

'I want a glass of water.'

'Go to sleep, Stella. That's enough for one day.'

'But –'

'No! I mean it. Do as you're told.'

She looked meaningfully at the hairbrush on the side table beside the bed. She was quite capable of dragging me out of the comfy bed, hauling me over her thighs, pushing up my nightdress and spanking my bare ass until it glowed hot and red. She would trap me between her legs, bare my buttocks to her blows, and spank me until she was finished. I would scream and cry and try to beat her off, but she would simply go on and on until she saw the pink turn to red and the red turn to purple. She was quite capable of beating me with the flat back of that hairbrush until I could not sit down for a week. And she was quite capable of making me stand naked with my face to the wall in a cold corner with only the glow of pain for company. She liked to watch the blemish fade from the white buttocks as she enjoyed her own private portrait of a punished girl.

I did as I was told.

The next morning we walked out of the house to discover that somebody had set fire to my beautiful Firebird. It was an ugly, burned-out, black shell. I loved that car.

'Right,' said Kit, as the tears ran down my face. 'That's it.'

From that moment on she would not let me out of her sight. She carried a gun and a knife at all times and she took to searching places as we arrived at them. She increased the security on the house – adding locks and bars to all windows and doors and installing CCTV. And she began to be more secretive about our activities. She would not reveal the address of meetings, for instance, and, when we did arrive, she would stand in front of me and cover me with her body until she was sure that the scene was safe.

It was like being the President.

She seemed to know what she was doing. She had the background, after all, in martial arts and competitive shooting. I felt that she would be able to fight, and I liked to have another pair of eyes looking out for me.

I was vulnerable and intimidated and she took over. I let her have this macho control. I enjoyed being led, protected, directed and driven. I felt safe with her and this turned me on. She was Machine-gun Mama and Dada and she knew what I liked.

Chapter Ten

Highway 19 leads to all the beauties of southwest Georgia. From Radium Springs to Ochlocknee, from Climax to Colquitt, some head for the peach-pie cook-offs, some go for the Rattlesnake Round-Ups. It is the land of the pecan and cotton, of swamp and savannah. Flat, humid, strangely exotic in its historical dress, it has a split – almost schizoid – personality.

Outback tribes made Georgia's shadow – an animus comprising the penniless and the desperate, the angry and the zealous; these species bred lone wolves and militia men who collected into skinhead nations and preached the New World Order. Any Phineas Priest would find a safe haven hidden in a bog. A nail bomb could be made from stuff bought at the hardware store.

Alspokane had managed to fall into the wilderness, for it was a dull little town with nothing to say for itself. Pitched haphazardly in the shadow of Albany, it was a diner-stop run-through on the route to Thomasville, a Southern city surrounded by pine-woods and plantations.

Alspokane had no peach blossom or folk art. It had no luxurious historic inn made to look like Tara in *Gone with the Wind*. There were no balsamic breezes or long blooming roses or bobtail quails. There were no dogwood or crape myrtles or events designed to let the visitor witness the traditional pursuits of cane grinding, tobacco spitting and greased-pig catching. The only thing Alspokane had was a nuclear power station known locally as 'ol' poison'.

An optimistic executive had once seen it as a tourist attraction and thrown open its doors to the public. The public failed to arrive. There were other things to do in Georgia – things that involved hang-gliding and scenic gorges and activities less likely to precipitate the arrival of a third leg. So 'ol poison' closed its doors and then closed down altogether, leaving the people of Alspokane to fend for themselves.

They had not done a good job. The local 'craft' of water-melon carving was an inadequate art dominated by crudely bludgeoned cyclops heads. The town clustered around the courthouse, which (appropriately enough) was the biggest building in the area, towering above the rotting clapboard façades of the *Christian Book Store* and *Dog Stop*. There were also three churches, a Greek-revival McDonald's and a trailer park that advertised itself 'AS SEEN ON THE JERRY SPRINGER SHOW'.

Kit and I and various members of the Porn Star Liberation League booked into the Lunker Lodge on Slappey Drive. It was a low wooden building of unkempt order surrounded by scrubby Mayhaw trees and several shanty homesteads, outside of which there were signs for 'CHEAP BARBECUE-SIZE GOATS'. A pile of uncarved watermelons stood on the porch and several rusting cars lay discarded in the yard. A huge gold-framed portrait of Jimmy Carter hung behind the desk and a glass dish full of peanuts lay on it.

There were two televisions in the foyer. One, silent, showed Aerosmith; the other, loud, had a show called *Christian Question Time*. This featured a member of the clergy fielding queries about fundamental issues. A pensioner in bottle-top spectacles noted that she was concerned about the verse in Leviticus which stated that those with defective sight must not approach any altar of the Lord.

'Where does that leave me and my Melvin?' She screeched, indicating an old man in bottle-top spectacles sitting beside her.

The manager wore dungarees, as if waiting for another remake of *The Postman Always Rings Twice.*

'You here for the trial?' he asked, indicating a photograph of Rowena Brocklhurst on the cover of his newspaper.

'Yessir,' said Kit.

'Best thing to happen to this town since Ellie-Mae Layfayette made the semifinals to Miss Universe – didn't win of course – boss-eyed the woman – but put us on the map, it did, with the TV crews and all. Sure helped make up for them closing down ol' poison when all the kids got, er, sick . . .'

He pushed the forms over the desk to Kit, who signed us in.

'You in that thur sex industry?' He asked.

'You could say that.'

'Well I don't mind who's doing what as long as there's a dollar at the end of it.'

He stared at her breasts for a couple of seconds, as if he was listening to a voice whispering to him from the deep shadow of her cleavage. Immersed in secret thoughts and licking the red lips that sat in the middle of a whiskered chin, he finally tore his eyes away from this restful region as a mother tears her reluctant children away from a beach.

'You be staying here long?' he asked.

'Long as it takes, I guess,' she answered.

That night the telephone rang seven times in our room. Each time Kit picked it up and each time the anonymous caller slammed it down. I smoked three cigarettes in a row and she didn't tell me not to. Then with sinister synchronicity, ABC showed a 45-minute 'special' documentary about the Disgust Brigade and their 'masked leader, the mysterious Cowl.'

The opening sequence showed several film clips of a figure identified as the 'Commander' of the Brigade's militia. It was difficult to tell whether he or she was young or old, black or white. In every shot the upper body was encased in a bulky, old-fashioned, leather flying jacket and the face was hidden by a balaclava. In one segment the terrorist was seen walking out of a meeting of the Vigilantes of Christendom in Mississippi, in another sitting on bench in Central Park wearing dark glasses and reading a book by Pat Robertson. In the final clip the leader was seen ambling confidently into the IRS building in Kalamazoo in order to place a bomb big enough to reduce the tax authority to rubble. This last action propelled the Disgust Brigade to a position of nationwide popularity and attracted an estimated 20,000 new recruits of all age groups and from all walks of life. The documentary noted that the Disgust Brigade were active in 35 states, had 230 operational fully armed militias and 806 chapters. They had published a book, *The Manifesto of God's Army*, and organised regular rallies designed to provoke the maximum reaction.

'This Christian Identity terrorist group has affiliations to white supremacists and gun lobbyists,' said the voice-over. 'It is empowered by clever propoganda and iconised by rebel youth.'

Rowena Brocklehurst and the Catholic Mothers appeared on the show in order to distance themselves from the activities of the Disgust Brigade. Interviewed at her home, and filmed in front of a large gold crucifix adorned with blinking fairy lights, Brocklehurst pointed to the Bible on the arm of her chair and said that, although she admired any adherence to the path of the

Lord, she was a lawyer and she believed that political progress must come not from breaking the law, but from making new ones.

A counterterrorist assault operative with his face blurred out stated that there was satellite evidence to suggest that Cowl's origins lay in Lebanon, where the brigade had worked with a radical Shia group based in the Bekaa Valley.

'So,' said a woman with frosted hair. 'Who is this silent soldier of the night? A zealot who believes that Christ cannot return to Earth until Satanic elements have been removed, or a highly trained terrorist fuelled by personal hatred and equipped with highly skilled know-lege of tactical operations. Is Cowl a man or a woman? Does this person actually exist? And if so, how has this clever terrorist managed to escape the legions of government agents who have spent many years and millions of the taxpayers dollars attempting to run him or her to ground? And finally, where is the leader of this outlaw army hiding now?'

'Where indeed?' I said nervously.

Kit hugged me close to her.

'I'm here,' she said. 'It will be OK. Don't worry.'

I wanted to believe her. I wanted to to have faith, but I could not. I was now genuinely frightened. The forces of threat were escalating and they were closing in, nearer and nearer.

Exposure had achieved our end. Leon was no longer demonised. He was now a nationally known figurehead with the power to appear on prime-time television and state his arguments. Washington was watching, as were the most influential federal judges and newspaper editors. The trial was going to be televised with a daily commentary by Judge Wendy. It was expected to achieve as high ratings as O J Simpson, as it promised the presence of some of the highest-paid professional sluts in the adult-entertainment industry.

The sidewalk outside the courthouse on Basinger Street was a carnival. Some people had arrived from out of state and queued for days, setting up sleeping bags and Calor-gas stoves in order to ensure that they were availed of a front seat in the public gallery.

'I bin here for three days now an' I hant had saw much fern since Dilly Dukewell gat the gas chamber,' one old man informed a Korean woman from PRTV. 'I just wish the wife was here to see it, the Lord restersoul.'

The people in the queue had attracted scores of local tradesmen who knew a captive audience when they saw one and plied the sedentary public with roasted pecans, sugar-cane sweets, attractive commemorative T-shirts, on-the-spot sermons, chilli-dogs, sodas, key rings and flamboyant exhibitions of fire-eating. These numbers were augmented the next morning by the arrival of television vans, lawyers, expert witnesses and protest groups working on behalf of both sides.

Trolldom now proliferated on the sidewalk. It was as if the square had become a landscape from a fantasy novel. The monsters of dreamscape, unreal, warty, misshapen and bizarre, had emerged from the abyss of death. It was as if one had walked on to the set of *Hellraiser III*. A child with a swastika on his forehead sat glumly in a stroller while, in front of him, 'the Cowboys for Christ,' jostled with, 'Aryan Youth.' Feminist cheerleaders pranced to Dixie and a grizzle-haired toothless entity insisted that exercise videos were pornography too. Everyone born with a mouth had arrived in Basinger Street to use it.

The Porn Star Liberation League staged a carefully planned entrance to gain the maximum attention. We rolled up in a motor procession that would have pleased the richest royalty. Givenchy, in leather catsuit, led on a Harley. Three police cars followed us, sirens silent, lights flashing. Kit drove me, Goo Lightly, Toyota and Pussy Willow in a gold and white 1963 Dodge Polara convertible. We had opted for a uniform look of tight yuppie suits with seamed stockings, white shirts, pencil skirts, tailored jackets, high, shiny, black court shoes and serious boxy handbags. Toyota was even wearing white gloves. Pussy Willow was not. She was wearing an engagement ring and a smug expresson thanks to the fact that she had finally extracted a commitment from Leon's bodyguard, Dennis.

'I'm gettin' married,' she lisped at the first reporter to approach her. 'Isn't it beautiful?'

I sat on the edge of the back seat of the convertible with my shoes on the seat, waving at the people like a sinister prom queen. We smoothed into the road outside the courthouse building. Kit stopped to let us out and then find somewhere to park the car. Toyota and Goo Lightly wove through the various television cameras that were recording the entrance and stopped to talk to the microphones that were shoved into their mouths. The crowd closed around the car as I stood up to climb out of it, slowly, and with concentration, as the manoeuvre involved a pencil skirt and four-inch-high heels.

Camera lenses prodded into my body; microphones surrounded my face; there was noise and voices and chaos. Then, as I stood up, a head and shoulders above the woman from PRTV and her cameraman, a crack split the air. At first I thought it was backfire as that is what it sounded like. It seemed to be nothing. Then there were several more cracks, a high-pitched scream and everyone fell to the pavement.

I had two seconds to wonder who they were firing at before I realised that it was me. A stabbing pain shot through my right arm, my head spun and I fell. There was a brief dizzying spell of pain, some heads bobbing, Kit holding me, and then nothing.

I awoke in the Hospital of St Mary and the Apostles. My right arm was bandaged. There was a tube in my wrist, wires, a salt drip, and a computer with flicking green and red numbers. The pain seered through my shoulder. I was in a private room. A corridor outside clattered with heels and trolley wheels. Kit sat beside me.

'You were shot,' she said.

I tried to remember, then it came – the crowd, the bang.

'Badly?'

'No. The bullet missed. It's a graze. But you were lucky. It was a tactical assault rifle and they think it was fired by a professional.'

'Who?'

'They don't know. Nobody was seen. They think it was fired from the roof of the courthouse and the assailant made off over the roofs, toward a waiting car, and then down the freeway. It would have been simple enough. The police suspect the Disgust Brigade, but they have no hard evidence.'

'What about Leon?'

'He's OK. But he's got the bodyguard. They've finished the opening speeches. The jury looks balanced enough; well, as balanced as you can expect in this wacko neighbourhood.'

'That's good.'

'Yeah. But I'm worried. There are a lot of lunatics out there. You know that. I know that. It doesn't necessarily stop here. What will they do when they find out they have missed? How am I going to protect you?' She took me in her arms and I realised that there were tears in her eyes.

I was too drugged with painkillers to register the full truth of what she said, but somewhere in the back of the dope and shock I knew that she was right, that this may not be over. She pulled away reluctantly.

'I've got to go, sweetie,' she said. 'The police want to ask me some questions. I think they want to know if there has been any history of this kind of thing.' She leaned over me, kissed me on the mouth.

'I'll be back soon.'

I leaned back in the pillow, aware that the day was about to stretch out long, slow and lonely.

A kind little orderly walked in with lunch – an apple, I think, and some soup. I was flicking the remote control between *Seinfeld* and my own self-pity when the room was considerably enhanced by the presence of a tall man wearing a stethoscope and a white coat. He was about 43 but no hint of middle age had contaminated his long lean body. He had dark-blue eyes, dark eyelashes, a long face, and the manner of someone who knows what they are doing, has been doing it for years, and expects immediate and unquestioning obedience. He walked tall, floated almost, confident that his presence was enough and there needed to be no noise or trickery to call attention to himself.

Every movement seemed to be organic to some greater purpose, but it was a purpose that was his own. This was not a man of the people: this was a leader. I wondered if he was some top surgeon who had wondered into my room by mistake. I wondered what he did at night, home alone, with his white coat and stainless-steel implements. His sexual charisma was such that I sensed it immediately and felt it, like a wild animal smells the scent of some far off mate exuding their pheromones in the distant forest. It wasn't a smell, exactly, not a man smell, anyway, after all we were in a hospital – the atmosphere was disinfected of all human origins. The scents were Mr Muscle and bleach and 'pine'. This feeling was more subtle than a smell, more unexplainable, more primal. I would call it the sixth sense but the sixth sense is supposed to warn of menace, and, in my experience, it never has. Quite the opposite.

In my experience the sixth sense smells out danger and propels the unsuspecting witch towards it, pushing her forward with dreadful force. She is powerless, tied to a conveyor belt smoothing ineluctably towards all the risks of new horizons. If she is lucky she will face the fear, and move on, triumphant, until she is trapped again by the subtle psyche that is her own best friend, worst enemy, better nature, who knows? I don't. Perhaps the Buddha does.

It feels like the instant rush of falling in love, but it isn't of course: the essence is animal lust. You know that. I know that. It means fucking, fighting and fleeing. It does not mean sunset and tequila and eternal youth. It means a couple of climaxes, standard affections, hard dick if you're lucky. It does not mean the silent beauty of mutual understanding, of unconditional compassion, of instant generosity. It's three weeks before you realise that their car is shit or they're a bore or they can only go a certain distance. Still, once you see it for what it is, it's good enough, and the modern-day harlot will take advantage of it, seize it and go with it. It doesn't happen everyday, after all, that a strict doctor eases himself into your presence and initiates the instant affection of sexual frenzy.

He was followed by a red-haired nurse of about 24 wearing a tight white uniform and a pair of white high-heeled shoes. The uniform, several sizes too small, eased itself tightly over her arse, causing it to wiggle as she walked; the buttons down the front strained to restrain her large round breasts. An upside-down watch jiggled on the end of the right one.

I noticed that her cream stockings were sheer and seamed. I wondered if she wore a garter belt, and, if so, whether it was function, white and cotton, or sleazy, of lace and ribbons. It was difficult to tell. Certainly her bush would be red and, I suspected, she would like me to spread her labia apart and lick her clit while she pushed her minge hard into my face and begged me to bring her to climax. I liked that idea. I liked the idea of diving between her legs with my mouth, inner thighs on either side of my face, nose down there, and her juddering about in that uniform, hair wild, starched little hat flung to the floor. She too had an air of efficiency, despite the fact that she looked like a debauched trollop.

'Nurse, you are wearing too much lipstick,' he said as they walked in. 'If it happens again you will be penalised. Do you understand?'

'Yes, Doctor.'

'I do not like women wearing lipstick. It is tarty and it does not suit the tone that a hospital ward should be setting.'

The doctor strode up to my bed, looked at my chart, made a mark with his pen, put it back in his top pocket, and stared down at me as if I was a naughty child and it had been my fault that I had got shot. That is what you get for playing with guns, he seemed to say, though, of course, he did not actually say it.

'Miss Stella Black?' His accent was British – the educated tones of middle England. You heard them in the army, you heard them at school. The voices were clipped and the speech used no unecessary words. He was not a man who wasted time.

'Yes.'

'You were lucky. You should be out of here in a couple of days, providing you do as you're told.' He looked down at me, unsmiling, his eyes piercing into mine and refusing to look away. I looked down first, shyly, at the long fingers of his hand, which were feeling the pulse on my wrist.

'Do you do as you're told, Miss Black?'

'Not very often,' I admitted.

'Well, you're about to start,' he said crisply.

He reached around to the back of my neck and undid the ribbons that tied the surgical gown. Then he pulled it down so that my breasts were exposed and placed the cold stethoscope between them. I breathed in sharply. My heart started to beat faster, palpitating almost, as he looked at his watch, smiling.

'Seems to be slightly fast. No dizziness?'

I shook my head. My nipples froze, erected, contracted into aperitif nuts, much against my will. I was not sure that I wanted to please this person. He had taken the control too easily. He looked at the chill of excitement constricting my skin and now grinned with genuine delight. Suddenly he was human as well as strict. I felt slightly disorientated. Perhaps I was getting a dizzy spell after all.

'Good girl,' he said. 'You're a brave girl and you're going to get better.' He stroked my cheek lightly and looked down at me with something very like love in his eyes. 'I am going to look after you. Prepare her, please, Nurse. We'll start with a rectal examination.

'But it's my arm that's hurt!' I protested

'Are you questioning my methods, Miss Black?' He was so tall and overpowering and authoritarian, I sank back into the bed, head throbbing, wishing that Kit was here to argue with this man, get rid of him, even. As it was I was in his power. There was nothing I could do. He was like some berserko Mills and Boon medical hero.

On the face of it he was the Dr Heartbreak of the romantic genre – brave in the face of medical emergency, attracted to Nurse Jessica but afraid to voice his feelings. The type who confesses his passion in the dispensary and hides a dark past. *The Doctor from Wales. Outback Doctor. Young Doctor Latham. Desert Doctor Frank. Doctor Luke's Return. The Marriage of Dr Brown. Nurse Friday Falls in Love.* You know the world. The consultant paedietrician always has capable arms. They sweep Nurse Lillian up and kiss her in the moonlight over the moors.

Only this medic wasn't kissing anyone. He was a patent perve and I dreaded to think what he planned to perform with his forceps and rubber tubing. He was not the type to place gauze gently on bruised skin. He was not of marital bliss, he was of mayhem in the morgue. If there was bandaging to be done, I suspected it would be around my mouth. There were two of them, and they were both a great deal larger than I. They could do as they pleased. Before I could register what was happening, the nurse had ripped back the sheets from the bed and flipped me over on to my face. The flimsy hospital gown, already half-undone, split down the back and revealed my spine and buttocks.

She placed four pillows underneath my stomach so that my bum was raised towards the doctor. She attached my ankles to a pair of leather straps attached to the iron posts at the foot of the bed. This served to spread my legs and buttocks far apart, revealing the orifice to my back passage as if it was an offering to be taken by whoever wanted it. My face was pressed into the cotton sheet of the bed and there was the smell of antiseptic and laundry. The surgicial gown fell from my body so that I was naked. The pain in my arm ebbed, thanks to the painkillers, and, for the same reason, I was more relaxed that I might have been otherwise, given these intimidating circumstances.

The nurse smoothed her fingers into a pair of latex gloves and spread Vaseline generously between my buttocks, softly kneading the flesh and gently massaging me as she did so. This was no perfunctory measure: this was foreplay. She eased the gel into my skin until it was oily, slipping her fingers down to my clit, then slipping one finger through the external sphincter and to the internal muscle. I wriggled my arse and groaned.

He spoke with matter-of-fact authority: 'If you move, Miss Black, I can assure you that there will be some pain. Please be a good girl. The nurse and I are never very kind to naughty girls – we don't have the time, you see. Or the patience. I have been known, Miss Black, to spank a naughty patient quite hard. Haven't I, Nurse?'

'Yes, Doctor.'

'Only the other day I had to put a certain Minnie Woodall over my knee, there and then, in the public ward with all the other patients watching. She had tried to wriggle out of an enema, Miss Black she thought she could question my authority, but the result was a smarting backside and a good tanning in front of all the other people in the ward. Public humiliation, Miss Black. I am sure you won't want that.'

The nurse contined to manipulate all the muscles of my posterior, now dipping two fingers slowly into the depths of my rectum.

'The anus, Miss Black, is a source of intense orgasmic pleasure. As I have written in my definitive study, *Rectal Health and Pleasure*, the muscles of the anus are all involved in the contractions of orgasm because the muscles of the pelvis region are all connected. This means, Miss Black, that the nerves of the pelvic floor are interconnected with the nerves of the vagina. The rectum should be seen as an extension of the vagina. You should go beyond your clitoris, Miss Black. The clitoral orgasm is the climax of a boring little girl, Freud's immature orgasm lest we forget.'

He stroked the back of my neck and hair but still the nurses fingers were causing me discomfort. I wanted Kit to come and get rid of them both.

'This procedure will show you the difference between the external sphincter and the internal sphincter. The external sphincter, Miss Black, is controlled by the central nervous system control. That means that your mind can control it, as you are trying to do now. The internal sphincter is controlled by the autonomic nervous system and is more difficult to control. It is full of tension. Knotted up, just as the neck or the stomach becomes knotted. This is the pain, Miss Black; this is what brings the tears into your eyes when the Nurse introduces her fingers into you.'

Gradually I let the internal anxiety go, surrendered to the warm greasy fingers of the nurse, allowed her to ease three fingers further and further up my back passage.

'Both sphincters are closely linked; let go of the external sphincter and you will help the internal muscle to relax,' he said. 'The external sphincter is connected to the pubococcygeus and I would reccomend Kegel exercises, Miss Black. Indeed, I will see to it that you are put on a regular programme and spanked hard if you do not keep to them. Kegel exercises will tone the pelvic floor and allow you to receive large objects through the skill of relaxation. And a large object is what you are going to get, miss. That is enough, Nurse.'

She had done a good job. My anus was open and ready. I was beginning to enjoy the flickering pleasure that passed between my butt and my cunt; he was right. It was all one. Clit was butt, butt was womb. And it was all beginning to need something. He stepped forward.

'You, young lady, have a beautiful behind.'

I heard him squeeze his fingers into his own latex gloves and felt them press into my back passage.

'The rectum is not a straight tube,' he said, still lecturing, as if I was a student taking notes in some classroom. 'They are as personal as fingerprints. Ah, there's your sigmoid.' Now he was inside me. I hardly knew how far. I was only aware that he was going further than anyone ever had before. He was determined and he was taking me with him while making sure that my mind was connected to the pleasure of new sensations.

'Breathe, please, Miss Black,' he said firmly. 'If you do not breathe I will spank you until you have learned to do so. I have found spanking to be an excellent way of encouraging anxious young women to let go of their silly anal retentions. And the one thing I can tell about you, Miss Black, is that you are a control freak. I can feel it in every muscle of your tight little arsehole.'

Jesus, I thought. He should meet Kit.

There was no pain now. Just him.

'The insertion of any object is a specialised skill. A wrong angle can cause a lot of pain. The person who sodomises is the person who must know what he is doing. And you will be glad to know, Miss Black, that I know what I am doing. I could fist you at this point, Miss Black. Certainly you are relaxed enough. I could force my hand, even my forearm into your rectum, beyond the rectum even. This could bond you to me for ever. But I do not believe in speed. The young woman who can cope with fingering is not necessarily the young woman who can cope with a man's forearm exploring her most private emotional regions.'

Now I was in pleasure. Now I wanted to journey to the final stage of this intercourse and abandon myself to the true trust of total vulnerability. I did not know this man. I did not know if there was love or safety or care or kink or cruelty or inanity. It could bring damage to my core, but I went forward, as any explorer steps into the dark knowing that to stay in the safe place is to starve or suffocate. Even die. Sometimes you just have to leap.

'Spread her buttocks further apart please, Nurse. I am going to sodomise her.'

The nurse stood behind me and pulled my cheeks apart with her fingers. I was as open to this stranger as I have ever been to anyone, even to Kit. We had played in this area, and I had let her have some of me but I had never let her have it all. Now I was splayed out. Anything could have got me but he was making me brave. And this was not a bad thing for a girl who had just got shot. He was a perverted practitioner but his medical theories had a strangely curative effect. He did not work within the code of any medical ethics; he was a mad buggering maverick, but he was giving me back my nerve and setting me on the road to recovery.

'Further apart, Nurse.'

Now I felt the oily tip of a very hard penis. Slowly he slithered through the external sphincter, easily and painlessly through the internal, fucking the back passage as if it was fucking the front, knowing all its nerve endings, enjoying its warm tightness pressing down on the nerves of his shaft. The climax did not come as usual from the button in the front, but from a much deeper place – a place that was difficult to explain, for it was the seat of the psyche somehow: the unknown timeless place where daddies lived and children played and there were no rules or time or shame or sadness.

He pumped slowly, not strict now, but a lover, whispering gentle encouragement, ensuring that I was still relaxed and still enjoying his presence in my undefended place. Then it all came out. I burst into tears as the calm euphoria burst into my pelvis. I could not believe what was happening to me. Well, it was difficult to believe.

I felt him shudder his own orgasm.

'Please put her back to bed, Nurse,' he said.

The nurse unbuckled the leather straps on my ankles and removed the four pillows from under my stomach. I collapsed face down on the bed. I was drained. I could not have helped myself even if I had wanted to. She gently turned me over, pushed me to the top of the bed, and tucked me smartly in. I was just awake enough to realise that he had left the room. I sank back into the pillows. When I awoke there was a hot cup of tea by the bed and a spray of flowers from Leon. My womb was satisified, there was a deep calm, and, for once the place did not smell of disinfectant. It smelled of lilies and roses.

I saw the doctor several more times. It was always the same. He would restrain me with gaffer tape or rubber tubing or the leather restraints, massage my rectum with gel, and slowly take me as he wished. Sometimes the nurse helped and watched, sometimes she did not. Sometimes he instructed me, sometimes he buggered me in silence. Often he came alone. Once he sat in a chair by the bed and made me go down on him, surgical gown slipping off my shoulders, tight lips pistoning on the swollen head. He could keep a hard-on for ever.

Usually, though, he would walk in with his clipboard and follow the same procedure as if it was a perfectly normal routine. Patient prostrate on hospital bed, white sheets, nylon screen, the sound of voices and trolleys in the distance, his dick hard up my arse, me crying, releasing.

I never got to know him. I felt that he had inspected my core. It was the closest I have ever been to anyone. But I never got to know him.

Kit refused to allow me to attend the rest of Leon's trial. She refused to let me go out at all. She picked me up from the hospital in a bulletproof limousine borrowed from Leon and locked me in our suite at the Lunker Lodge. We had three rooms: a bedroom with a double bed and a crib day bed for a child, a television dining area with a small stove, and a bathroom with an old-fashioned standing bath and a tarnished brass shower unit that made a noise like falling buildings. There was a framed photograph of John Wayne chained to the wall.

The view? The back scanned over scrubland to a swamp; the front saw the courtyard of the motel: crumbling wooden doors, rotten wooden panes, rusting pick-up trucks, edentate nomads passing through to who knows where to do God knows what. The other inhabitants were rootless families, adulterous couples, small-time whores and a very old woman who had lived there since 1973 and insisted that she had once met Gregory Peck.

I was made to stay behind while Kit went out to

attend to the various activities connected to the Porn Star Liberation League. The hours were long. I only had chat shows and old movies and shopping channels for company. I ate watermelon and take-out ribs and Cherry Garcia. And watched more TV.

And so Kit became the ultimate authority. She fed me, dressed me, bathed me, and I let her, partly because I could not be bothered to resist, mostly because I liked it. I liked her pushing my legs above my head and powdering my cunt; I liked sitting on her knee when I was sad and hearing her whisper into my ear. I liked it when she told me to go to the loo or to clean my teeth or to eat up. I liked it when she fed me.

Sometimes there was a scenario and I would end up in the corner with a burned bottom and red face, having cried and spat and tantrummed. Once in frustration I threw a plate against the wall and it shattered. She thrashed my arse with a pizza paddle and sent me to bed. I couldn't sit down for two days. By the end of the first week I was putting on weight on my stomach. She made me wear my hair in bunches, brushing the style each day, and fixing them herself with elastic bands. And she made me wear baby-doll pyjamas, little cotton dressing gowns, frilly panties, short pinafores whose hemline sat just below my arse, puffed-sleeve shirts, tiny shorts, ra-ra skirts with pie-crust frills, ankle socks and little Mary Jane shoes with buttons.

I was beginning to look younger and I was beginning to act younger. Slowly she was turning me into the child that she wanted. Slowly I was becoming her very thing. And, as always, I was abnegating. That ultimate thrill. To abscond from oneself. Fab foreplay is not necessarily to be fucked. The exile from selfhood is enough, an erotic reward in itself. I would lie on the day bed semi-naked, legs akimbo, hair stuck to the forehead from the heat, sucking my thumb. I would eat candy and read magazines. I would demand things, spoiled. Sometimes I got them and sometimes I did not.

I saw them on the television, of course, while she was out. They were all there, in between Penelope Pitstop, Scooby Doo and Marge Simpson. Penelope Pitstop had a nice life. She was always being abducted and tied up. The car, a pink convertible with a parasol, was perfect. She was a Southern belle, a millionairess and a proper modern woman. I wanted Dr Ken. I nagged and nagged for hours. I nagged for so long I drained myself of all energy so when she did finally buy him I had lost interest. The chase was over. The lust had gone. The want was the thing; the gratification was a bore. I didn't even bother to take him out of the box.

She was furious. She shouted at me and took him straight back to the shop. But I didn't care. Dr Ken – I told her he was a git. Tattoo Barbie was way cooler. So I refused to eat the supper, which meant that I wasn't allowed pudding, which meant I sulked and kicked the furniture and whined and was told not to whine. Finally she made me bend over the small dining table with my knickers pulled down to my ankles and my skirt above my waist. She didn't touch me. She merely made me stay there, air against my cheeks, in silence. After ten minutes I had worked myself into a fantasy frenzy of need. I was wriggling and complaining. My cunt was wet and it was empty and I was bored of my butt being in the air. I didn't like her any more. I didn't want to do as I was told. I wanted her to thrash me as hard as her right arm would allow. I wanted her to fist me. I wanted attention. But she was clever, the bitch, and she left me there. She ignored me and refused to touch me.

After that I shut up. I didn't like that.

And so we played. Spanking, fingering, licking. My dummy doubled up as a butt plug.

'Wash your hands before you sit down.'

'No you may not.'

'What did I say about please and thank you?'
'Do as you're told.'
'Elbows off the table.'
'Do you want to go to bed early?'

I liked the tension that preceded punishment, the silence that told me I had gone too far. She would stare at me coldly for an eternity, when there were no more words or arguments. The line had been crossed. She would get up with great calm deliberation, take a beer slowly out of the fridge, stare at me some more, and I would look up at her below my fringe, pouting, not giving in. Angry.

Sometimes she would go and get the hairbrush herself; sometimes she used a paddle; sometimes I was told to go and get the tawse. Sometimes I was made to undress in front of her, slowly stripping for her, panties slipping down the legs, nightie falling off the body, easily, slowly, with cheek. Then I would turn around and wriggle my arse at her. She liked that. She liked the sleazy lap-dancing child who didn't care that she was heading for the punishment that she richly deserved.

Sometimes I was more reluctant and had to be dragged by the hand to the place of punishment. She was physically much stronger than I, as strong as a man, in fact, and a great deal stronger than many. She would throw me over the back of the chair, over the bed, over the table, over her knee. I was always wet after all this. So was she. Sometimes my pelvis would burn with her punishments and I would fight to get into her pants, ripping the zip down, forcing her out, diving into her minge, wanting her, also wanting some of the control back and knowing her clit was a way to get it. An easy way, sure. But a way. She would lie flat and I would go on all fours, naked, white except for the freshly reddened cheeks, my face deep in her crotch, making her come.

Then, if I was lucky, she would push her hand into

me and somehow the pain of the punishment, the tingling of the clit, the warm deviant satisfaction of shadowy ideas made into reality – all these would combine, and I would scream into climax and collapse on her neck and cry that I loved her I loved her I loved her. We were very close.

I didn't always want to be beaten. It hurts, after all. Threat, anyway, can be as good as a touch. But once she decided that my arse was hers I had to go with it. There were moments when I regretted the game, when I was just humiliated and began to wonder where I was, who I was and where we were going. Sometimes I just lay on top of her – she, fine in black girdle, I naked except for the frilly high-waisted panties – and I would suck on her tits while she stroked my hair. I would suck on her tits as if I wanted to eat her. I went out of my way to provoke her so that I was never good, always naughty. She had to attend to me all the time or I would find something to cause a reaction. This was her fault. She had made me needy and dependent on her.

Once when I was bored, I pissed on her lap and she went mad. The wet stain seeped into her jeans. I laughed and then I got it. She lost it. I swear that hairbrush came down on me one hundred times; my entire bottom and thighs were crimson. I was sobbing and howling by the fifitieth stroke, by the hundredth I knew I would never do anything bad *ever again*. And she was cross. There was no make-up after this thrashing. I was sent crying to bed.

I sobbed long and loud, longer and louder, on and on, trying to make her come to me. Then I turned the light on and sobbed some more. I sat up in the bed, arse enflamed, little baby-doll nightie rumpled, hair knotted, red in the face, tears falling down my cheeks, howling at her to come to me, but she stayed in the sitting room. I could see the light. She would not come.

I became hysterical. I left the present and went out

there. Time slowed down. I just screamed and screamed and screamed and I did not know who I was any more. I thought she had gone for ever. I was alone. I was going to die. I ripped a rag doll to pieces, crashed a glass, and went on wailing for her.

Aaaaaaaaaaaa!

And at last there she was, a dark figure against the door.

'Shh, now that's enough.' She took me up but I did not have the satisfaction of success. I had pushed myself too far out. I had no petty emotion, just need and upset and plain primal sobbing from deep within, the emergent pain from a space that I did not even know existed.

'Shh, baby. That's enough. I'm here.' She rocked me, allowing me to weep and snivel all over her. The convulsions ceased. I clung to her as if I was never going to let her go again. I began to forget the bullet that had nearly killed me. I was no longer so scared. I had entered the scene. There was no door marked EXIT. I disengaged from the threat of the guns and the hate out to get me. I had been shocked by the physical power of prejudice and by the violence of strangers; it is difficult to accept hatred and it is difficult to believe evil. Easy on the TV. Very, very hard in real life. It's not like a car crash; there is none of the fate of an accident; this assault was personal. Paranoia was not a delusion. I could have become very nervous, but Kit locked me into drama and gave me a strange freedom from the effects of trauma. I lost myself to the purity of play as she turned me into her baby doll.

Chapter Eleven

Leon's trial came to an end four weeks after it had started. There had been a parade of 'expert' witnesses, some with hair, some without, all testifying for and against legalised profligacy. A doctor announced there was tangible evidence to suggest that pornography was a necessary release to repression and an aid to public health, while a political-science professor arrived from a university in Wisconsin and said that *Biker Bitches from Hell* exceeded all acceptable community standards.

Several hatchet-faced women pointed out that Leon Lubrisky had flagrantly flouted all the suggestions so sensibly set down by the Meese Commission, while a rambling defect quoted gospels and said that eating shellfish was a lesser abomination than homosexuality. He had started to throw prawns into his mouth when the ambulance arrived.

The Oscar-winning director Ivan Standof said Jed Blacksnake's work was art; so did the critic of a leading New York newspaper who had written reviews to prove it. Everyone had their say.

The judge, a 63-year-old ex-teacher, was blessed with a sense of humour that he had honed during his years teaching ten-year-olds. He doubtless felt that he had returned to school, such was the silliness and showing off that characterised the courtroom atmosphere.

His attitude was one of cynicism and disbelief. He stared at both defence and prosecution as if they were throwing paintballs at each other and he was not beyond actually rolling his eyes and staring heavenwards like the saints of so many religious depictions. Kit told me that he spent most of his lunch breaks on his mobile phone laughing with his wife and fixing to see Meg Ryan movies at the Cineplex.

The television camera (to Leon's delight) once caught him putting his hands over his ears when some particularly overwrought witness started to actually thump a bible.

Nevertheless, Judge O'Connor took copious notes when the salient and relevant legal points were made by both Rowena Brocklehurst (wearing shoulder pads, acrylic and an ozone-defying patina of lacquer) and Leon's team of sixties liberals.

His attorney, Miles Foreman, who had begun his career defending the Weathermen, told the jury that First Amendment freedom was not supposed to be discriminatory in its effects. Freedom was available to everybody, from serial killers to Quakers. Those who decided to take that freedom away from someone else, took that freedom away from themselves and started to build a prison for all.

This was not a matter of religion, he said, glaring at the prosecuting team. This was a matter of law and common sense. It would be dangerous to set a precedent based on prejudice and ignorance when the state of Georgia had fought so hard and won so many triumphs in the battle for human rights.

Finally the judge had his say, and say it he did. He told the jury that he felt that the laws on which the trial had been brought were tenuous at the least, oblique in their meaning, old-fashioned in their foundation and obsolete to the mores of contemporary society. They were, however, the laws, as written, and should be respected as such. Nevertheless, he did not think that Leon Lubrisky had broken them in his capacity as chief executive officer of Pleasure Dome Inc.

The jury took some time in their deliberations, leaving everyone to worry that there would be a hung vote. Rowena Brocklehurst's arguments for the sanity of society had been lucid and she appealed to the protective mother in every woman.

The lawyers huddled, smoked and whispered. Leon sweated and yelled down his mobile phone. I received daily reports from Kit and 24-hours-a-day drama on Court TV.

The reason for the jury's thoroughness was finally revealed. They were spending some time watching Leon's videos and reading Pleasure Dome publications such as *Super Nubie*, *Tittie Bitz* and *Anal Amateurs*. After fifteen hours of this 'research' they achieved enlightenment and re-emerged into the courthouse with their conclusion.

Not guilty.

The world went mad.

Leon was carried crying out of the courthouse.

Rowena Brocklehurst said she would appeal.

Miles Foreman said she wasn't very appealing.

A jury member said that he had never enjoyed himself so much in his life; the whole thing had been even more fun than the last family holiday to Disneyland and a great deal cheaper. Now an agent had booked him to do a round of chat shows and meetings with studio executives.

The news was headline stories all over America, beating down a new war in Syria and an old one in Pakistan. Photographs of Leon and the Porn Star Liberation

League appeared on wires and there were interviews with all concerned.

Leon, triumphant (and now staying in the grandest hotel in the county), announced that he was going to hold a celebration party at the Obediah Mansion, the historic antebellum estate on the outskirts of Alspokane.

He planned to invite a thousand people. There were to be side shows, burlesque shows, fireworks, fun fair, hot-air balloons, Roman orgies and stars flown in from both coasts.

'I will build the biggest Jacuzzi in the world,' he told CNN. 'It will have to be patrolled by Air-Sea Rescue. It will go into *The Guinness Book of Records*.'

I started to plan outfits. It was to be my first night out for weeks. I hadn't seen any of the friends. I hardly remembered what they looked like.

There were several choices. I could be simple sleaze in stripper spikes and gold lamé hot pants or I could be sultry chic in an off-the-shoulder 50s number and some pearls that one of the pop stars had bought me.

I was easing myself into a fuchsia satin with a low back and whalebone teamed with red silk stilettos when Kit returned.

She allowed me to flounce around in front of the mirror for a couple of minutes as she enjoyed some arcane sadistic moment. Then she said, 'You're not going to that party.'

'Yes, I am.'

'No, you're not. It will be a scrum. There will be no way to protect you in the event that any assailant should manage to get into that place. We won, Stella. That is dangerous in itself. The law did not work for them. Who knows what goes through the heads of these Christian warriors? They could do anything and they could be anywhere. They could easily gain access to Leon's party. The guest list will be enormous – the police will never be able to guarantee security.

'These people are terrorists. They have false passports and fake ID and they know how to disappear. If they want to come to this party they will. They will nibble a canapé one minute and shoot you in the head the next. Do you want that, Stella? Do you want to even live with that knowledge? You're not going, and that is that. I've said what I have to say. You will do as you're told. That is my final word on the matter.'

I eased the red stiletto off my foot and flung it very hard at her head.

Then I screamed. No words. Just a loud female screech of utter inarticulate vexation.

I had had enough.

I had been cooped up, controlled, bullied, dominated, brainwashed, mind-fucked and spoon-fed. I had not seen anyone apart from Kit for three weeks. I wanted out. I wanted out of the hotel room, out of the relationship and possibly out of the country.

I had had enough.

I wanted my self back. I wanted the recalcitrant spirit who owned a fabulous car and could apply nail varnish while driving it. Now the Firebird was burned out and so was I.

I didn't want to be her plaything any more. My arse was sore. I felt out of synch with reality and I had had enough of primal catharsis. I wanted to get on to the Next Thing. The next thing might be my career, it might not. It might be art, it might not. It might be hot-rod racing in Nevada, it might not. I did not know and I did not care. But I wanted to get away, travel down new roads, find new men, study new women, eroticise exploration. America beckoned. She was unfathomable. A country that no one could ever know.

So I lost it and yelled and told her that it was not her decision to make. It was my decision to make, my responsibility to take, and my risk to face. I would do as

I pleased, and she should either accept this idea or pull away from the relationship.

'You can fuck off,' I said. 'I'm going to Leon's party and there is nothing you can do about it.'

We were standing opposite each other across the small kitchen table.

She stared at me, furious and dangerous. She had long played with the power of anger – she had an actress's control of emotional interplay, and she knew how to use it.

Slowly she walked around the table, stood in front of me and stared down at me, intending to intimidate me, intending to provide a calm space where I would feel threatened and begin to appreciate the mistakes that I was making.

And once, not so long ago, I would have succumbed. For she could make me melt just like that. A cold glare and I was hers. I would offer myself up for the punishment of her hard hand, or the lick of the whip of her choice. My white flesh would be hers to spank, my every opening would be hers to finger and lick and taste and manipulate. I would prostrate and meld as if she was some enlightened being who knew the greater good. She held me with the pure strength that is the charisma of authority. I was the follower in the tribe, doing a frenzied dance to drums, fervent to her will and possessed by reverence. She was a hex-hag, but there had been ecstasy, the ecstasy of the entranced. I had been enticed by her hoodoo charms. I had become absorbed and entrenched and I had trusted, but, having been comfortably engrossed, I now felt afflicted. Some invisible ligature was tightening around my neck and I was struggling to breathe.

I stared up at her, carried into courage by fury.

'I'm going!' I repeated.

'We'll see about that,' she said, and slapped me in the face.

Her hard hand cracked against my right cheek and the tears sprang into my eyes. My head rang and I staggered but I did not fall.

Once, the pain would have hit my stomach and seeped between my legs. Once, need would have made me hers in a matter of nanoseconds. The trigger was delicate. A slap was foreplay. A bad girl needs to be given boundaries. Once she has learned them she receives love and sex. They are the rewards for obedience. It had worked. My, *how* it had worked. She had given me a moral integrity that I could not find for myself and assuaged the guilts that I hardly knew I had. She had allowed me to play with fire and the primal scream and all the erotic possibilities of uninhibited drama. In some ways she had made me free, but in too many others she was imprisoning me.

This minute was full of fear and rage: fear that something was actually dying inside me; rage that I had allowed it to happen and that she, the great warrior, Kit the Protector, committed to saving my life, had not seen that. In fact, it was she who was destroying me. Slowly and ineluctably, she was killing me, more slowly than the bullet of a gun, sure, but killing me nonetheless.

God, those black eyes, flashing. Those breasts, huge, angry, motherly. I could have fainted but I slapped her back, not as hard – I was smaller, after all, and slapping had never been my métier. But I slapped her and the sting rang against her cheek.

Surprise momentarily disorientated her. She touched her burning face with an expression of disbelief.

'You ungrateful little bitch,' she snapped. 'After all I have done for you. I have devoted my life to you and you think you can just pull out when you feel like it? Do you think you can just throw people away like Coke cans? You're worthless, Stella. You have no honour and no integrity and you are going to end up alone . . .'

I was ready to retort that I would rather be alone than

bullied by an insane control freak, but she walked smartly out of the room, slammed the door and locked it.

She had locked me in. Again.

I stood staring at her, the sting still ringing on my cheek, tears in my eyes, shaking with fury.

I kicked the leg of the table quite hard with my foot and then, superseded by the feeling, turned it over altogether so that all the cutlery and china smashed to the floor.

This prison was not going to contain me any more.

I had a platinum credit card. I had a lipstick the colour of blood. What more did I need?

I worked fast because I did not know how long it would take her to cool down, come back, and try to gentle me back into submission. I knew from past experience that this would not be hard. I did love her. Leaving her was not going to be easy.

I looked around at all the symbols of our relationship. Kit's books about Berettas, my books about Jane Russell. Kit's knee-high leather boots; my marabou mules. Kit's endless supply of black lace plunge bras; my satin thongs. The photograph of us lying on the Firebird. A crumpled poster for *The Ordeals of Emmeline*. Bullets lying on the bedside table. A CD compilation of the best Southern swamp music. Her skull ring (real ruby eyes). My Tiffany earrings.

We had had a good time but I refused to allow myself to go there. Instead, I took up the chastity belt, which was lying on a chair, and threw it symbolically into the rubbish bin, where I hoped that she would find it when she returned.

Bitch! I thought.

I slithered out of the evening dress and into a tiny black miniskirt that was split up the side and allowed movement. I grabbed a push-up bra (a girl needs cleavage even when escaping – remember that, my lovelies, tell your grandchildren, it's really worth knowing because you never ever know when you may have to run), sleeveless T-shirt, leather jacket and a darling pair of soft, brown, leather sling-backs that no one, and I mean no one, could have left behind. Then I pulled open a drawer.

Kit's belongings lay in chaos. I had never understood her untidiness, being quite an orderly soul myself. But she always flung things about, left them where they lay, picked them up to wear them but probably not otherwise.

Bras and stockings lay in a tangle of elastane straps and nylon ganglia intertwined with silver belly chains and satin nickel handcuffs. Underneath this geologic layer there was a dildo harness, several grip panels from discarded revolvers, an ejector alignment pin, a can of WD-40, a gunsmith screwdriver set, a trigger lock, a pair of shooting glasses, the snaky leather belt with which she had once lashed me for sleeping with her mechanic, and a bowie knife in a pony-skin holster.

Scrabbling around in this jumbled regalia of Kit's life I finally found what I was looking for and pulled out her Smith and Wesson pistol. It was a single-action model, tiny and light, more of a plinker than a real man-stopper, but it would serve its purpose, at close range, anyway.

It was all I needed. Well. That, the Joy, the lippie and a new life.

I pushed the gun gently into the back of the waistband of my miniskirt where it sat, tight, and hard and comforting, like a man's morning erection, pushing towards one with semi-conscious determination.

Ready now, ready to go, almost expiring with the urge to leave, I attempted to dismantle the ancient wooden window frame and remove the pane. This was weak, but it was not completely rotten and it refused to submit to my frantic wrenching.

Finally I gave up, took the handle of Kit's whip, smashed the glass and, wearing her leather gloves, carefully picked out the shards that sprang from the frame like teeth.

I sniffed the leather of the darling shoes then, carefully, sling-backs in one hand, I climbed through.

The late afternoon was warm and sunny. No one was about. A couple of turkeys gobbled about in the back yard. A radio delivered a hysterical sermon from some invisible niche of millenarian holiness.

I walked quickly towards the edge of the swamp.

Free at last.

Chapter Twelve

The Ogeechee Swamp. This was no small marsh. This was a wetland wilderness the size of a small county. I had wondered out, ignorant and innocent, as an unknowing tourist might wander on to a Yorkshire moor or a snowbird camper from Nebraska might circle eternally in the Mojave desert.

Bogs and islands spread for miles in a tangle of slash pine, blackgum and loblolly bay. A sodden jungle of warm wet vegetation procreated with moist fecundity over warm peat and oozing mud. Everything was the temperature of blood. There was the smell of damp and of methane. Towering cypress trees trailed Spanish moss, which hung down as tenuous strands of grey lace and tangled with the white flowers of the climbing heath that clung inside the bark.

The swamp had remained stagnant since some arcane geological gestation had caused its putrid flood, and man had made no mark. It was a sprawling mossy grotto and it all looked the same. Here were tall ferns and floating spores, glossy lily leaves and matted vines, but there were no signs. No helpful rural landmarks, man-made or nature-borne, were of use to navigate. There were no creek carvings or animal nestings.

Shadowy, green, wet, hot. I was surrounded by the moist heat of vulgar growth and slow decay. The climate clung to me like a wet garment.

The lakes ran as black as ink, creating a glossy surface on which the crisp clear reflections of the sky and of the vegetation were mirrored with crystalline accuracy, like realist paintings. Duplicate landscape floated on a surface under which all the swamp myth lurked. It was made of decay. Matter mouldered at the bottom of the tannin mess; it was where the zomboids bred and the sprites sprang and strange lights were seen.

I could not guess what supernature had bred in this primordial nexus. It was a black lagoon and unsightly creatures came from it.

And soon I realised. This eternal lake could swallow you up as easily as one of the phallic flesh-eating pitcher plants swallowed up a darting bug by luring it to its funnel-shaped leaves with promise of gooey nectar, then snapping its leaves closed to make a prison.

Even in the swamp there was sadism. Nature's bullies and victims endured a lifetime of survivalist struggle. Here there were mothers who deserted children and daughters who fucked fathers – there was all the psychosexual cruelty of amoral anomaly. That fat 'gator would eat her baby – eighteen foot the woman, the *el lagato* of Spanish sailors, monster of the Mesozoic area, she would eat her baby as soon as look at it, great overbite snapping down on the small head and swallowing the progeny whole.

All around there was mayhem and atrocity. A horror show lurked within the tangled vegetation; no moss was innocent, no snake free of blame. The gaudy swamp iris was armed with Borgia poison; the red-tailed hawk would peck the eye out of a small squirrel. It was a deviant burlesque of delinquents, feathered, scaled, clawed and otherwise. You could hear the snort of the feral pig, the screech of the owl, the rustle of the skink in the undergrowth, the flapping of wings through leaves, the throaty orgasmic growlings of reptiles mating.

The marshland was a downtown club where all organisms were locked into a combat of mutual destruction and carrion was the currency. The green-briar vine had made itself smell of rotting flesh in order to attract the flies who fed on putrefaction; they were like some necrophiliac nymphomaniac who had smothered herself in formaldehyde to attract a morgue attendant of similar inclinations. Try not to imagine that particular date.

Gaudy allurement and sophisticated ritual. Bodies modified to attract mates; behavioural abnormalities designed to escape death. There were no rules for perennials and predators. Everything went in this mire. Biology was psychopathology wallowing in the mud of the slough and Nature's id knew no boundary. It made me realise that Kit and I were not weird. We were natural.

I had not even thought what I was going to do or where I was going or how I was going to get there. I had vaguely thought that somewhere beyond the peat and plush there would be a one-pump town or minimart or a man in a van ready to drive me away. Away from Kit. Away from porn. Away from the life that was now sucking the sprite out of me.

I had forgotten how to direct myself. I was floating hopelessly in a stagnant land. I stepped carefully on to peat batteries that shuddered underneath me, like giant muddy waterbeds. I had to carry the shoes. I caught my foot in the scrambling root of a tree, the heel broke and I fell down. So now I was barefoot. And bare feet provide all kinds of terrors in a swamp: there are parasites that can climb into you and plants that will paralyse you.

Buzzing feeders swarming on squelching goo are of no comfort to the bare skin of a person who was beginning to wish that she had stayed where she was. I should have developed a more sensible course, stolen Kit's car perhaps, or at least waited until she returned, so that some real-life plan could have been made, some proper severance that would aid sensible closure rather than abet confusing exploration.

There was no sign of civilisation. I lost all sense of direction as I wondered about in plushy moss and floundered among trailing creepers. The sun speckled through flickering leaves; the head of an alligator floated above the dark-brown murk. I was a drunk in the hothouse at Kew – staggering, looking for the door marked EXIT, wanting to scream for a man in a uniform.

I was exhausted. I was hot. I was thirsty. I sang into a soft moss on a bank and tried to restore myself. I could walk no further. I simply did not know what to do. Then some gaseous exchange ignited in the mud and a small volcano burst forth in an explosion of methane. The noise made me jump. Looking over to the direction from which it came I saw a shallow skiff moored to a bunch of reeds.

After slowly making my way towards it, the ground trembling underneath my feet as I did so, I stepped into it and lay down. It rocked gently, like a crib. The sun speckled down through the shivering canopy. There was cocoon warmth. I planned to cast off and float down the blackwater stream. At least this would be quicker than staggering barefoot in the snarl of roots and undergrowth that matted the marshland. Water had a direction and there was the possibility that humanity would live at the end of it.

I made this plan, but I did not keep to it. Exhausted by the row with Kit, disorientated by the heat and endless wandering in the swamp, I went to sleep.

* * *

I awoke to find a man standing thigh deep in the water and staring down at me. He was about six foot, 35 years old and he looked like Gabriel Byrne. He was wearing a white shirt and khaki chinos and he carried a rifle.

Life did not seem to have touched him, yet here he was, moving in a primordial sludge, at odds with all I knew about swamp people. The hokey mamas and grizzled edentates who had passed through the motel tended to reflect their origins; certainly they were proud to trace their heritage to the times when the Seminole Indians hid themselves to escape Confederate constriction and were followed soon after by other outlaws – escaped slaves, army deserters, convicts, and a tribe simply known as the goat people.

The marsh sapiens tended to be old and etched and odd, as keen to make a kebab out of a snake as to discuss the healthful effects of the swamp willow. They led unruly groups of unruly pigs and tried to sell you possum skins. They could tell you where a raccoon lived but they could not tell you where the supermarket was. They reflected the nature in which they lived. They were wild and maverick and untouched by modernity. No cosmetics met the women's skins, no new cars sat in remote-controlled garages. They drove horse-drawn trailers piled with hay and they spent the evenings shooting bobcats. The swamp people moved in a module made by the marsh and existed in the mores that it made.

This new stranger did not. He was an exotic, transplanted by some unknown hand, and he was still waiting for his roots to take.

'You're lucky you didn't fall out,' he said. 'You'd be mummified if a 'gator didn't get you first. It's dangerous to close your eyes out here . . . Where are you goin' anyway?'

I didn't know the answer to this. I struggled to recall

some plan – I had a credit card. I didn't know much more.

'Er. I got lost, but I can't go back,' I said.

'Problems at home?'

'Yeah.'

'Come with me, then. I only live down there. It's round the corner. You would have reached it if you had floated downstream . . .'

'My mother said I shouldn't talk to strangers.'

'Well, we better get to know each other, then.'

He smiled, cast the boat off from the bank, and pushed it slowly down the river with the oar.

'You from round here?' I asked.

'From hereabouts . . .'

I wanted to ask him a lot more, of course, for the mysteries that he carried were almost tangible. He wore unanswered questions proudly as if they were tribal jewellery prized in a magical mating rite. He was not sullen, but neither was he effusive. I lapsed into silence. I was tired.

He knew the waterways and the currents and navigated them easily, smoothing the boat down the black mire as easily as some could smooth a convertible into a parking space. Occasionally a weed snarled progress and he would slash at it with the knife that he kept in a holster hanging from his belt, and I enjoyed watching the biceps undulate as he did so, strong survivor easing the endangered beauty to the safety of his castle.

I wondered if my eye make-up had smudged. I wondered what his name was. I wondered how soon it would take us to make out.

But I was weak and, half an hour or so later, when the boat did finally stop in tangled reeds that led to a clearing, I felt I could go no further. I did not say anything, but he sensed it, and, saying nothing, he simply lifted me out of the boat and carried me with my arms around his neck.

I nestled against his neck and smelled him and he had that smell that can make one love a person. I can fuck a man who smells wrong but I cannot love one.

He smelled right.

The fight had drained out of me. I could hardly speak now. He laid me gently on a little bed in a tiny room in a wooden cabin and left me lying on top of it.

I slept for twelve hours.

The next morning, of course, I did not know where I was. It took me five minutes or so to register life and then to explain the unfamiliar location. The head swirled and the scenes played past as confused biopic full of Kit's wild face and motel furniture and being shot in the crowd.

I seemed to have thrown all the parts of me away and now there was nothing else. I was going to have to walk back on to the plain and gather them back, like an old vagrant picking up litter. I jolted upright. Awake now. I was wearing a little pair of black lace knickers and the sleeveless T-shirt. My skirt and leather jacket were on the floor. The handbag was by the side of the bed. I checked it. Credit card, lipstick, Joy, gun. All were present and correct.

This new place? The walls were wooden, the floor was wooden, the decrepit bed was old and made of iron. A window showed a view to some shivering trees. On the wall there was a wagon wheel and a black-and-white photograph of an old man engaged in a friendly relationship with a horse.

I walked out.

A door opposite was open and, pausing, I gazed into his empty bedroom. Who wouldn't? Who doesn't? Who can resist inspecting another person's life? But it was a monastic cell and it revealed very little about its occupant. There was an old-fashioned iron bed similar to the one in my room. A plain green candlewick bedspread.

A bedside cabinet on which there was a paraffin lamp and a bible. There were no other books. No other things at all, actually, except a hairbrush, shaving things and some loose change. The tableau described a person who needed little in the way of external entertainment, who did not cling to the past, and who was clean and ordered in his personal habits.

I padded into the kitchen. It had shelves full of striped blue and white china and a stove on which old-fashioned saucepans stood in piles. A cafetière of coffee stood on a sideboard. Somewhere there was toast and bacon.

He was outside sharpening his knife on a stone with firm strokes.

He looked up and smiled a smile that would melt the Queen of Narnia.

'Hullo.'

'Hullo.'

'Hungry?'

'Uh huh.'

'You sit right there.'

I did.

I sat on the wooden balcony at a table and I stared at the stranger's homestead while he fried bacon on the stove inside.

A circle of feeble structures met in a clearing like a collection of street drunks who had come across each other in a downtown AA meeting. Thrown together in a haphazard conglomerate of wood and metal, they were the constructs of DIY ineptitude. The past builder with the hammer should not have bothered. Window frames were out of line, nails were irregular and, in some cases, the walls had collapsed under the weight of the roof.

This ageing collection had obviously been there for some time, as vegetation had begun to take it over without resistance. Plush worts and gaudy perennials climbed high and clambered through the windows and doors. Moss-covered gables and holes of various sizes provided habitat for various faunae, not least several turkeys and a colony of raccoons.

Piles of dried crops lay on the earth, as did twisted metal and other discards of arcane origins. Some huts were thin, some low, some high, though all were basically built to the rectangular design of basic sheds. The appearance of their exteriors bore no evidence of the function of their interiors. They were like men. Their clothes did not reflect their true nature. I had been a porn queen long enough to know that inside every shivering polyester tracksuit there is a man who thinks he is Rambo.

I recalled that the outbuildings that surrounded the motel were of similar design and tended to be full of potatoes and rusting farm equipment, though there was also a hog gallows of which the owner was most proud, insisting it was historical and attempting to exhort money to look at it.

This hamlet seemed to reflect the lifestyles of the locality, though the inhabitant did not. There was no immediate sign of the nature of his profession and I could not help wondering whence his means sprang and what he did all day, here in the mushed foliage of the deserted swamp.

He said his name was Matt but he did not ask me what my plans were or who I was or where I was going or why.

So I did not ask him these questions either.

I had arrived in his present for reasons that I could not explain because they were inexplicable. Life had stopped in the swamp. There was no day, date, time or season. There was no television and no newspapers. Kit was miles away. The porno slut of my alter ego lived elsewhere in a legacy of glossy photographs and digital formats. All that was left of the other life was a small blue bruise from where that other life had tried to murder me.

'My shoe is broken,' I said, as this matter seemed to be of primary importance.

'I'll mend it,' he said. 'If you want clothes you could look in the box by your bed. There are a lot of things in there . . . Some of them might be useful. This house has a good way of producing what is needed when they are needed – I found a scythe the other day just when I was about do some cutting back . . . You look in that box and take what you like.'

'Thank you.'

'You're welcome, ma'am . . .'

He was right. The box contained a lot of things that a girl might need, and a lot that she might not but might want anyway. It was a trove full of antiquarian treasures and vintage booty.

The owner of the box had been a woman with dreams. There were piles of *Film-Fan* magazines whose scrumpled yellow pages displayed 50s cheesecake shots of everyone from Frenzy le Carr to Kool Gak. Coiffured deities of yesteryear, pronounced in their retro-sexuality, hunks and harlots posed in swirling ball gowns and striped bathing suits, all décolleté necklines and chignon, always the one foot in front of the other to make that leg line that we know and love and sorely miss.

I hoiked the pile of magazines out and put them to one side to read later. A layer of tissue paper revealed a collection made by a loving hand whose owner had time on her hands and knew how to find the best. This wardrobe, perfectly preserved and smelling of dried lavender, included daywear, evening wear, nightwear and an unidentifiable time of day that I could only assume was between bath and bed – an hour when some women of bygone days lounged on a sofa with a glass of champagne while wearing a negligée and toenails.

These things, no doubt, were the 'something more comfortable' that lucky people slipped into.

There was a pale-green soufflé dress with an underskirt made of iridescent sequins; there was a spotted bikini with a ra-ra skirt; there was a print cotton playsuit with a tiny top, there were two fur coats and several straw picture hats. At the bottom, in soft balls of hand-stitched sensuality, lay silk underwear, nightdresses and seamed stockings.

I was trying on a jet Deco-style necklace with antique silver clasp when I noticed that he was standing at the doorway.

'You have a beautiful neck,' he said.

I blushed for the first time in twenty years. I don't know what came over me. I cannot remember the last time that I was embarrassed. Or shocked. I'd spent months talking gooey facials with the sleaze stars of LA. I'd seen and been every contortion and puckering and arbitrary spurt that you can imagine. I was as comfortable nude as I was clothed and I had allowed an audience of millions to inspect parts of me that most people reserve for their doctors.

I had exposed myself in every sense of the word. There should not have been anything left because no solemn secrets lurked at the bottom of the psyche ready to be manipulated by old guilts. But the subconscious can throw up old flotsam. Bits of the past float to the top, as corpses eventually float to the surface of a river. One can only stare in bewilderment.

I knew humiliation because I had played with it, experienced it and walked through it. I had known subjugation and subjection and interesting levels of agony; I had frisked in the darkness with no fear and I knew how draw on all the reserves of carnal psychodrama in order to make the most pleasure.

Sometimes I thought I had seen and done it all.

But here, suddenly, in a swamp with a man called Matt and a dressing-up box and the encrypted codes of new realities, genuine mortification had come suddenly upon me, slinking upon my body as a flush, suppressing me with inexplicable shame and making me small.

He caught me off guard. I was momentarily unprotected. I did not have the useful shield of the porn queen (she had no place in a deserted marsh, after all; who would care about her?); I was not the slinky miss who did as she pleased. Some flying seconds had swept me up in their quantum spurt and, for a moment, I was no one, my mind was not on anything, I was immersed, childlike, in the present whimsies of an old dressing-up box.

The focus had slipped as I chose a new disguise and he had been there to peak underneath the shiny veneer that guarded the soul.

Who thought about necks any more? Necks were something that held the bra up.

I'd spent months talking cunt and cock. I had forgotten the subtleties of the erogenous zones. Now I knew there were thighs, and arms, and mouths, and toes. And necks. Patches of discreet flesh could be tormented with the simple act of deprivation.

I unclasped the necklace with my eyes lowered and placed it carefully in some tissue paper.

I could not look at him and neither could I stop my face flaring crimson.

It was as if some virgin maiden of yore had entered my body and taken me over in order to have a laugh.

He noticed my blush and smiled.

'I've embarrassed you.'

Blue eyes dazzled with amusement, and, in there, somewhere, lurking deep, I thought I saw a glint of cruelty. It died as soon as it ignited and I could not study clearly for I was discomposed with effort of clawing back my dignity.

Did he want me to shed everything and walk towards him, all disguises discarded?

I could not place his accent. The dialect proved no identifiable locality. Sometimes it was as if he was from the South, sometimes I thought I heard the Middle East.

'No,' I said flushing more, flushing so much now that I could hardly see and I was beginning to hate myself. 'No, you haven't.'

What was it? Simple subtle sexual desire? Why then did I not flirt and seduce as always? Why this sudden sensitivity to invisible impropriety?

Head down, furtive, back to him, wishing he would go away for ever, I rustled about in the pile of garments to find something appropriate to wear for the day. Silky camis. Blouses. Straight-cut 50s trousers.

I looked up. He was still standing there. He showed no intention of moving.

The crimson ebbed. I gathered my weapons up again and girded myself for mischief.

I let him have it, slow and easy.

I let the chiffon evening dress drop to the floor and I stepped out of it as if it was a pool. Then, as if I did not know he was there, I shimmied into a pair of silk camiknickers and a plunge bra. Ensuring that he saw it all, the orbs of the cheeks, the tits, the tone of the biceps, the neat ankles, making sure that he saw all this, I eased smoothly into a pair of tiny gingham shorts and a gypsy blouse that simply fell off the shoulders without any effort whatsoever.

He stayed where he was, leaning up against the jamb of the door, looking but saying nothing.

I sat in front of the little dressing table and brushed my hair.

The neck was there.

I was there.

Why didn't he come to me?

I glanced covertly into the mirror to look at him.

The doorway was empty.

Jesus. Was this man going to fuck me or not?

I don't know if you have ever known what it is to receive innocent reverence. Worship is an outmoded concept, after all, associated less with romance and more with celebrity stalking. The sensations of courtly love where troubadours knelt in awe at the wonders of deified beauty cannot exist in a culture of gratification.

I had been adored by the metropolitan clodpolls who crept about in the fandom of porn, but this was different. This was an echo of a past where the exquisite frustration of unconsummated lust leaves the dancers trembling at the sight of a tiny tendril of hair or an eyelash behind a fan.

If touch is taboo, sexual drama heightens to a frenzy of unfulfilled desire. Everything is too much. The natural excitement of delayed gratification can be more exciting than the faux rules made by the permissive sophistication of fetish play. It is as if a society without taboos must impose its own leather restraints in order to enliven its bored romantic psyche.

I enjoy a good flogging as much as anyone and I had always got what I wanted. I knew how to fuck but I did not know how to kiss. I knew how to talk dirty but I did not know how to wait.

I decided that he must be a gentleman. Who can remember what they are like? They died a long time ago. Killed in the 60s at around the time the Panthers were shot. No one bothered to campaign for their conservation. No one bothered to round them up and put them in a reservation. They are not even remembered on a commemorative stamp.

He exuded desire but he would not touch me or make any sign. He complimented me and cared for me but he did not submit to me. And so he created a vacuum that I abhorred. I became frenzied, sometimes desperate. I did not know what to do. My stomach was knotted with dissatisfaction and need. I was bad at this waiting game. I am too impatient and too basically honest. I like hard penetration and then on to the next thing.

So I followed him round like a lamb as I tried to read a sign of his thoughts and impose myself on his plans. The Stella super-seduction techniques had never failed in the past. But it was a fixated effort. I was always conscious. I wanted to reveal all and wave it like flag, but I knew that discretion was my voodoo. A little cleavage, some thigh, the toned shadow of the upper arm. I put myself on show but I did not show, you know, the thing. Cunning. Invisible. Magic.

I followed him around as he wandered around the huts and sheds engaged in tasks of maintenance.

The outhouses of the homestead were full of the hallmarks of old lifestyles. A rusting still that had been used to make moonshine was an alchemical disarray of old bath and rubber tubes. A furnace to boil sugar cane stood next to a loom for cotton. There was a stuffed possum, a corn crib and a blackened smokehouse. One shack was merely full of old dusty bottles full of turpentine.

And over the next day he would tell me the swamp tales of strange lights and mythical creatures and how the juices of various plants could heal a wound.

He was very good at hunting. Everyday he would catch a fish or shoot down a bird from the sky. I would watch him follow the prey with his gun. He never missed.

He knew how to cook a bird in a box and make a trap out of string.

We drank tea pulled in handfuls from a coarse sack full of rough dried leaves. Sometimes he melted sugar cane on a pot on the stove and made a strange kind of fudge.

He said he had lived in the swamp for some time and did not need much.

'What's in here?' I said one afternoon, pushing a door to one shed that was firmly locked.

'That? I dunno. I think the key is lost to that one,' he said. 'Come back to the house and I'll make gumbo . . .'

Still he made no move.

I did not tell him who I was or what I did or where I had been. He did not ask and I wondered if this was because he knew anyway. He could have seen my face in a magazine, or my cunt on DAT, or heard about me through the news. Fame is a skittish thing: one man can know everything about you, but his neighbour only wants to meet Leonard Nimoy.

He never opined or judged or revealed. His whole being seemed to be of the present and it was a present without sex.

I could only think of the invisible barrier between us, unfathomable and unexplainable, that seemed to exist for no point.

I longed for the touch of his hand on my skin, a hug full of affection, some passion of physicality.

Was he gay?

Was he dysfunctional?

Was he human?

Was I in love?

I had run through a lucky life doing much as I pleased. The breeds of those who like to call themselves masculine had tended to place their parts into my hands with enthusiasm and even gratitude. The wildlife came. I moved in porno and around Hollywood – these are urbane geo-cities where the barrios have no boundaries. Anything goes. No one says no. A girl gets it when she wants it. In LA it is easier to get laid than it is to get a taxi. Now, though, in this muddy lagoon, a challenge had arrived in the form of resistance. The sweet smell of unavailability scented the air. Uncertainty? It's a form of foreplay, I suppose.

If Kit had been with me she would have said that

Matt's polite neutrality lay in disinterest, that I neither aroused nor inspired him, and, though her imaginary words rang in my head, I could not believe them.

If he did not want me why then did he stare at me with unblinking and unashamed eyes, not even bothering to avert his gaze when I caught him watching me, brazen in his base instinct? If his senses were dull why then did he serve my every whim? Tell me that I was beautiful? Refuse to let me out of his sight? Say that his life had changed for the better now that I was here – things were warmer, livelier, more exciting. His detachment was mystifying, but I knew, I knew this man wanted me.

On the seventh evening, released by four glasses of red wine, I blurted out the question that, as far as I was concerned, had subsumed the atmosphere since the minute he had found me on the boat in the swamp.

'Shall we make love?' I said, staring at him from under my fringe and sipping a glass of wine with the glossed lips of a perfectly pert hussy.

It was about 6.30 p.m. and I dropped it casually into the conversation in the same tone of voice one would maintain to talk about the weather to a stranger.

It was a neutral suggestion, a comment almost, rather than an invitation loaded with intent. There was no passion, no demand, no hint of reprimand. It was flung out as a free-floating idea.

I was wearing a tiny pair of white shorts. My legs were smooth and brown. I stretched them out in front of me in order to better appreciate the patina of 'Crimson Dawn' that licked the toenails.

He was sitting next to me on the sofa and his body jolted as if he had walked into an electric fence.

He laid his glass of wine carefully on a leather chest next to the sofa.

'What?'

'Shall we have sex?' I said.

He looked genuinely surprised and then slightly frightened.

'Sex?'

'Yes. You know. Fuck.'

'I will not have sex with you,' he said.

'Why not?'

He stammered.

'There are things you will never understand.'

'Try me.'

He sighed.

'Three years ago I promised the Lord of my Understanding that I would never again have sexual relations and I have kept to it. I do not want to break my oath.'

I groaned inwardly. So that was why the Bible was in his bedroom. The man had got God.

'How do you know that the Lord of your Understanding wants you to be celibate?'

'He told me so, in a clear voice.'

'In a clear voice? What did he say?'

'The wages of sin is death.'

I had always found the wages of sin to be lucrative; indeed I had been paid $800,000 for my last porn movie, but I said nothing. He was looking at me as Adam must have looked at Eve, the fallen woman beguiled by the serpent and set to bring God's land to ruin.

'The Bible teaches us that we should have a pure mind,' he said. 'A person should not give himself over to sinful thought . . .'

I edged my body closer to him so that he could see down into the crack of my cleavage and smell the Joy exuding from my every wanton pore. He might have God, but here was temptation, good and proper and ready to perform every act in the Devil's repertoire.

'What about love?' I whispered.

'Separation from the love of our Lord is for all eternity. I have taken a solemn oath. You will have to respect that.'

Respect it? I wanted to laugh out loud. *Respect* it? As far as I was concerned the Lord had removed a handsome man from the market of pleasure and placed him in an absurd delirium where reality was made of the political machinations of organised religion. Respect it? I think not.

But it sure was a challenge.

I stretched with feline flexibility and edged closer to him.

I stroked his cheek very gently with one finger.

He looked into my eyes, on to my breasts, on to my thighs, back into my eyes.

I placed my mouth two millimetres away from his lips.

And, slowly, as slowly as one must creep up on a bird so that it will not fly away, with all the stealth of a natural-born minx, I eased my fingers on to his crotch and felt the satisfying pulse of a burgeoning erection. Gently I pressed my hand down on his groin, pushing my fingers into the warm curves. I massaged him with gentle determination. The swelling grew bigger and bigger under my hand, straining against the zip of his trousers.

He closed his eyes and groaned.

The man was nearly mine.

'You could try to convert me,' I said, licking my lips.

I went for the top of the zipper, ready to worm my fingers into the flies, bring that celibate cock out and lick its head until it did not know whether it was in heaven or hell.

But he rallied. Defiant zeal won through.

'No!'

He pushed me roughly away from him.

I nearly fell off the sofa.

'Hey!' I said. 'Watch it!'

'Get away from me, you Jezebel! You harridan of hell. Thou shalt not stimulate the lust in me. Get away!'

Fear and anger contorted his features, which were now red and ugly.

'Get away from me!'

He stood up, strode out of the room, and left the house. His glass of wine shuddered as the door slammed and fell off the chest. A 1998 Merlot oozed over the floor like blood.

Mustering some dignity, I retired to my bedroom, where I packed my few possessions. I knew now that I had to go. I planned to leave first thing in the morning, before he was awake. Disappointment flared as resentment. I did not want to see him again.

I fell asleep, only to wake with a jolt at 4 a.m.

Life flashed into my head with frantic intensity. I was very awake. Outside, in the night, the darkness was churning.

Tyres crunched over the gravel and earth of the backyard. Headlights flashed beams of gold over the walls of the bedroom and there was the shout of men's voices. The noise was akin to that made when the dustbin men arrive at 5 a.m. – but they were not dustbin men. They were tall figures wearing combat jackets and they were unloading wooden boxes from the backs of several vans.

Matt, armed with a torch, was guiding them to the hut that he had claimed was locked.

They were there for an hour or so, piling boxes, crunching with their boots, smoking cigarettes and muttering to each other. Then, one by one, they got back into the vans and disappeared throughout the clearing towards the road that led out of the swamp.

Ten minutes later I heard him return to his bedroom.

Heart thudding, I rose slowly out of my bed and crept across the room. The yard was clear and all the men had gone.

Having eased myself into my miniskirt and shovelled

on a crumpled silk blouse, I paused by his doorway to ensure that he was asleep.

The door to the hut was ajar. Pushing it with a whine of the hinge, I entered. The floor was piled high with wooden boxes. One was open. There was straw and, as I bent nearer, I saw that it contained a sub-machine gun.

Newspapers strewn across the floor displayed the headlines made by the Disgust Brigade; there were stories about terrorist atrocities and photographs of blood-spattered faces.

I started to tremble as the dreadful realisation began to poison me.

Matt was Cowl, Cowl was Matt.

As the blood pumped hard into my head I looked up to see a man's face staring at me. I nearly screamed. But it was not a man: it was a ghastly mirage created by shadow. Something was hanging on one of the hooks behind the door. I edged close and shone the torch. It was a black balaclava.

I was about to turn, leave the outhouse and run straight into the swamp, when the light of another torch shone straight into my face so that I could see only the yellow radius of the beam and a shadow behind it.

'What do you think you're doing?'

It was Matt's voice. It was low and it was very nasty.

'You're Cowl,' I snapped. 'Jesus. You bastard. You tried to kill me!'

He moved in closer so that now I could see the features in the dark behind the torch.

'I lead the Christian warriors to the path of truth,' he said.

'You're a fucking nutter.'

'And you . . .' he said pushing me hard up against the wall. 'You pervert your own body – the body that is the temple of God. You are unclean!'

I dropped the torch.

He squeezed one hand around my throat.

His mouth pressed close to my face and I could feel his breath.

The blood pumped in my neck. I felt dizzy and I thought I was going to collapse.

'You're going to help us,' he said. 'I knew who you were all along, Miss Stella Slut, whore of the damned. But now you are going to help the righteous brothers of the true faith. You are going to be a martyr to our cause – the final testament of our mission. You will die in our honour.'

His fingers tightened around my neck.

I reached into the waistband of my miniskirt.

'I think not,' I said and shoved the nose of the Smith and Wesson into his stomach.

He looked down, saw what it was, and stepped back.

'You move and I'll blow your colon to Atlanta,' I said. 'Try reading St Luke with no stomach, matey.'

'You wouldn't . . .'

'Try me.'

He didn't.

He sat in the chair like a lamb.

'Take off your clothes,' I said.

'What?'

'Take off your clothes or I will shoot you dead. And I owe you a bullet, you know. An eye for an eye and all that shite . . . I owe you a bullet and I'm about ready to give it to you.'

He removed his clothes like an old uncle playing strip poker at Christmas. The shirt first, then the socks, then the belt, then the jeans, until he had eased himself down to the white Y-fronts.

I stood over him, thighs akimbo, and pointed the gun towards his groin.

'Everything . . .'

He eased his underpants down his thighs to his calves. They dropped as a pool on the floor around his ankles.

His cock hung down, thick and fat and brown.

I inspected it closely, lifting it gently with the barrel of the gun, as one lifts a dead animal in the woods with a stick. It was shrivelled and limp. Nearly dead. 'Nice dick,' I said. 'What a waste.'

He started to say the Lord's Prayer under his breath.

'You sit there like a good lad,' I directed.

I bound his hands behind the back of the chair with some twine from one of the packing cases.

Then I stood underneath the bare bulb that hung from a single wire from the ceiling, spreading a golden shaft of light into the darkness as a spot makes a circle of light on the stage of a theatre.

It was my spot. And I used it well.

'You watch me, you motherfucker.'

I had learned lap dancing from the most highly paid exotic dancers in America and I knew what I was doing. Givenchy. Toyota. Pussy Willow. They had taught me everything they knew. I could contort myself into every gyno posture in the sleaze-tripping repertoire.

'You watch me until you come . . .'

His body was slumped into the chair. He was naked. He was bound. He was in his own hell. But his eyes burned into me. I could feel them, but I could not see them, for my own were on his groin.

Still holding the pistol in one hand, I gyrated my hips, rotating slowly and with bestial provocation six inches away from his face. Lifting up the black cotton of the skirt, I eased my panties down and pushed my shaved pussy towards his mouth, rudely offering it to his unwilling lips, close enough for him to smell the excitement.

And then, demented chorine slithering to an invisible sleaze track, I turned around and bent over so that all he had were the two round orbs of my buttocks, the lewd black cleavage of my arse, the smooth lips of my pussy, which then opened out in full carnal display as I splayed out my legs in the scissor position of the insolent coryphée.

There was no escape. He was forced to stare at my bare ass shaking shamelessly, my anal opening offered up to him, my cunt so close he would have been able to smell the salty excitement of my lips. He got it all. If it had been Nevada, it would have cost him five hundred bucks minimum.

Min-ee-mum.

I oozed and moved to the unseen sound of invisible burlesque – somewhere out there, there should have been a sax player named Sonny and a percussion section with tailgating brass and all the jazzy whine of a low-down strip track in some cococabana come-on joint.

And all the time I covered the righteous punk with the gun and kept an eye on his groin. I would not let up. He had no place to go.

Finally, as I went down on all fours for the third time, and I was the dirtiest nudest dog you could ever see, finally as my own fingers went into my excited, wet, revengeful pussy, I saw that dick thicken. It grew, it blossomed, it stood straight up. The Christian warrior began to moan. The Christian warrior began to fall from the path of righteousness and enter the realm of the damned.

But I did not let up.

Oh, no.

I know how to get a cock good and hard and I know when it is about to burst its juices.

I went on. I wanted him hard. I wanted him so hard he would beg for it.

The veins threading the side of the purple stem now swelled up like junkie seams begging for a fix. The helmet glowed pure and red. He started to whine and tremble. His pelvis shuddered. Boy, did he want it! But his hands were tied. If they had not been he could have relieved himself. But he was restrained. His hard-on had no place to go.

I nearly laughed out loud.

But I did not.

I teased him.

Splayed over him, I dipped down and touched the throbbing tip of his dick with the candid wet of my feckless vulva, kissing his nerve endings with peccant misconduct. I dipped up and down on him, giving him the promise of everything and tainting him with nothing.

'Admit it,' I snarled. 'Admit it. You want it. You want to fuck me hard, you motherfucker. You'd do anything.'

Suddenly and without warning he burst into loud and noisy tears.

'Yes! Yes! Please fuck me. Make me come. I can't stand it any more . . .'

He stamped his feet on the dusty ground.

'Please!'

Now he was begging and sobbing, his body a seizure of guilt as he was forced to succumb to vice.

His painfully purple penis looked as if it was ready to launch itself out of his groin and split his body clean in half.

'Please, please fuck me,' he moaned.

I leaned slowly forward and kissed him very lightly on his mouth. The lipstick would be there long after I had gone. He would smell me long after I had gone.

I picked up the panties that I had dropped on the floor, turned my back on him and walked out of the room.

'Goodbye, Daddy,' I said. 'Trust the Lord.'

I could still hear him begging as I reached the edge of the swamp.

LOOK OUT FOR THE ALL-NEW BLACK LACE BOOKS – AVAILABLE NOW!

All books priced £7.99 in the UK. Please note publication dates apply to the UK only. For other territories, please contact your retailer.

BURNING BRIGHT
Janine Ashbless
ISBN 978 0 352 34085 6

Two lovers, brought together by a forbidden passion, are on the run from their pasts. Veraine was once a commander in the Imperial army: Myrna was the divine priestess he seduced and stole from her desert temple. But travelling through a jungle kingdom, they fall prey to slavers and are separated. Veraine is left for dead. Myrna is taken as a slave to the city of the Tiger Lords: inhuman tyrants with a taste for human flesh. There she must learn the tricks of survival in a cruel and exotic court where erotic desire is not the only animal passion.

Myrna still has faith that Veraine will find her. But Veraine, badly injured, has forgotten everything: his past, his lover, and even his own identity. As he undertakes a journey through a fevered landscape of lush promise and supernatural danger, he knows only one thing – that he must somehow find the unknown woman who holds the key to his soul.

Coming in February 2007

THE BOSS
Monica Belle
ISBN 978 0 352 34088 7

Felicity is a girl with two different sides to her character, each leading two very separate lives. There's Fizz – wild child, drummer in a retro punk band, and car thief. And then there's Felicity – a quiet, police, and ultra efficient office worker. But as her attractive, controlling boss takes an interest in her, she finds it hard to keep the two parts of her life separate.

Will being with Stephen mean choosing between personas and sacrificing so much of her life? But then, it also appears that Stephen has some very peculiar and addictive ideas about sex.

GOTHIC BLUE
Portia Da Costa
ISBN 978 0 352 33075 8

At an archduke's reception, a handsome young nobleman falls under the spell of a malevolent but irresistible sorceress. Two hundred years later, Belinda Seward also falls prey to sensual forces she can neither understand nor control. Stranded by a thunderstorm at a remote Gothic priory, Belinda and her boyfriend are drawn into an enclosed world of luxurious decadence and sexual alchemy. Their host is the courteous but melancholic André von Kastel; a beautiful aristocrat who mourns his lost love. He has plans for Belinda – plans that will take her into the realms of obsessive love and the erotic paranormal.

Coming in March 2007

FLOOD
Anna Clare
ISBN 978 0 352 34094 8

London, 1877. Phoebe Flood, a watch mender's daughter from Blackfriars, is hired as lady's maid to the glamorous Louisa LeClerk, a high class tart with connections to the underworld of gentlemen pornographers. Fascinated by her new mistress and troubled by strange dreams, Phoebe receives an extraordinary education in all matters sensual. And her destiny and secret self gradually reveals itself when she meets Garou, a freak show attraction, The Boy Who Was Raised by Wolves.

LEARNING TO LOVE IT
Alison Tyler
ISBN 978 0 352 33535 7

Art historian Lissa an doctor Colin meet at the Frankfurt Book Fair, where they are both promoting their latest books. At the fair, and then through Europe, the two lovers embark on an exploration of their sexual fantasies, playing intense games of bondage, spanking and dressing up. Lissa loves humiliation, and Colin is just the man to provide her with the pleasure she craves. Unbeknown to Lissa, their meeting was not accidental, but planned ahead by a mysterious patron of the erotic arts.

Black Lace Booklist

Information is correct at time of printing. To avoid disappointment, check availability before ordering. Go to www.blacklace-books.co.uk. All books are priced £7.99 unless another price is given.

BLACK LACE BOOKS WITH A CONTEMPORARY SETTING

- ❑ ALWAYS THE BRIDEGROOM Tesni Morgan ISBN 978 0 352 33855 6 £6.99
- ❑ THE ANGELS' SHARE Maya Hess ISBN 978 0 352 34043 6
- ❑ ARIA APPASSIONATA Julie Hastings ISBN 978 0 352 33056 7 £6.99
- ❑ ASKING FOR TROUBLE Kristina Lloyd ISBN 978 0 352 33362 9
- ❑ BLACK LIPSTICK KISSES Monica Belle ISBN 978 0 352 33885 3 £6.99
- ❑ BONDED Fleur Reynolds ISBN 978 0 352 33192 2 £6.99
- ❑ BOUND IN BLUE Monica Belle ISBN 978 0 352 34012 2
- ❑ CAMPAIGN HEAT Gabrielle Marcola ISBN 978 0 352 33941 6
- ❑ CAT SCRATCH FEVER Sophie Mouette ISBN 978 0 352 34021 4
- ❑ CIRCUS EXCITE Nikki Magennis ISBN 978 0 352 34033 7
- ❑ CLUB CRÉME Primula Bond ISBN 978 0 352 33907 2 £6.99
- ❑ COMING ROUND THE MOUNTAIN Tabitha Flyte ISBN 978 0 352 33873 0 £6.99
- ❑ CONFESSIONAL Judith Roycroft ISBN 978 0 352 33421 3
- ❑ CONTINUUM Portia Da Costa ISBN 978 0 352 33120 5
- ❑ DANGEROUS CONSEQUENCES Pamela Rochford ISBN 978 0 352 33185 4
- ❑ DARK DESIGNS Madelynne Ellis ISBN 978 0 352 34075 7
- ❑ THE DEVIL INSIDE Portia Da Costa ISBN 978 0 352 32993 6
- ❑ EDEN'S FLESH Robyn Russell ISBN 978 0 352 33923 2 £6.99
- ❑ ENTERTAINING MR STONE Portia Da Costa ISBN 978 0 352 34029 0
- ❑ EQUAL OPPORTUNITIES Mathilde Madden ISBN 978 0 352 34070 2
- ❑ FEMININE WILES Karina Moore ISBN 978 0 352 33874 7 £6.99
- ❑ FIRE AND ICE Laura Hamilton ISBN 978 0 352 33486 2
- ❑ GOING DEEP Kimberly Dean ISBN 978 0 352 33876 1 £6.99
- ❑ GOING TOO FAR Laura Hamilton ISBN 978 0 352 33657 6 £6.99
- ❑ GONE WILD Maria Eppie ISBN 978 0 352 33670 5
- ❑ IN PURSUIT OF ANNA Natasha Rostova ISBN 978 0 352 34060 3

❑ MAD ABOUT THE BOY Mathilde Madden ISBN 978 0 352 34001 6
❑ MAKE YOU A MAN Anna Clare ISBN 978 0 352 34006 1
❑ MAN HUNT Cathleen Ross ISBN 978 0 352 33583 8
❑ MIXED DOUBLES Zoe le Verdier ISBN 978 0 352 33312 4 £6.99
❑ MIXED SIGNALS Anna Clare ISBN 978 0 352 33889 1 £6.99
❑ MS BEHAVIOUR Mini Lee ISBN 978 0 352 33962 1
❑ A MULTITUDE OF SINS Kit Mason ISBN 978 0 352 33737 5 £6.99
❑ PACKING HEAT Karina Moore ISBN 978 0 352 33356 8 £6.99
❑ PAGAN HEAT Monica Belle ISBN 978 0 352 33974 4
❑ PASSION OF ISIS Madelynne Ellis ISBN 978 0 352 33993 5
❑ PEEP SHOW Mathilde Madden ISBN 978 0 352 33924 9
❑ THE POWER GAME Carrera Devonshire ISBN 978 0 352 33990 4
❑ THE PRIVATE UNDOING OF A PUBLIC SERVANT ISBN 978 0 352 34066 5
Leonie Martel
❑ RELEASE ME Suki Cunningham ISBN 978 0 352 33671 2 £6.99
❑ RUDE AWAKENING Pamela Kyle ISBN 978 0 352 33036 9
❑ SAUCE FOR THE GOOSE Mary Rose Maxwell ISBN 978 0 352 33492 3
❑ SIN.NET Helena Ravenscroft ISBN 978 0 352 33598 2 £6.99
❑ SLAVE TO SUCCESS Kimberley Raines ISBN 978 0 352 33687 3 £6.99
❑ SLEAZY RIDER Karen S. Smith ISBN 978 0 352 33964 5
❑ STELLA DOES HOLLYWOOD Stella Black ISBN 978 0 352 33588 3
❑ THE STRANGER Portia Da Costa ISBN 978 0 352 33211 0
❑ SUMMER FEVER Anna Ricci ISBN 978 0 352 33625 5 £6.99
❑ SWITCHING HANDS Alaine Hood ISBN 978 0 352 33896 9 £6.99
❑ SYMPHONY X Jasmine Stone ISBN 978 0 352 33629 3 £6.99
❑ TONGUE IN CHEEK Tabitha Flyte ISBN 978 0 352 33484 8
❑ TWO WEEKS IN TANGIER Annabel Lee ISBN 978 0 352 33599 9 £6.99
❑ UNNATURAL SELECTION Alaine Hood ISBN 978 0 352 33963 8
❑ UP TO NO GOOD Karen S. Smith ISBN 978 0 352 33589 0 £6.99
❑ VILLAGE OF SCRETS Mercedes Kelly ISBN 978 0 352 33344 5
❑ WILD BY NATURE Monica Belle ISBN 978 0 352 33915 7 £6.99
❑ WILD CARD Madeline Moore ISBN 978 0 352 34038 2

BLACK LACE BOOKS WITH AN HISTORICAL SETTING

❑ THE AMULET Lisette Allen ISBN 978 0 352 33019 2 £6.99
❑ THE BARBARIAN GEISHA Charlotte Royal ISBN 978 0 352 33267 7

❑ BARBARIAN PRIZE Deanna Ashford ISBN 978 0 352 34017 7
❑ DANCE OF OBSESSION Olivia Christie ISBN 978 0 352 33101 4
❑ DARKER THAN LOVE Kristina Lloyd ISBN 978 0 352 33279 0
❑ ELENA'S DESTINY Lisette Allen ISBN 978 0 352 33218 9
❑ FRENCH MANNERS Olivia Christie ISBN 978 0 352 33214 1
❑ THE HAND OF AMUN Juliet Hastings ISBN 978 0 352 33144 1 £6.99
❑ LORD WRAXALL'S FANCY Anna Lieff Saxby ISBN 978 0 352 33080 2
❑ THE MASTER OF SHILDEN Lucinda Carrington ISBN 978 0 352 33140 3
❑ NICOLE'S REVENGE Lisette Allen ISBN 978 0 352 32984 4
❑ THE SENSES BEJEWELLED Cleo Cordell ISBN 978 0 352 32904 2 £6.99
❑ THE SOCIETY OF SIN Sian Lacey Taylder ISBN 978 0 352 34080 1
❑ UNDRESSING THE DEVIL Angel Strand ISBN 978 0 352 33938 6
❑ WHITE ROSE ENSNARED Juliet Hastings ISBN 978 0 352 33052 9 £6.99

BLACK LACE BOOKS WITH A PARANORMAL THEME

❑ BURNING BRIGHT Janine Ashbless ISBN 978 0 352 34085 6
❑ CRUEL ENCHANTMENT Janine Ashbless ISBN 978 0 352 33483 1
❑ THE PRIDE Edie Bingham ISBN 978 0 352 33997 3

BLACK LACE ANTHOLOGIES

❑ MORE WICKED WORDS Various ISBN 978 0 352 33487 9 £6.99
❑ WICKED WORDS 3 Various ISBN 978 0 352 33522 7 £6.99
❑ WICKED WORDS 4 Various ISBN 978 0 352 33603 3 £6.99
❑ WICKED WORDS 5 Various ISBN 978 0 352 33642 2 £6.99
❑ WICKED WORDS 6 Various ISBN 978 0 352 33690 3 £6.99
❑ WICKED WORDS 7 Various ISBN 978 0 352 33743 6 £6.99
❑ WICKED WORDS 8 Various ISBN 978 0 352 33787 0 £6.99
❑ WICKED WORDS 9 Various ISBN 978 0 352 33860 0
❑ WICKED WORDS 10 Various ISBN 978 0 352 33893 8
❑ THE BEST OF BLACK LACE 2 Various ISBN 978 0 352 33718 4
❑ WICKED WORDS: SEX IN THE OFFICE Various ISBN 978 0 352 33944 7
❑ WICKED WORDS: SEX AT THE SPORTS CLUB Various ISBN 978 0 352 33991 1
❑ WICKED WORDS: SEX ON HOLIDAY Various ISBN 978 0 352 33961 4
❑ WICKED WORDS: SEX IN UNIFORM Various ISBN 978 0 352 34002 3
❑ WICKED WORDS: SEX IN THE KITCHEN Various ISBN 978 0 352 34018 4

❑ WICKED WORDS: SEX ON THE MOVE Various ISBN 978 0 352 34034 4

❑ WICKED WORDS: SEX AND MUSIC Various ISBN 978 0 352 34061 0

❑ WICKED WORDS: SEX AND SHOPPING Various ISBN 978 0 352 34076 4

BLACK LACE NON-FICTION

❑ THE BLACK LACE BOOK OF WOMEN'S SEXUAL FANTASIES Edited by Kerri Sharp ISBN 978 0 352 33793 1 £6.99

To find out the latest information about Black Lace titles, check out the website: www.blacklace-books.co.uk or send for a booklist with complete synopses by writing to:

Black Lace Booklist, Virgin Books Ltd
Thames Wharf Studios
Rainville Road
London W6 9HA

Please include an SAE of decent size. Please note only British stamps are valid.

Our privacy policy
We will not disclose information you supply us to any other parties. We will not disclose any information which identifies you personally to any person without your express consent.

From time to time we may send out information about Black Lace books and special offers. Please tick here if you do not wish to receive Black Lace information. ❑

Please send me the books I have ticked above.

Name ....

Address ....

....

....

....

Post Code ....

Send to: Virgin Books Cash Sales, Thames Wharf Studios, Rainville Road, London W6 9HA.

US customers: for prices and details of how to order books for delivery by mail, call 888-330-8477.

Please enclose a cheque or postal order, made payable to Virgin Books Ltd, to the value of the books you have ordered plus postage and packing costs as follows:

UK and BFPO – £1.00 for the first book, 50p for each subsequent book.

Overseas (including Republic of Ireland) – £2.00 for the first book, £1.00 for each subsequent book.

If you would prefer to pay by VISA, ACCESS/MASTERCARD, DINERS CLUB, AMEX or SWITCH, please write your card number and expiry date here:

....

Signature ....

Please allow up to 28 days for delivery.